HEARTS OVER FENCES

An Equestrian Romance

TONI LELAND

Hearts Over Fences
©2004 Toni Leland

ISBN 1-887932-68-2
Library of Congress Catalog Number: 2004113519

This book is a work of fiction. Any references to historical events, real people, or real locales are used fictitiously. Other names, characters, places, and incidents are the product of the author's imagination, and any resemblance to actual events or persons, living or dead, is entirely coincidental.

Printed in U.S.A.

Parallel Press is an imprint of the Equine Graphics Publishing Group

Acknowledgments

No author really writes alone. Though the story may be unique, the details grow from a wide range of sources–mostly other people. I owe many thanks to those who've helped me form this story into something readable.

To first readers, Katie and Mitzi; Jenny, for setting me straight on my heroine; Philip for advice about physical therapy; fellow author and friend, Bob Bennett, for insight into the construction trade; Art, Janet, Ellen, and Holly for final proofing; University of Kentucky College of Agriculture for a fabulous place to research land issues; and finally, to Lexington, Kentucky for being such a beautiful and exciting place in which to set a tale.

For Bob,
Plotter Par Excellence

&

In memory of Pzaz
A great horse

One

The bold headline leaped off the front page of the *Herald-Leader*, and Beth Webb grinned. Adjusting her wire-rimmed reading glasses, she pored over the feature article.

$6 Million Equestrian Facility Hosts Exhibition Today
"Lexington, KY — National and world champions will thunder across the rolling green fields behind Highover Gate Equestrian Center, the dream-child of well-known venture capitalist, Bethany Webb. The new three-and-a-half-mile cross-country course is the first phase of a unique training and show facility that will see completion by the end of the year.

"Local investor Tim Trent voiced confidence in Webb's ambitious undertaking, emphasizing the need for a first-class horse show facility to soak up the overflow from the Kentucky Horse Park."

Beth frowned. "Dammit, Tim. Why do you always have to be in the spotlight?"

She scanned the remainder of the article, satisfied with the detailed coverage. Today was her "show them the money" phase, the proof that her investors had chosen wisely and could each confidently hand over another two hundred grand for the second phase of Highover. She laid the newspaper aside and carried her coffee mug out to the flagstone terrace. Just above the hills to the east, the sky wore a thin ribbon of bright pink, but directly above it, a heavy blanket of rain clouds threatened to smother the promise.

"Nuts. Just what I need."

Thirty minutes later, Beth's bright yellow Miata whizzed down the long driveway toward the main barn. Several horse trailers were already parked in the field, and handlers were working with horses in the warm-up paddock. At the end of the lane, the dark skeletal outline of the new dressage arena and barn contrasted against the pale gray sky, and her stomach jigged with pleasure and pride.

Inside the estate's original barn, the lights blazed and the air hummed with morning activity. Beth hurried to her office, determined to check every detail of the day one more time. She had too much at stake to leave anything to chance.

Hal MacGregor appeared about an hour later, his brown eyes twinkling from beneath bushy red eyebrows, his gravelly voice echoing a hint of Scotland.

"Mornin', Lass. Ready for your big day?"

She grinned mischievously. "Oh, Aye!"

He chuckled, then his expression sobered. "Are ye sure about ridin' in this event?" His expression reflected apology. "Ye haven't a chance against the big boys."

"I know, but that's not my goal. I just want to be part of the excitement. The next phase of construction starts on Monday and, after today, I won't have much time to ride."

Beth fiddled with the chinstrap on her black velvet riding helmet as she watched a horse and rider cross the finish line.

"First call, Miss Webb."

Her pulse quickened and she drew in a deep breath, nerves instantly on edge. Nodding to the event official, she nudged her horse toward the starting area. A quick glance at the vast gray sky sent a murmur of tension through her chest. Low, dark clouds were rolling in from the north, and the temperature had dropped noticeably in the past ten minutes. With any luck, the rain would hold off until she'd finished the course.

Two riders waited ahead of her, and Beth narrowed her eyes with curiosity at a vaguely familiar man astride a muscular gray Irish Draught. The rider's broad shoulders filled out a perfectly tailored hunter green jacket, and his thigh muscles rippled beneath tight tan breeches. Add his excellent posture, and he was the picture of equestrian perfection. As though feeling her scrutiny, he turned and looked at her. Embarrassed to be caught staring, she looked away, feeling warmth creep across her cheeks.

Hal's voice rumbled into her thoughts. "Ready?"

She nodded, an eddy of anticipation and apprehension swirling through her head.

He patted her mount's shoulder. "Lassie, ye'll do fine."

She watched him amble away. *A prize find, that one.* Her campaign to hire the finest instructors in the country had targeted the famous world-class jumping instructor. Through him, she'd hooked up with a former Olympic dressage rider and two world-champion equitation instructors. With a state-of-the-art, fully accredited training facility and the best equestrian educators, on completion, Highover Gate would be the crème de la crème.

She scanned the horses and riders milling about the grounds, then let her gaze sweep across the magnificent, gently-rolling green pastures. From there, her gaze drifted to the specially-constructed VIP viewing boxes where her investors were assembled, sipping champagne Mimosas. *I'm on my way.*

"Hal MacGregor your coach?"

The nearness of the soft drawl startled her, and she nearly lost her balance. Brilliant green eyes scrutinized her from barely four feet away, while the handsome guy astride the equally handsome horse stared boldly, a sly smile playing about the corners of his mouth.

Regaining her composure, she leveled a cool look at the stranger and nodded. Her stomach did another little dance—his impudent smile unnerved her.

He saluted. "I'm Brett Hall from Louisville."

"Ah, yes, the one who's chasing Wegner's crown."

Another charming grin. "Yup, and gaining fast."

The loudspeaker crackled through the air, *"Number 962. Karen Allen."*

He straightened up in the saddle. "Gotta go—I'm next up."

He wheeled his horse around, then threw her a quick, tantalizing look over his shoulder before trotting toward the starting gate, his body moving in exact rhythm with the horse's stride. She watched him check in with the gatesman, her thoughts moving into business mode. She could do worse than having Brett Hall at the event. Familiar important names would shine in the newspaper account of the day, and she wanted every possible advantage to publicize Highover.

Hall moved up to the starting line, and Beth's butterflies returned. Annoyed, she closed her eyes and tried to concentrate on regaining her mental composure for the rigorous course ahead, hindered by his cocky grin still floating in her mind's eye.

Brett watched the current rider cross the finish line. The complicated course would be tricky, but he loved the challenge of a new pattern. An Olympic designer had laid this one out. Though this event was only an exhibition, Brett's determination to be the best still coursed through his head. There were too many national champions and Olympic hopefuls gathered there, and *he* had an aggressive reputation to protect.

Treating himself to one last glance at the aristocratic looking fair-haired woman astride the big bay Trakehner, he erased all thoughts from his head, except those he needed to dominate the field.

Beth watched the gray horse streak across the grass and launch himself over the first fence of the course. As he disappeared around the bend, she considered Brett Hall's obvious talent. *I'll bet Wegner is looking over his shoulder all the time.*

Hal appeared, solemnity creasing his weathered face.

"Ye'll probably cross the finish line soaked, from the looks of those clouds. Mind the Glen Trail if the rain starts—it'll be slippery as the devil."

He patted her knee, then climbed into his golf cart and drove toward the access road to watch her ride from a position midway through the course. She looked up again at the threatening sky, then leaned forward and smoothed her hand over her horse's sleek neck.

"Here we go, Paso. Be a good boy for me, and there'll be treats at the barn."

The big horse bobbed his head and chuckled deep in his throat, affirming her belief that horses understood every word their handlers spoke.

"Number 702. Bethany Webb."

The tinny announcement sent a surge of excitement swirling

through her chest, and she drew in a deep breath. Paso moved forward immediately at her gentle knee pressure. They waited at the starting post, muscles and nerves singing with both apprehension and anticipation. The starting gun cracked, Paso shot forward like a bullet, and Beth lost herself in the exhilaration of the ride.

It no longer mattered that it might rain, or that so much hinged on the day's event. Her body became a part of the powerful horse beneath her, flowing with his stride, lifting as he soared over obstacles, then melting back into a single entity that moved at breakneck speed through the open countryside. Her focus became Paso's as she guided him over the rough terrain and through a stream.

The first drops of rain fell as Paso sailed over the hedges, just before the woods–and Glen Trail. Within seconds, the sodden skies unleashed a torrent, reducing her visibility to almost nothing. *I need to slow down!* The potent desire to show well in the event countered her instinctive thoughts. Paso had his head and gave no sign of slowing his pace in the downpour. Horse and rider charged into the woods.

Narrow and winding, Glen Trail snaked through the forest for about a quarter-mile. A tree lay across the path, but Paso easily jumped it, landing solidly without breaking stride. The rain streamed down Beth's neck, soaking her shirt, chilling her to the bone. Then, as quickly as it had started, the downpour stopped and the sun knifed through the trees, dappling the glistening ground with patches of gold, and she relaxed a little.

Suddenly, Paso lowered his head and grunted. Tiny beads of cold sweat crawled across her scalp–they were going down, and there was nothing she could do about it. As she plummeted to the ground, brown and green and wet and gray whirled around her in a crazy kaleidoscope. Soft mud oozed up around her body, then a bolt of lightning surged through her back. A split second later, twelve hundred pounds of horseflesh crashed down on top of her, crushing the breath from her lungs. Stars spun through her view of the world as she sank into darkness.

Two

B rett stood in the finish paddock, grinning with satisfaction while he removed his riding helmet. So far, he'd beaten the best time of the day by eighteen seconds. He glanced up at the gray sky, now punctuated with scattered patches of blue. *And,* he'd lucked out on the rain.

A petite television newswoman in a bright yellow slicker thrust a microphone toward him. "Brett, what do you think of this new facility?"

"It's a little premature to judge the whole thing, but the cross-country course is fantastic."

"Do you have any plans to make Highover Gate your training headquarters?"

He chuckled, reaching for his horse's reins. "Right now, I'm concentrating on getting through this season...so, if you'll excuse me, I need to cool down my horse."

"Thank you, Brett Hall..."

She turned to face the camera, her voice fading into a murmur as Brett led his steaming mount across the field toward the horse trailer. He glanced around at the expanse of lush property that seemed to go on for miles, and his sharp mind focused on the future. Highover Gate already employed world-class instructors for every discipline. According to a detailed article he'd read in a sport horse magazine, when the project was completed, the facility would have an indoor formal dressage arena, both an indoor and open-air show-jumping arena, a driving concourse, and over four hundred stalls. *Training here might not be such a bad idea.* He toweled the sweat from

Rex's neck, thinking that Highover Gate Equestrian Center was an ambitious undertaking for the young woman who'd organized it. He paused in mid-swipe, trying to remember what the article had said about her age–thirty-two, or thirty-six. *I wonder what she's like. Probably a hardhead to have become so successful.*

The horse snorted impatiently, and Brett's thoughts refocused on the grueling Longines Royal British Eventing Grand Prix at Hickstead, just four weeks away. The highest level riders–including national champion Stephen Wegner–would vie for top honors. Already, the idea of competing in the prestigious equestrian event made Brett's heart pound with excitement. As a first-time exhibitor at that show, he'd need to be prepared, even if it meant training nonstop until then.

A loudspeaker echoed across the grounds, interrupting his thoughts and he stopped to listen, but the trailer was parked too far away for him to pick out the words. Given the urgent tone and the length of the muffled announcement, it was clear there was a serious problem. A second later, the on-site ambulance raced along the access road toward the far end of the course. The flashing lights and forlorn wail of the siren sent a chill across his shoulders.

He stowed his tack in the truck, then headed back across the field to find out what had happened.

Beth opened her eyes to a hazy filigree of dark trees against brilliant blue sky. A crushing weight pressed her legs against the hard ground, and her dazed brain struggled to comprehend her whereabouts. Suddenly, the weight lifted, then urgent voices penetrated her foggy confusion.

"Easy, don't move her. The medics are on the way."

She turned her head, trying to locate the source of the words, and her gaze came to rest on a chocolate-brown mound lying beside her.

"Paso! Oh my God! Paso!"

She struggled to sit up, but strong hands held her firmly, and a familiar accent softened the edges of her confusion.

"Easy, Lass. Don't move. The ambulance is on the way. You're gonna be all right."

"Let go of me! I want to see Paso!"

Hal's hands maintained their firm, but gentle restraint. His kind face, eyes filled with sorrow, shimmered into her line of vision.

"Ah, Lassie. I'm so sorry. He..."

Screams from somewhere far away echoed through her head. *A dream, only a dream–please*. Tears streamed down her temples into the mud beneath her head, then blessed darkness swallowed her.

Brett approached a group of people gathered next to the VIP enclosure.

"What happened?"

A rangy woman in riding clothes responded. "Not sure, but it might be the owner."

The air thumped with vibrations, and they all watched solemnly as a white helicopter with a red cross on its belly glided over the crowd, then dropped slowly behind a grove of trees at the far end of the course.

He walked away, his chest tight with heartfelt sympathy for the unfortunate equestrian who'd been injured–a fear experienced by every rider on earth.

Three

Three Weeks Later

B eth glowered at the small woman in white standing beside her. "Don't!"

Looking straight ahead to the open French doors, she reached down to the wheels on either side of her and grasped them firmly, then struggled to steer the wheelchair forward in a straight line.

"I don't need you, I am *not* an invalid."

The visiting nurse's tone hummed with pity. "Bethany, I know this is very hard for you, but please don't be stubborn. You've only had the chair for one day. Let me help until you get the hang of it."

The woman's kindness sent tears racing to Beth's eyes, further infuriating her. She blinked them back.

"I'm sorry I snapped, but I'm so damned frustrated. Why won't this thing move where I want it to?"

Why can't I just stand up and walk? Why did this happen to me? The floodgates opened, and she could no longer control the tears. A few minutes later, she regained her composure, donned a brave smile, and pointed toward the doors to the terrace.

"Would you please push me over there? I'd like to sit outside for a while."

During the time she'd lived there, Beth hadn't spent much time on the elegant terrace. Now, from a different vantage point, she absorbed the breathtaking view with a new appreciation. The panorama of rolling emerald-green hills stretched to every horizon. Dark brown fences divided the seemingly endless expanse into neat green squares, uninhabited now at dusk. Her eyes burned again as she envisioned the magnificent horses that grazed there during the day.

A large clump of trees in one of the farthest pastures drew her gaze, and her heart wrenched as the pain washed over her for the millionth time. Her beloved Paso lay within the shelter and solitude of that dark stand of trees. She closed her eyes, trying desperately to think of other things, but she could not erase the horror of her last moments with him.

The telephone rang inside the house, bringing her back to the present. She reached for the chair wheel. *I'll figure out how to drive this thing if it kills me.* She pulled and pushed and, suddenly, the chair spun smoothly through a half-circle.

The nurse smiled from the doorway. "See? You can do it. You just need some practice."

Beth exhaled sharply from her efforts. "Who was that on the phone?"

"Dr. Kellart, checking to see how you're doing. He'll stop by tomorrow."

She pushed hard on the wheels, and the chair zigzagged toward the door. "I'll be here."

Surgeon Dave Kellart arrived around Noon on the following day, a charming and optimistic smile brightening his freckled face. Beth liked him very much, despite the unfortunate circumstances of their meeting. She appreciated the fact that he was honest and open about her injuries, and always offered a glimmer of hope that the future would be promising—hope she desperately needed.

Paso's death had been a devastating blow and, coupled with her partial paralysis, the stress was taking its toll. Her mental state had deteriorated significantly since the accident, and she seemed unable to control her emotions. The endless days had melted into weeks of disconnection and frustration.

Kellart ambled over and dropped his lanky body onto the ottoman next to her, then bent down to roll up the cuff of her linen slacks. She frowned at a pale stain on her knee, the result of yesterday's coffee mishap, and realized how rumpled her clothes looked. Had it been one day, or two, since she'd changed? Maybe he wouldn't notice.

The doctor examined her right leg, the skin criss-crossed with red scars from the reconstructive surgery. His skilled hands moved softly across the area he'd rebuilt three weeks before.

He gently pressed her shin while he watched her face. "Still hurt here?"

She winced. "Just a little, but it doesn't ache as much now...I just wish it worked."

His face brightened into a smile. "It will, soon–I think you're ready to start working with a physical therapist." He rose from the ottoman. "We'll have you out of that chair in no time."

She looked through the French doors to the pastures beyond, carefully avoiding the secluded corner and Paso's grave.

Defeat rang in her ears. "When can I ride again?"

The smile faded from Kellart's voice. "Ah, Beth, let's take it one thing at a time. I can't promise you anything this early." He hesitated, then plunged on. "You might never regain enough control and balance to ride safely again."

Numbed by the prognosis, Beth stared up at him, silently denying the words.

Sympathy defined his features. "I'm *really* sorry, but I just can't give you false hope. All I can offer is the possibility that the nerves will mend, given enough time."

Despair flooded into every recess as she tried to comprehend the prospect of a life without riding.

Kellart squeezed her shoulder gently. "I'll have my nurse schedule you for an appointment with a physical therapist in town. The sooner you start rebuilding your muscle tone and strength, the sooner we'll know."

"I'll do whatever it takes."

A few minutes later, she grappled with the wheelchair until she was able to maneuver it back to the French doors. She mulled over the surgeon's words. *He's not optimistic about my full recovery. I can tell by the way he acts.* Her throat tightened painfully, as the unacceptable vision settled itself into her future.

The telephone was Beth's only access to the barns and daily activities. Daily reports from the instructors and the construction supervisor confirmed that her life's work continued without her. A looming depression threatened to engulf her and quench the very spark of her soul. Losing her favorite horse–and the harsh probability that she'd never ride again–sent despair at her helplessness coursing through every thought. She could manage only the simplest personal tasks, and required other people to shoulder the burden of her existence. For someone who'd spent her life as a mover and shaker, the situation was intolerable, and her resilient nature was fading as surely as the peonies in her garden.

She hadn't been at home much during the past year. Her life had been immersed in the serious business of building Highover Gate, spending every waking hour in the office, planning and consulting, commanding and cajoling, trying to wear all the hats, and driven by her dream. Since the accident, she spent most days in her cozy study, furnished with comfortable chairs and an overstuffed sofa. Cherrywood bookcases covered the walls, forming ribbons of color and texture with hundreds of neatly lined volumes. A small Scottish-style gas fire, faced with Spanish tile and fronted by a fieldstone hearth, completed the homey feel of the room.

In the silence, she looked down at her useless right leg and drifted again into an abyss of dismal thoughts, scenarios that sent Highover Gate tumbling to the ground. In the past, after every plummet into the depths of discouragement, she'd managed to crawl back up to just within reach of her sanity. But, as the days dragged by, each melancholy episode became harder to manage, and the tenacious spark of her determination grew dimmer with the passage of time.

She heaved a sigh of resignation and maneuvered herself to a spot that provided a good view of the television. With the touch of a button, burnished cherrywood cabinet doors whispered aside, revealing a built-in home theatre system cleverly concealed in the wall. A flick of the remote, and the large dark screen leaped to life, permanently tuned to ESPN. Today, the station featured show jumping somewhere in Southern California.

A huge tabby cat launched himself onto her lap, his motor rumbling as she stroked his soft fur.

"And how is Mr. Felix today?"

The cat turned around several times, trying to find just the right spot before settling down for however long she might stay put. The cell phone chimed and she muted the sound on the television, then cringed at Tim Trent's familiar condescending tone.

"Hello, Beth. How is everything?"

"Just fine. What's up?"

"I'd like to stop by this afternoon, go over some things with you."

Oh, crap. Now what? She swallowed the urge to tell him she was busy.

"Sure. Anytime."

She slipped the phone back into her pocket and stared at the pantomime on the television screen. After months of repressed hostility during the investment discussions, and his constant nit picking, Tim's suddenly affable manner was unsettling. The skin on her neck crawled, jolting her from the timid thoughts. She could handle Tim Trent—always had. This time would be no different, but she needed to get her wits about her and stop feeling sorry for herself. She needed to be back in control.

She refocused her attention on the magnificent horses sailing over stone walls and elaborate gates. The camera panned to the crowd gathered in the brilliant California sunshine, then quickly zoomed in on a chestnut Hanoverian as it tumbled to the ground beyond a hog's back jump. The crowd gasped collectively, and Beth held her breath as the rider flew through the air and landed flat on his back, some ten feet from the horse. Someone helped the rider up, the horse struggled to its feet, and a groom led it away. Images of her own fall crowded into her thoughts, followed by a cold feeling oozing through her gut. She waved the remote, and the screen faded to black as the door chime echoed through the house.

The muffled voices of her housekeeper and a male visitor drifted closer. Brushing a strand of hair back over her ear, she glanced again at her clothes, wishing she'd taken the time to change. She shrugged and assumed what she hoped was a businesslike smile as her visitor stepped into the room.

Timothy Trent III. Old money, foundation family, ruthless business magnate—all packaged into a deceptively good-looking and quietly arrogant man. A condescending smile barely changed his smooth mask, and one eyebrow lifted just enough to send a tiny crease across his tan forehead.

A prickle of irritation crawled up her neck. She felt vulnerable with him towering over her.

"Good to see you, Tim. Have a seat."

He shook his head. "I can't stay long." He casually leaned a hip against the back of the sofa, then crossed his arms. "Beth, the board has some concerns."

Her gut clenched, her brain instantly on alert, but she kept her tone light. "And what might those be?"

"I'll be frank. The project is approaching the second phase–the big one–and we've heard nothing from you about who'll do the work. I–uh, the board members are uncomfortable with having only barn employees onsite as supervisors."

"Tim, I receive updates every day. I know exactly what's going on."

"That's fine, but we're talking hundreds of thousands of dollars here and, frankly, I don't think it's reasonable to have proxy management."

"Is the board questioning my ability?"

"No, *I* am. A board member should take over until you're capable again."

"What you mean is, *you* want to take over, right?"

Tim cocked his head, and the eyebrow drifted upward again. "I'm the most qualified to supervise."

A blast of anger sent adrenaline pumping through her system. "Let me tell you something, Timothy. You may be a big-time developer, but you don't know squat about managing a project. I can still think. I didn't damage my head, just my ability to move around freely–which is temporary.

She glowered up at him. " And since when does the board meet behind my back?"

His aristocratic features oozed disdain. "Since our six-million-dollar-investment went into limbo."

"Before you get too smug about taking over, you'd better read your contract again. *I* control this project. You and the board can meet until the grass turns purple, but unless you have clear proof that the project is in trouble, your threats are nothing but smoke."

He glanced at a gleaming gold watch peeking from beneath a

crisp white French cuff. "Don't be too sure."

With a curt nod, he turned and left the room.

She watched the perfectly tailored suit disappear into the hall, heard his leather heels tap across the parquet floor in the foyer. The heavy front door echoed its closure and, for a moment, she listened to her heartbeat thudding in her ears. She felt a little sick, then the adrenaline subsided, and her pulse began to slow. The incident jolted her into the reality of her situation. She had to let all the investors know she was fully in charge again. The barracudas she'd gathered to fund Highover Gate were circling and would like to have her for breakfast. Obviously, they didn't know her very well.

The housekeeper peeked into the study. "I'm ready to leave. Anything you need before I go?"

Beth's fingers fluttered a goodbye. "I'm fine, Jean, thanks. I'll see you tomorrow."

Beth couldn't imagine what she'd do without her housekeeper, especially under the current circumstances. Jean Kramer, a motherly woman in her late fifties, had looked after Highover House part-time for the past six years. She was married to a cranky alcoholic, and her ne'er-do-well, thirty-something son lived at home. Between the two, poor Jean was always knee-deep in laundry, cooking, and cleaning, but she always made light of the situation, saying that working for Beth was a "busman's holiday"–and the only thing keeping her going.

The cell phone rang, and Beth smiled with pleasure at the Massachusetts-coast accent burbling into her ear.

"Hey, Doll. Whatcha doin'?"

James Trent had been her closest friend since grade school.

"Trying to calm down after my shouting match with your brother."

"Uh-oh. I was going to stop by in awhile, but maybe it's not safe."

If anyone could cheer her up, it would be Jamie.

"That would be great–I need some human company."

He chuckled. "Right-O. See ya in a few."

Beth cringed inwardly at how aggressive her tone sounded. "Tell me what Timmy's up to."

Jamie's handsome face clouded. "And Good Afternoon to you, too."

"Sorry, I'm a little cranky today."

"I noticed. How's the leg coming along?"

She recognized the dodge, and steeled herself for an argument.

"Getting better. I start therapy on Thursday...Jamie, please tell me what Tim is doing behind my back."

"Jeez, Bethey, I'm just his brother, not his keeper. I don't know. Hell, I hardly ever see him."

She sighed. "Okay, I'll ask someone else."

Jamie picked up her hand, his gaze earnest, his tone soft.

"How about I drive you to your physical therapy appointment?"

She smiled sadly and nodded, immediately glad he was with her. She'd grown up with his adoration, mostly taking it for granted, but always pleased to have his loyal support. Sometimes, though, she felt guilty that her feelings for him weren't the same as his.

He squeezed her fingers. "I'll see what I can find out about Timmy's skullduggery."

Beth doodled nervously while she waited for Jake Biggs to answer the phone. He was the oldest member of the board, and had been in the banking business before his retirement. A long-time friend of her uncle, Jake's involvement in Highover Gate had evolved from his interest in horses, and Beth knew she could count on him for just about anything.

"Bethany! Good to hear your voice. How are you doing?"

"Pretty good. Jake, has the board decided I'm unfit to continue managing this project?"

"Hell, no! Why do you ask?"

Relief seeped into her muscles, and she closed her eyes, surprised again at how anxious the whole incident had made her. Minutes later, Jake's reassurances boomed through the phone.

"Ignore him. He's a hotshot, but we need his money."

Four

The following morning after breakfast, Beth went straight to her desk to get things back on track. Dismayed, but determined, she stared at the stack of papers she'd ignored for the past ten days, always telling herself she'd get to them right away. *What have I been doing?* She threw a quick glance toward the television, and the open space where her wheelchair fit perfectly. *Wasting time feeling sorry for myself, and look what it's almost cost me.*

Tim's smug expression drifted into her thoughts, and she snatched up a thick folder filled with construction bids for the second level of Phase II–the open-air show jumping stadium. Two local companies and one firm from Cincinnati had placed bids on the job. She glanced at the response date, only two days away. Tim was right–she'd waited until the last minute on this one. Then she frowned, feeling justified. After all, she'd just come home from the hospital two weeks ago. Anyone would understand that. *Anyone but Tim Trent, that is.*

Pushing away the personal turmoil, she opened the folder and scanned the paperwork, reviewing the board's comments and choices. She needed to act quickly for the winning bidder to start on time. She glanced at the calendar–even if she called them today, it would leave only one week until the scheduled groundbreaking. This was just the sort of slipup Tim hoped for.

She picked up the phone and dialed the first-choice Lexington company, her brain spinning a plan. She could jump-start the process by faxing a go-ahead, then mailing the acceptance letter the same day.

After a brief delay, the manager of the company came on the line.

"Miss Webb, I'm surely sorry, but another big job opened up and we hadn't heard from you, so we took it."

Her shoulders slumped. That left her with the board's second and third choices, Cincinnati Construction Company, or Barker Brothers, a small outfit in town. The Ohio firm had done extensive work on the Horse Park; the local Lexington company's bid was competitive, but they had no relative experience. Because of her own preoccupation with her personal life, her choices had dwindled to almost nothing. She picked up the phone again, praying that the Cincinnati company hadn't also accepted another job.

Crippled or not, I have to get back on top of this thing, or I'll be reading headlines about the failure of my dreams.

The week passed quickly and, by Thursday, Beth eagerly looked forward to a day out of the house, even if it was only for a therapy appointment. Her frame of mind had improved tremendously with the newspaper announcement that Cincinnati Construction Company would break ground for the jumping arena on the following Monday. She watched the scenery roll by, thinking about her close call with disaster. It had reinforced her lifelong belief that you only succeeded by your own efforts.

Jamie's voice intruded. "I see in the news that you're busy stirring up a hornet's nest."

She cocked her head. "What are you talking about?"

"Hiring an outside firm over a local? Not very good PR."

"Jamie, business decisions have to do with getting the right people, or equipment, or skill to do the job–not supporting the good-old-boy-network."

"Beth, sometimes your naiveté amazes me. You're not living in LA anymore. There's an unspoken loyalty factor in a small town. You ought to know that–you've lived here long enough."

"Not with six-million dollars in the pot. Which reminds me, did you find out–"

"Beth, I can't get involved. Pain-in-the-butt or not, Tim's my brother. Please don't ask me to spy on him."

Jamie's tone caught her off-guard, and warning signals raced through her head. She looked out the window, not knowing how to respond.

A minute later, they pulled up in front of the clinic. Jamie had barely closed the car door before Beth began urging her chair toward the ramp that rose to the entrance.

"Hey, let me push you."

He leaped forward and reached for the handles, but she shook her head.

"Jamie, I can do this. I'll never be able to manage by myself if everyone wants to push me all the time."

She struggled for a minute, finding the effort of moving the heavy chair up the small incline a bigger task than she'd anticipated.

Jamie whispered through her hair. "But, Hon, you won't need this thing forever, so why not take it easy and let us pamper you a little?"

His warm hands massaged her shoulders, tears burned her lids, and she blinked furiously. *The last thing I need right now is a red nose and puffy eyes.* Resigned, she allowed him to push the chair into the clinic.

While they waited, Jamie regaled her with the latest escapades of his current horse trainer, an aging Lothario with an unbelievable reputation. Jamie raised Standardbred harness horses on his breeding farm, situated about eight miles from Beth's place. As her old friend talked, her mind drifted into memories of the past.

Beth's aunt and uncle, with whom she'd grown up, had been good friends with Jamie's parents, years ago. When Jamie was ten, his family had moved from Massachusetts to Kentucky, and she'd become fast friends with him, their common love of horses the greatest bond. Older brother Tim, on the other hand, showed no interest in horses, in fact, thought they were stupid animals, and spent most of his adolescent years harassing her.

By their senior year, Jamie was totally smitten with her, and had made it clear he thought they would marry someday. Now, fifteen years later, they were still like brother and sister. And Tim was still badgering her.

"Miss Webb? Mr. Reed will see you now."

A woman in lavender scrubs stood by an open door. Jamie jumped up and deftly maneuvered the wheelchair toward the open door, making motorcycle noises as he steered around corners and into the hall. Beth rolled her eyes with embarrassment as they passed the surprised medical assistant.

Jim Reed stood up from his desk as she entered the office. He was a tall, slim man with a warm, friendly smile.

"Hello, Bethany, come on in." He turned to Jamie. "I usually have my first conference with the patient alone. Then, family members or friends can be involved after that. Would you mind waiting outside for a little while?"

His disarming smile took the edge from his words, and Jamie nodded, squeezing Beth's shoulder gently before he left the room.

For the next half-hour, she answered questions and talked about the accident. Her efforts to remain dry-eyed disintegrated when he asked her to describe the mishap in detail. Reliving her sudden somersault into the air—and the reminder that her favorite horse had died in the fall—were too much. She fought the tears, but lost.

When she regained her composure, Jim leaned forward and looked into her face, compassion spreading over his features.

"Beth, I can help you walk again—there's no question about that—but it will take some time. Dr. Kellart feels the damage *is* reversible. Exercise and retraining the muscles will be the keys to your recovery."

His distorted features danced in her pooled tears. She blinked and nodded, hearing the unspoken *"But...,"* waiting to hear the rest.

He continued. "That will be the easy part. What I'm seeing here is another, more complicating factor, one that could keep you from succeeding. The emotional blow of losing your horse has obviously taken a strong hold on your state of mind. Add the stress of your business venture, and the fear that you'll never ride again, and you have the formula for failure. Your depression will be the stumbling block you'll have to overcome to succeed with your therapy."

Her tears started again and, for the first time in her life, she felt incapable of helping herself. But, the battle would be hers, and hers alone. Did she have what it would take to win it? Her thoughts flashed back over the last ten years. She'd pursued and attained her dreams through sheer tenacity and hard work. *Is this any different? Can I do this on my own?*

The therapist's soft voice interrupted her sad thoughts.

"Beth, I'm going to refer you to a specialist over in Louisville. This guy is one of the best physical therapy and rehabilitation technicians in the industry. *And...*" He paused for effect. "His area of expertise is the psychology of equestrian injuries, and retraining. If anyone can put you back into the saddle, it will be him."

Five

Jamie grinned like a kid skipping school. "Wow! A day in the big city every week. We'll have a blast!"

Beth smiled and shook her head. "Always the party-guy. Don't get your hopes up–I have no idea how I'll feel at the end of a session. You might have to carry me home on a stretcher."

The blocky SUV nosed through the midday traffic, then headed out the Paris Turnpike toward the green hills to the east. Beth sighed, soaking up the beauty of the landscape–the stage on which the biggest part of her life had been played.

After her parents had been killed in a private plane crash when she was very young, her aunt and uncle had welcomed her into their home and hearts. She'd become the child they'd never been able to have. Uncle Earl had worked as the barns manager for a huge Thoroughbred farm, and Aunt Ida had taught fourth grade at a local elementary school. Together, they'd provided a wonderful warm and loving home for Beth, a priceless gift that even her inherited fortune couldn't buy for her.

Jamie's teasing tone interrupted her thoughts. "Lost in the back pasture?"

She blinked. The car was stopped in her own driveway. She gazed up at the large, elegant house she inhabited with the housekeeper and Felix. The place had never seemed lonely before, but since the accident, she'd rattled around in two rooms, solitude her constant companion. *If I don't do something about this situation, I'll be a pain-in-the-butt for the rest of my life.*

As if he could read her thoughts, Jamie reached over and picked up her hand, sincerity smoothing his features.

"Bethey, listen to me. I know you like your privacy, but why don't you let me move in for a while so I can look after you? You won't have to be alone, and I'd be right here if you needed anything."

Oh, God, here we go again. Every so often, Jamie tried to convince her that being together in some personal way would be a good thing. She always rejected the idea, a thought lingering around the fringes of her mind that someday there *might* be a special someone to share her life, if she ever had a chance to draw a breath. But so far, her drive to build a stellar career–then her Highover Gate dream–had eclipsed her personal life. Success, not people, had energized her. The years had passed, and that special person hadn't materialized. Or if he had, she hadn't recognized him. Life had been taken up with a routine she loved and, deep in her heart, wasn't sure she'd ever want to share, or worse–give up.

She smiled fondly at Jamie, not wanting to hurt his feelings. "Let's wait awhile and see what this fancy new therapist has to say. You know I love you and appreciate your concern, but I'm not quite ready to take such a big step."

His face crinkled into a smile at the faint possibility that she might actually let him into her life.

She leaned over and brushed her lips lightly against his cheek. "Thank you for being here for me."

His face glowed with unabashed love, and her heart softened. *I could certainly do worse than Jamie Trent.*

Early Monday morning, Beth opened the front door for the site boss from Cincinnati Construction Company. He whipped his cap off and bobbed his head as he stepped across the threshold.

"Miss Webb, I'm Dan Cornell."

She shook his hand and gestured toward the door. "We can talk in the dining room."

Cornell spread the blueprints over the mahogany table, started asking questions, and Beth concentrated on the project plans. Thirty minutes later, she sat back in her chair, satisfied that she'd made the right choice.

"Dan, I'll give you my cell phone number. If you have *any* problems or questions, please call me. I'm hoping to be back in the barn office in a week or two, but until then, I'll be supervising from here."

He nodded and entered the information into a tiny pocket organizer. When he looked up again, she saw a question in his eyes.

"Is there something else, Mr. Cornell?"

"Well, uh...Mr. Trent said–"

Her blood sizzled, and she tried to keep her tone civil. "You are to report only to *me*. Is that understood?"

"Yes, ma'am. Completely."

When he'd gone, she rolled out to the terrace, her thoughts sharp with frustration. Regardless of what she might have to do, she would not allow Tim to insinuate himself into a position of power. She'd have to be aggressive about staying in touch with Cornell. The low growl of earth-moving equipment drifted on the soft morning air, further kindling her determination. *I should be down there where I can keep track of what's going on.*

The inside phone rang, and she spun the chair around to return to the study, just as Jean appeared in the doorway.

"A Mister Barker for you."

Beth winced at the rough snarl that grated through the phone.

"Can you give me one good reason why you hired an Ohio company over a hometown business?"

"Excuse me, Mr. Barker, is it?"

"Yeah. Barker Brothers Construction."

She thought for a minute, figuring how best to respond to his hostility. She didn't really owe him an explanation, but she wanted to diffuse the uncomfortable situation.

"I understand your disappointment at losing the bid, but we have to consider all aspects of each company, and choose the one with the broadest capabilities. I–"

"We've been in business for thirty years, and can do anything Cincinnati can do. And cheaper. I think you just wanted the prestige of a big-time name, that's what I think."

Recognizing the futility of trying to argue, she continued her explanation anyway.

"Mr. Barker, our decisions were well thought-out. Your firm has no prior experience with equestrian facilities, and that was the deciding factor. There *are* some other phases of the project that you're welcome to bid on."

"Nah, I'm not wasting any more time on you blue-blooded snobs!"

Beth winced as he slammed the phone down.

On Thursday, Beth half-listened as Jamie drove toward Louisville, rambling on about all manner of things. One of his least appealing traits was the need to keep a conversation going at all times, and she finally tuned him out. She'd always used the private silence of a drive to review current issues, and so much was happening now that her thoughts jumped from one facet to another, trying to gather the pieces into something manageable.

Jamie's voice penetrated her musings. "I suppose this guy will want me to wait outside, too?"

A mock scowl distorted his face, and she laughed. "I suppose, especially since you're just the chauffeur."

The scowl turned into a true frown, and she immediately regretted the careless comment.

"Sorry, just teasing. You know what I mean. These medical types don't want any interference from anyone."

Jamie's chipper smile returned. "Yeah, they all think they're God."

An involuntary shiver ran through her as they pulled up in front of a large, turn-of-the-century home that had been converted into a clinic. *You'd better hope this one is, if you want to ride again.*

Inside, she handed the referral card to the receptionist, who passed a clipboard and pen over the counter.

The woman's tone was brisk. "Fill out these forms, both sides, then take a seat. We'll call you."

Beth stared in disbelief. *Take a seat? Is she kidding?*

A moment later, a young man in a green lab coat stepped into the waiting room.

"Beth'ny Webb?"

Jamie rose from his chair, but Beth shook her head.

"I can manage. You wait here. Read something interesting and give me a full report."

She winked to dull the sting of her words, but Jamie was like the proverbial duck—the rebuff rolled right off his back. As they moved down a narrow hall, the assistant made small talk about the unseasonable bad weather, his Kentucky accent so thick with rural twang that she had to listen closely to understand him. At the end of the corridor, he motioned her into a large office.

"SeeBee'll be right with ya." He smiled and closed the door behind him.

She looked around at the stark, ugly office furniture that looked so out of place in the once-beautiful room. The high ceiling had been fitted with fluorescent fixtures that robbed all warmth from the soft rose-colored walls and deep mahogany woodwork. Computers and books cluttered the desktop, and framed diplomas and certificates formed a mosaic on two walls. She gazed at the gray institutional carpeting, sure that beautiful hardwood floors lay beneath it. *Such a waste.*

A glance at her watch sent a sigh through her chest. She'd been sitting there for at least ten minutes, and she was not very good about waiting. She spied several framed photographs sitting on a bookshelf behind the desk. They looked like horse-show photos, but she was too far away to see any detail. *Probably pictures of patients.* The click of an opening door interrupted her speculation, and a strong voice preceded its owner.

"Hi. Sorry to keep you waiting. I—"

The air stilled, and astonishment pressed her deep into the chair, as Brett Hall's handsome face lit up with a surprised and charming smile.

Six

S ilence thickened the air further as Beth's new therapist moved into the room and offered his hand. "Hel-*lo*, again."

Warmth moved up her neck, and her voice cracked. "Hello."

A softer expression replaced his sassy smile. "Let me re-introduce myself. I'm Connor Hall."

She tilted her head. "I thought your name was Brett."

The smooth tanned cheeks creased with a smile again, and he looked a little embarrassed.

"That's my middle name. I only use it when I'm competing." He shrugged his shoulders. "It helps keep my personal activities separate from my professional life—which is *very* important."

She watched his mouth as he talked, fascinated by the way his lips moved with each word. He turned his attention to her chart, while she continued her assessment of his finely chiseled features, reminiscent of something she'd seen in a museum once, possibly in the Greek section.

He looked up at her again, his eyes softening with sympathy.

"I read about your accident in the paper. It blew me away, knowing I'd been right there, talking to you before it happened...I understand you lost your horse. I am *so* sorry."

Her throat tightened at the sharp reminder, and her words came out in a hoarse whisper. "Thank you."

As Connor guided her through some mental exercises to help her relax, his soft, reassuring voice caressed her mind. Ambition had driven every day of her life, and since the accident, she'd spent her days in pain, on medication, or completely disconnected. Long ago, she'd forgotten what it felt like to relax. After fifteen minutes with Connor, Beth felt as though she could float up out of the chair and walk away–an amazing feeling.

He came around the desk and motioned toward the door. "Let's go to the weight room and see what kind of muscle tone you have."

As soon as she saw the intimidating contraptions that lined the walls of the exercise room, her light euphoria skidded to a halt. The room looked more like a torture chamber. Connor pushed her wheelchair back into a stall-like contraption with weights and pulleys on each side.

Kneeling down, he gently grasped her right ankle and removed her foot from the footrest. A delightful tingle ran across her bare skin at his touch. As he flexed her foot up and down, she watched the top of his head. His wavy dark blonde hair shifted slightly with his movements, and a sudden urge came over her to reach out and touch it. The impulse startled her, and she closed her eyes, amazed at her unusual thoughts.

Connor's hands slid up under the hem of her slacks and massaged her calf muscles. Another ripple of pleasure spread through her, and she let out a little gasp.

His head snapped up, his face sharp with concern. "Did I hurt you?"

"No, I'm just ticklish."

Embarrassed, she looked away from his questioning gaze. He returned to his work with her legs, and she allowed herself to slip back into the delicious state she'd enjoyed, moments before. His gentle touch awakened new sensations and thoughts that both delighted and frightened her.

After repeating the massage on her other leg, Connor nodded. "Looks as though your muscles still have pretty good tone. They loosened up quickly with stimulation."

That's not all you stimulated. "What's next?"

"We'll see what you can do on your own."

He pushed the wheelchair over to a raised platform about the size of a twin bed. Instructing her to hold on to his shoulder, he slipped his arms around her waist and under her knees. In one swift movement, he swung her up onto the thickly padded table. The sensation of his arms around her snatched at her breath, and she closed her eyes briefly as he carefully settled her on the mat.

After adjusting the pillow beneath her head, he straightened up and smiled. "Comfortable?"

She nodded, watching his muscular arms ripple as he propped a barrel-shaped pillow under her left knee, his movements deft and confident. *He certainly seems to know what he's doing. That's encouraging.* She thought about the exciting sensations she'd just experienced at his touch, and she smiled to herself. *In fact, I might really enjoy this.*

Connor stepped back from the platform. "Now, I want you to slowly lift your lower leg as far as you can, then slowly lower it."

She managed to lift the leg almost straight, but a second later, it turned to lead, thudding onto the table, the muscles quivering with the exertion. She looked at Connor, but could read nothing into his expression as he removed the pillow and placed it beneath her right knee.

He stepped back and nodded. "Okay, let's try the bad leg."

She struggled to lift the leg, but nothing happened.

"Try again."

The second attempt was equally futile. *Oh, God, I can't do this.* She felt tears pooling in the corners of her eyes. One sneaked down her temple and into her hair, and she squeezed her eyes tightly, trying to stop the flow.

Connor's voice drifted through her despair. "That's good, you're doing great. Try one more time."

She strained, but the truant muscles in her damaged leg wouldn't budge. The tears came faster, then she felt soft fingers gently brushing them away. Mere inches from hers, Connor's eyes were filled with compassion as he sought to comfort her, and, for one instant, she wanted to feel his arms around her again.

Connor watched Beth maneuver the wheelchair awkwardly down the hall. His hands felt clammy, and his pulse ticked insistently, just below his ear. The brief intimate moment in the exercise room had really thrown him. He could still feel the sensation of her silky hair and the softness of her cheeks. How could he be so unlucky? Bethany Webb was an intriguing woman, and she'd been on his mind more than once during the past month. He shook his head in disgust. Now, she was his patient. His mental tirade stopped. As Beth entered the waiting room, a good-looking man jumped up from the chair, his expression an open acknowledgment that he adored her.

Well, so much for that. Surprised by his own disappointment, Connor returned to the office to write up the first session with his new patient.

Beth's face felt puffy and uncomfortably warm as she wheeled into the waiting room.

Jamie's smile dissolved into concern. "Are you okay? What's wrong?"

She smiled grimly. "I've just spent the most discouraging hour of my life."

"What do you mean?" He propelled the chair toward the entrance, quizzing her further. "Didn't you do any exercises or anything?"

The memory of Connor's face, just a breath away, appeared in her head. Jamie repeated his question, and she closed her eyes. *Why can't he just shut up for a minute?* She suppressed an irritated sigh.

"Jamie, I haven't walked in over a month, I have *no* muscle tone or strength, and my legs won't do anything. How enthusiastic should I be?"

The silence behind her confirmed that the sharp retort had wounded him. Immediately contrite, she turned a little so she could see his stricken face.

"Jamie, I'm sorry. I'm just...I'm frustrated and..."

She stopped. That was about it–there wasn't much else she could say.

He caressed her shoulder affectionately. "It's all right, Hon. I think I understand. But, look at it this way. You've only just started down the road to your recovery. You can't expect miracles the first time out."

He was right–it would take time and patience, no different than building a group of investors. The ridiculous comparison sent a ripple of mirth through her head.

Jamie insisted on having lunch before they returned to Lexington, and an hour later, she felt better. Jamie was, indeed, very good for her spirits, and she considered his offer to stay with her. Lately, she'd had too much solitary time on her hands. *It might not be a bad idea, at least for a while. I'll think about it tonight.*

As they drove through town, they passed a huge billboard, advertising Barker Brothers Construction. A ruddy-faced, chunky man with small dark eyes stared out at passersby, his overly enthusiastic smile making him appear ready to pounce.

Beth glanced over at Jamie, noting his smirk. "Okay, you were right about the hornet's nest, but he's such small potatoes, I'm not worried."

"Just be careful about burning bridges, my dear."

Beth's answering machine announced four calls, and she hit the play button. The insurance company, again. Aunt Ida, asking about brunch on Sunday. Dan Cornell with a brief progress report.

The fourth message caught her attention instantly. *"Hi, Connor Hall here. I forgot to give you the home exercises to do between clinic sessions. I'll be in Lexington tomorrow. I'll just drop it off, if that's okay with you. Give me a call, or leave a message with my service. Thanks."*

The prospect of seeing him again so soon sent a quick flush of pleasure through her thoughts, followed by reality. *This won't work. My relationship with him is strictly professional and has to stay that way.* But, serious doubts aside, she was excited to see him again.

Her thoughts turned to Jamie. Was it fair to let him think something might finally come of their relationship? She told herself that he knew how she felt and, in the long run, he was practical about most things. On the self-serving side, whom else did she have to rely upon? Her aunt and uncle were too old to care for an invalid. Her chest froze in mid-breath at the word. *I'm not going to be in this wheelchair forever. I couldn't bear it.* The thought of forever prodded her over the edge of her indecision and, closing her eyes and taking a deep breath, she picked up the phone.

"Hi, Jamie. Long time no see."

She suddenly felt awkward, unsure of how to start the conversation, but his cheerful voice on the other end of the line removed her hesitation and she dived in.

"Listen, I've been thinking about your offer to stay here for a while. It's probably a good idea, at least until I get back on my feet, so to speak."

He was thrilled beyond words–a rare happening. He quickly recovered and began babbling, promising to start packing right away.

"Whoa! I need to have Mrs. Kramer prepare the guest cottage and plan some meals. Why don't we aim for Sunday?"

She felt a little guilty about stretching the truth. In reality, she wanted just a few more days to herself.

Jamie's enthusiasm sparkled through the phone, making her wonder, again, if she was making a mistake. She did *not* want to hurt him.

Seven

Connor double-checked the trailer hitch and yanked hard on the safety chain, then scanned the sky. Faint pink glowed on the eastern horizon, and he glanced at his watch. He'd be in Lexington by six-thirty–plenty of time to set up, exercise his horse, and prepare his own head for the competition.

As he started the truck, he glanced down at the sheet of paper on the passenger seat and shook his head.

"Pretty lame excuse, Bud. You could have just mailed it to her."

The truck inched away from the barn, and he looked in the rear-view mirror to check the trailer one more time, then his thoughts moved to the long day ahead.

Beth jockeyed the chair up to the patio table where Jean had set the breakfast tray.

"Mmm. Smells delicious...Thank you."

The housekeeper beamed. "Do you need anything else?"

"Yes, the guest cottage needs to be ready for company by Monday. Jamie is coming to stay until I can take care of myself."

The older woman's worn features softened. "Oh, Miss Webb, I'm so glad! I've worried about you here all by yerself, no one to help if you fall or somethin'. I'll do it right away."

Beth smiled as Jean bustled off down the hall. *What a gem. Too bad her life will always be taking care of other people. I wonder if she ever knew any happiness when she was young.* The thought reminded Beth of her own youth, passing quickly. The fast-track career, followed by the excitement of her steady advance toward her ambitious dreams, hadn't afforded any time to worry about a solitary life. Now, a dull pain lodged in her chest at the prospect of being alone forever.

Felix appeared, pushing his head softly against her leg.

"I know, Baby-Cat. I'm not really alone."

She smiled at her furry companion, then brushed aside her unsettling thoughts and checked the starting time for the events at the Horse Park. There weren't many television programs that could hold her interest, but she thoroughly enjoyed the professional equestrian events. A moment later, her thoughts turned to Connor, and the memory of his athletic body and sexy charm dominated her attention. She'd left a message with his answering service, confirming she'd be home, but had no idea what time he might arrive.

"Felix, you'll have to move. I think I'd better freshen up, in case he shows up early."

Brushing her chin-length honey-blonde hair, she critiqued her image in the mirror. An oval face with fine features and wide-set hazel eyes held traces of her emotional state, and pale gray circles marred the delicate peach-toned skin beneath her eyes. Tiny smile parentheses appeared at the corners of her mouth. She wouldn't win any beauty contests, but she still looked pretty good, considering the drain of the past six weeks.

A small flutter moved through her chest. *Why am I so nervous? He's only coming to drop off the exercises.*

Hal's Scottish brogue rolled through the phone, feeding Beth's homesickness for the barn.

"Mornin' Lass. How are ye t'day?"

"I'm fine, a little tired from my therapy session."

A quick replay of her brief excursion in Connor's arms flashed through her head, then she pushed away the distraction and focused her attention on business.

"How's the dressage arena coming along?"

"Excellent. The roof's almost finished, an' the boys are starting to frame the stalls in the barn. Long as the weather keeps, they'll be finished on schedule."

She thought ahead to the future when Highover Gate could host competitions sanctioned by the United Stated Dressage Federation. She had no doubt that the Olympic size arena and attached stabling area would be very appealing to the organization.

Hal's voice intruded on her daydream.

"The jump arena is leveled, an' the site boss tells me they plan to start buildin' the grandstand next week. They can't do anything more on the arena until the ground settles a bit. This crazy weather, though...I canna remember such a wet spring."

Beth nibbled the inside of her lip. The constant rain had thrown her meticulous plans and schedule out of whack, but it would have to stop at some point. She hoped.

"What about the stone wall?"

"The mason came 'round this mornin'. The quarry will deliver the fieldstone this afternoon."

She fairly shivered with delight. "God, Hal, I'm so excited I can't stand it! I wish I could be down there with you. I need to get back into the fray."

"In good time, Lassie. You just concentrate on gettin' well... I'll handle the rest."

She struggled with the overwhelming urge to cry, something she'd never done, and now did regularly since her accident. Hal's excited tone quelled the threat.

"Whoops! I almost forgot to tell ye the great news–Sammy Ferra wants to make Highover Gate his home base."

Minutes later, she stared with unseeing eyes at the dressage riders on the screen, while her busy brain mulled over Hal's news. Attracting high-profile riders like Sammy Ferra proved that Highover Gate was gaining visibility and credibility.

Beth had been glued to the television for over two hours and felt a little groggy. A discreet cough brought her back, and she glanced away from the scores that had just appeared on the screen.

Jean stood in the doorway. "I'm done in the cottage. Do you want to see it?"

"Yes, we can do that after I eat lunch. Thanks."

She turned back to the TV. The scores had disappeared, and a reporter was interviewing one of the riders while the dressage session broke for lunch. She muted the sound and moved to the French doors. She gazed at the perfect day for riding, not a cloud in the bright blue sky, then her last wet moments on Paso sprang into her thoughts, and she struggled with the pain in her heart.

Beth's frustration braided through her chest as she struggled to guide the wheelchair over the rough cobbled path to the guest cottage.

Jean's tone had a motherly quality. "Can I help?"

Beth recognized that her fierce pride could be a detriment sometimes, causing her to resist help, even when she couldn't do something by herself. Connor had counseled her that she'd never recover if she tried to be too independent. She tried to relax and accept the situation, at least for the time being.

"Yes, please."

The small cottage was spotless, and Jean had even placed a vase of fresh lilacs on the dresser. Their heady perfume filled the room with spring, and Beth's heart curled with longing for what she was missing.

An hour later, she sat in front of the television again. Felix appeared from wherever he'd been sleeping and muscled his way onto her lap. As she watched the dressage riders skillfully guide their mounts through the test pattern, she grew drowsy. After falling asleep twice, she flicked off the television and glided down the hall. Felix bounded ahead, tail high, anticipating a cozy nap with his mistress.

Mrs. Kramer had left for the day by the time Connor arrived. Beth opened the door, smiling shyly. He stood there for a moment, gazing at her with open admiration, and she flushed with pleasure. He stepped through the door and, in one stride, stood beside her wheelchair. He pulled her up into his arms and held her close. She inhaled deeply, delighting in the sensations spreading through her body. He nestled his face in her hair and whispered her name. She lifted her lips to his, and closed her eyes as his mouth covered hers.

Beth sat straight up on the bed, her heart thudding against her ribs. Blinking away her confusion, she looked at the bedside clock.

Five o'clock–she'd been asleep for over two hours. Her pulse raced and her neck felt damp. *What a dream!* Shaking off the last vestiges of sleep, she sighed and eased into the wheelchair. At the dressing table, she stopped to comb her hair. The flush across her cheeks gave her face a look of fulfillment, as though she'd just been lost in the throes of passionate lovemaking. Still warm and tingling from her dreamy adventures, she slipped back into the imagery of the fantasy.

An instant later, an alarming thought interrupted her whimsy. What if he'd come by while she was sleeping? Disappointment flooded over her like a rainsquall, leaving her more disturbed than she'd felt in days. When she returned to the study, the dressage events had finished for the day, and a golf tournament was in the first round of play. Disgusted, she tossed the remote onto the couch, then pushed herself out to the terrace to sulk. In moments, the rolling hills and her beautiful garden had their usual calming effect, and she relaxed a little.

Jean appeared in the doorway. "Miss Webb, I'm leavin' now. Yer supper's in the warmin' oven and there's fresh biscuits on the counter. You need anything else?"

"No, I don't think so...Did anyone come by while I was resting?"

The housekeeper shook her head. "Nope. Nary a soul."

Irritation followed the brief feeling of relief. Where was he? It was getting rather late to be dropping in.

Connor whistled appreciatively as he drove up the long, curving driveway in front of Beth's large plantation-style house. He glanced at his watch and frowned. *Five-thirty. I hope it isn't too late to come calling.* Cleaning up after the event had taken more time than he'd planned, and traffic in town had been heavy. Checking his reflection in the rearview mirror, he smoothed down his still-damp hair, then jumped out of the truck. He'd almost reached the door when he realized he didn't have the exercise instructions. Feeling like a dope, he trotted back to the truck, then back to the house.

Exhaling sharply, he pushed the brass doorbell button and waited. His anxiety disappeared with Beth's lovely smile.

"Sorry I'm so late. The traffic was crazy leaving the Horse Park."

"Oh, were you there to watch the Champagne Run?"

Caught off-guard, he stammered. "Uh, no...I was *in* it."

She looked totally surprised. It obviously hadn't occurred to her that he might be riding in the event. But then, why would he expect her to be thinking about *him*?

They still hovered in the doorway and a second later, Beth backed her chair out of the way.

"Please, come in and tell me everything. I slept through most of it."

More disappointment crept into his head. Flustered, he looked at the now-crumpled sheet of paper in his hand, then grinned as he offered it to her.

"Here, sorry it's such a mess."

Her head dipped as she examined the sketches and instructions on the page, and vivid memories assaulted him. The silkiness of her hair as he'd brushed away her tears of frustration during that first session. How tantalizing her firm body had felt in his arms as he'd lifted her onto the exercise table. Images he'd been trying to block out.

Suddenly, he saw her amused expression and felt self-conscious. "Uh, if you have any questions, you can just call me."

Oh for Pete's sake, stop acting like a smitten schoolboy!

She grinned, laid the paper on her lap, then turned her chair around. "Let's go into the study."

Dropping onto the soft couch, Connor looked around the room. There was clearly more to the woman than met the eye. He glanced at her, unable to picture her as a wheeling-dealing financial wizard, but Highover Gate was proof of her expertise.

Beth's soft voice interrupted his musings.

"Would you like something to drink? Beer? Scotch? Lemonade?"

"Beer sounds great. Will you join me?"

"I haven't had any alcohol because of my medication, but maybe I could cheat, just this once."

She started to turn the chair around, and Connor leaped up.

"I can get it. You don't have to–"

A serious frown tightened her fine features. "I have to do things myself when no one's here, why not now?"

Thoroughly embarrassed, he returned to the sofa and watched her move into the hall, her self-sufficiency obvious from the set of her shoulders. His gaze moved around the room again, examining the contents more closely. Beth's patient information card indicated she was single, but he knew nothing else about her personal life. *No evidence of a man staying here on a regular basis. I wonder just where that guy I saw in the waiting room fits in.*

The thoughts hit him hard and he exhaled sharply. The visit wasn't a good idea—he had no business being there. How could he remain objective and professional as her therapist, if he had personal thoughts about her? *I need to leave before the situation goes any further.*

A large cat stalked into the room, giving Connor a wide berth.

"Well, hello, kitty." He leaned forward to pet the cat, but the wiley feline deftly sidestepped the outstretched hand, giving Connor a disdainful look. *God, even the damned cat knows I shouldn't be here!*

Beth returned, balancing a small tray with two longneck bottles of lager and two frosty mugs. Her face was flushed with the effort, and Connor knew he couldn't insult her by leaving immediately. At least, that's what he told himself.

He chuckled. "Hey, how did you know Australian beer is my favorite?"

"Haven't you seen the commercials? How could I go wrong?"

He met her gaze as he lifted the froth-topped mug into the air. "Here's to the future."

Eight

B eth struggled to keep her churning thoughts under control as Connor lounged back on the couch and made himself comfortable. Seeing him against the backdrop of her home was both intriguing and unsettling.

He took a long swig of beer, then sighed and closed his eyes. "Ahhh, what a treat. I really needed this...today was pretty grueling."

She leaned forward, eager to hear about the event. "So, tell me, how'd you do?"

"Well...I placed second." A sly look sneaked across his face as he drew out the suspense. "Behind Stephen Wegner."

"That's fantastic! He's a formidable opponent."

Pride danced across Connor's features, then he leaned forward and scrunched up his face like an old wiseman, his voice rasping across his words.

"Well, Dearie, his days are numbered. I'll not rest until I've beaten him."

She burst into laughter at his comical approach to an ambitious dream. Stephen Wegner held all the national titles in eventing. Unseating him would require an outstanding horse, an incredible rider, and unswerving dedication. She tilted her head and gazed at Connor through narrowed eyes. *And you might just be the person to do it.*

He suddenly looked embarrassed, quickly finished his beer, and stood up.

"I need to leave. I have to be at the park very early tomorrow for the cross-country session."

While she watched him shrug into his windbreaker, it finally came to her that he could have mailed the exercise instructions, but he'd used them as an excuse to visit her. Seeing the relationship in a different light, her earlier disquiet returned.

He started for the door, then turned back. "Hey, thanks for the beer. I'll see you at the office next week, right?"

"Right. Good luck tomorrow."

"Thanks. I'm gonna need it."

When he'd gone, Beth sat in the silence of the study that, only moments before, had rung with laughter. She felt hollow, as though she hadn't really known the meaning of being alone. She gazed out the windows at the gathering dusk. *I'm glad Jamie is going to be around.*

The drive back to the motel gave Connor time to do some serious thinking about his predicament, and his thoughts played on fast-forward. Something about Beth Webb made him feel important and protective. Not just her disability—something else he couldn't pin down.

His thoughts rewound to his childhood. Both his widowed mother and his older sister had been tough, proud women who'd never considered accepting help from anyone. In the coal shanties of southern Kentucky, it was do for yourself or fail, and Connor's youth had been overshadowed by his mother's domineering personality. So far, as an adult, he'd failed miserably to provide the strong, nurturing persona that most women wanted, and his bulldog determination to rise above his poor beginnings had eliminated any desire for involvements that might jeopardize his goals. Beth Webb could definitely be a problem.

Beth rose late the next morning, and settled in for a day in front of the tube. Felix raced across the room and bounded up to the back of the couch, then launched himself into the air, landing with a thud and disappearing down the hall. She laughed out loud, watching the antics of the crazy cat. Within seconds, he was back and eagerly chasing an imaginary mouse around the edges of the bookcase.

"A little too much catnip this morning, Mr. Felix?"

The tabby stopped in mid-stalk and gave her a reproachful look for scaring off his prey, then sat down to wash his face. The feline entertainment apparently finished, Beth turned her attention to the television. The endurance event was about to move on to the cross-country portion, and she was eager to see Connor in action. The rider ratings came up on the screen, with Connor ranked fourth in a first-round field of fifteen.

She thought about the previous night and her pulse quickened. For a short time, she'd been able to distance herself from her wheelchair. She'd thoroughly enjoyed his company—an exciting new friend, instead of the professional who would help her walk again. *I have to believe in him, trust that he has the skills to help me.* She remembered the feelings that had accosted her on that first office visit, and again the night before. *No, I have to stay focused on my recovery. Nothing else.*

On the screen, Connor appeared in the vet box, and her good intentions flew out the window. She leaned forward, watching closely as the officials checked his horse's vital signs.

Ten minutes later, Connor's horse moved smoothly and evenly, approaching each obstacle with a measured gait and seamless transitions, sailing effortlessly over the first three. Beth held her breath as horse and rider galloped toward a large rock formation flanked by a water hazard.

"Easy...*easy!*"

His red jacket formed a blur as he guided Rex over the jump. The horse landed hard, obviously not completely prepared. Beth winced, then exhaled softly, watching the pair finish the course. Something didn't seem quite right about the rest of the ride, but she couldn't put her finger on it. The ratings appeared on the screen again, and Connor's score included one fault for hitting the water. *That must be why Rex landed so hard. He was a little off balance.* Still, Connor's rank moved from fourth to third. *He must feel good about that.*

Sunday dawned bright and glorious, and Beth looked forward to brunch with her Aunt Ida and Uncle Earl. As soon as Ida stepped through the door, she started her mother-hen act.

"You're so pale from being cooped up, you could pass for a ghost." She clucked her tongue, glancing around the large foyer. "Bethany, I hate thinking about you all alone in this huge house. You must be terribly lonely, now that you can't follow your usual routine."

Uncle Earl intervened. "Now, Ida. Leave her be–she's a grown woman. She has lots of friends. If she wants company, I'm sure she can have it."

Beth smiled indulgently. "Auntie, I'm fine, really I am. Mrs. Kramer takes good care of me during the day, and Jamie is moving into the guest cottage this week."

"Hmmm. Are you two finally planning to get together, then?"

"Ida!" Earl's tone meant business. "Leave her alone and let's get going. Our reservations are for ten-thirty."

Though her aunt's sincere meddling would have irritated most young women, it didn't bother Beth. Aunt Ida and Uncle Earl were her people–the only family she'd ever known–and she adored them. No matter what she'd done or wanted, their love and support through the years had been firm and constant.

From the back seat, Beth studied her aunt's silvery gray hair, and a surge of love threatened to explode her heart. She caught her uncle's eye in the rearview mirror, and he winked. They'd always enjoyed a quiet bond, an understanding that helped them weather Ida's exuberant and sometimes overbearing personality.

The restaurant at Gratz Park Inn in Lexington had been the family's traditional Sunday brunch spot since Beth could remember. Elegant and quiet, it was the perfect setting for a leisurely meal. As they worked their way toward a table at the back of the room, several long-time Thoroughbred owners greeted Earl.

Beth gazed fondly at the first "man in her life." During his younger years, he'd been wooed by the best, but had remained staunchly loyal to the farm that had given him his first chance at a career in professional barn management. Despite many generous financial offers, he'd stayed at Fenwick Farms until his retirement a few years previously.

Her heart filled again with thanksgiving that her life had been blessed with these wonderful people. Suddenly, her right leg started to quiver and jerk, as though it were attached to a puppeteer's string. She pressed down on her thigh, willing the strange spasms to stop. In a few moments, the leg felt normal again and she made a mental note to mention the episode at her appointment on Thursday, in case it was important.

Thoughts of Connor brought a warm flush to her cheeks and she smiled, caught up in anticipation of seeing him again.

"And just who is *that* secret smile for?"

Her aunt leaned close, inquisitive eyes searching for an answer.

"Oh, I...uh." She stopped, then laughed nervously. What could she say? She certainly couldn't tell them she was daydreaming about her physical therapist.

Salvation came with Hal's familiar voice. "Lassie! Yer lookin' great this mornin'!"

Without thinking, she rose and started to step forward to hug the man who'd shepherded her around the cliffs and through the valleys of riding. Her leg began to jerk violently and she sank back into her chair, her heart thumping against her ribs.

Her aunt's voice shrilled. "Bethany! Don't do that! You'll fall. My goodness, what's the matter with you?"

"I have no idea. I guess I forgot I can't walk."

What was meant as a joke came off poorly, if the sober faces around the table were any indication.

Hal settled into the chair beside her and reached for her hand. "It'll come, Lass. It'll come."

While the family enjoyed the restaurant's famous King Crab Cakes and Eggs Royale, washed down with strong coffee, the conversation turned, as always, to horses. Beth listened to the spirited banter and smiled. *Once in love with horses, always in love with horses...I guess I ought to know.*

Though she'd had little time to ride during her stellar career in Los Angeles, dreams of owning her own training facility had germinated in her subconscious, blossoming into ambitious plans to design the best show site in the country. Once she'd made the decision to go for it, she'd sunk hundreds-of-thousands of dollars into the purchase and development of the old Winston estate on the Paris Turnpike.

When the venture capital group had finally materialized, her life had then been consumed by consultations with the top course designers in the industry and discussions with architects, lawyers, and accountants. She'd invested her entire future into Highover Gate so she could immerse herself in what she loved best–riding. In one wet, terrifying instant, that future had been put into jeopardy.

"Honey, what is it?"

Her uncle looked concerned.

"Oh, nothing."

Ida jumped in. "Oh, yes, there is something. I know that look. What is it?"

Beth glanced apologetically at Hal. "I was just thinking what my life would be like if I can't ride again."

He reached over and touched her hand.

"Lass, you have to believe that you *can* ride again. If yer already thinkin' about what you'll do instead, well then, it's as good as finished."

She saw the disappointment in his kind eyes and knew she sounded like a quitter. She'd never walked away from anything in her life.

"I know. I'm just feeling a little sorry for myself this morning." She smiled. "I *am* working with a physical therapist now, but I guess it's too early to see any progress."

Hal's face brightened and his accent came through stronger than usual.

"That's great! Is this person any good? 'Cause there's a guy in Louisville who's the best of the best when it comes to horse-related injuries. And he's an excellent rider, t'boot."

"Is his name Connor Hall?"

Hal's face crinkled into a huge smile. "Why, yes! Ya know him?"

Her heart thumped a little. "That's who I'm seeing. Is he really good?"

Hal sat back in his chair. "Oh, aye, he's the best." A sly wink. "I'll be seein' ya back in the barn by winter. Mark m' words."

Her heart soared with renewed hope. She desperately wanted to ride her horses again, be back in charge of her world, and if Connor Hall could make that happen, she'd love him forever. ❖

Nine

B eth couldn't wait to get home. She'd thoroughly enjoyed the morning, but somewhere between the last two cups of coffee, she'd started thinking about the show jumping portion of the Champagne Run, which had started at Noon.

Uncle Earl wrestled the wheelchair open and helped her into it, muttering under his breath about the "darned contraption." Thanking him again for a wonderful morning, Beth waved goodbye to her aunt and closed the front door, her thoughts already on the horse event.

A horse and rider flew across the green course, and Beth's gut tightened into a cold, hard knot, the scene snatching her back to her own last ride, and tragic fall. A lump rose in her throat and a moment of sorrow crept through, but she abruptly discarded the emotion when the rankings came up on the screen. She scanned the list for Connor's name, but it wasn't there. What had happened? She knew he'd entered the event.

Knuckles rapping on wood interrupted her mental threshing. Jamie stood in the doorway, holding a large duffel bag and wearing an impish grin.

"Jamie Trent, reporting for duty."

She laughed at his elaborate salute. She was genuinely happy to see him–it would be good to have some company.

Jean appeared. "Shall I take him on over to the cottage?"

Beth muted the sound on the television. "Yes, then would you fix us some lunch?" She looked at Jamie. "We can eat in here. I'm watching something at the Horse Park."

A mock scowl darkened his features. "So I'm doomed to watch horses on television all day?"

She threw him a wry smile. "See you later."

Alone again, she restored the sound as the camera switched from riders in the field to the broadcast booth at the Horse Park.

"Today's events are in full swing. So far, the only bad news is Brett Hall's withdrawal from the show jumping today. If you were watching yesterday, you'll remember that Brett had a very good time in the cross-country, but his horse pulled a tendon at one of the obstacles, and Hall scratched "Rexford's Nomination" from today's event. Too bad, 'cause Brett Hall has been breathing down Stephen Wegner's neck this year, and..."

Beth switched off the set, relief and sympathy flooding through her thoughts. *What a shame. He was so close.* She tried to imagine how he might react to the cruel disappointment, but without knowing anything about him, it proved futile. Her thoughts drifted to Hal's enthusiasm earlier that morning. *If Connor is the one who can help me ride again, then nothing will keep me from doing that. Nothing.*

She moved to a small desk in the corner where she'd left the crumpled sheet of instructions. The exercises seemed simple, and it looked as though she could perform most of them in her wheelchair. *I'll start my first session this afternoon, when the horse show is over.*

Her gaze moved through the French doors, irresistibly drawn to the dark clump of trees in the far pasture, and her throat closed up. *No! I'm not waiting until after some damned television program. I owe you that much, Paso.*

Jamie returned to the study less than thirty minutes later.

Beth raised her eyebrows. *"That* was quick."

He dropped into the soft couch cushions and ran a hand through his unruly brown hair. "If you don't mind, I think I'll go back to the cottage after lunch. I'm really not into eventing, you know."

"No, that's all right. I've changed my mind. I need to start my therapy exercises, and thought I'd do that after we eat."

"Good...Say, listen, I was thinking. Would you like me to drive you down to the barn later? You can see how the construction is progressing, talk to Hal and Cozy."

Beth's heart thudded to a brief halt, then started thumping. She hadn't been to the barn since her accident. Was she ready for the familiar beloved smells and atmosphere of her favorite place in the whole world? Was she ready to face Paso's empty stall?

Jamie leaned forward and softly touched her arm. "Bethey, you'll have to go back down there sooner or later." He sat back again. "But, if you don't feel up to it, we can go another time."

Her heart rate had slowed to something near normal, and she managed to choke out a response.

"No, you're right. It's been almost eight weeks–it's time." She took a deep breath. "I'll be ready around five."

After lunch, Jamie retired to the cottage, and Beth retrieved the exercise sheet. The two warm-up exercises were easy, bolstering her positive attitude and filling her with the rush of success. By the end of the fourth exercise, however, her optimism had turned to mud, as she struggled to work with muscles that hadn't functioned properly in weeks. The final exercise required her to lie down, so she headed for her room. *When I finish, I'll just have myself a nice nap–I'm so good at it.*

As she pushed herself up and out of the wheelchair, her damaged right leg began to shake violently, threatening to buckle. Lurching forward, she aimed for the bed, clutched at the slippery satin spread, and slithered to the floor.

She sat there for a minute, watching her right leg jump and jerk as though it were possessed by demons. She pressed firmly on her thigh and waited for the spasms to stop. In a few seconds, the movements diminished and the leg ceased quivering. Completely drained, she leaned her head against the bed and eyed the wheelchair, which had rolled back about six feet. *Now what? How am I going get up from here?*

The cat appeared from nowhere.

"What d'you think, Felix? Which would be harder? Struggle to the chair, or try to crawl up on the bed?"

The pudgy ball of fur sat down and began grooming his hind leg, apparently not interested in her dilemma.

"Thanks a lot, Bud."

She reflected for a minute. Only hours ago, she'd vowed she would ride again, that nothing would stop her. If she were to be true to that promise, then she'd have to find a way to help herself right now.

Using both hands, she lifted the dead weight of her right leg and scooted it as far to the left as she could. Then, she picked up the left leg and lifted it up and over the right one. Eight weeks in a wheelchair had built up her arm muscles, and she counted on that strength to help her. She rolled over onto her stomach, then planted her hands firmly on the floor. Pushing up with every ounce of strength, she found she could only lift her hips a scant inch off the floor. Her arm muscles began to quiver, and she knew there was no way she'd be able to get up on her own.

She slumped down onto the soft carpeting, her heartbeat jangling in her ears, her breathing ragged and heavy. Hot tears burned her cheeks as she spiraled into a whirlpool of exhaustion and defeat.

The heavy blanket of sleep fell away slowly as Beth opened her eyes. It took her a moment to realize she was on the floor, then she remembered why. Maybe she could crawl over and reach the telephone.

"Oh, my God! Beth!"

Jamie leaped through the door and dropped to his knees beside her, his face white with fright. "What happened? Are you okay?"

She nodded, and he slipped an arm beneath her shoulders and helped her to a sitting position.

"Are you sure you're not hurt? Maybe I shouldn't be moving you."

She closed her eyes. "Jamie, I'm *fine*. I just slid down the side of the bed, I didn't really fall."

He pulled her close, and stroked her face and hair, his words shaking with emotion. "C'mon. Let's get you back into your bed."

Recalling her earlier determination, she recoiled at her brief surrender to discouragement. *No one ever said this would be easy. I just need to keep at it.*

"No, I want to go to the barn, like we planned. Help me into the chair."

He looked doubtful, but didn't argue, scooping her up into his arms and settling her gently into the seat.

Beth's eyes focused straight ahead as the car idled down the long lane leading to the main barn. Panic rose in her chest, but she resisted the urge to ask Jamie to turn back. The dark red-brown building had white-framed paddock doors and windows, and a white cupola on the north roof rose against the blue sky, an antique running horse weathervane headed west, a silent and still sentry.

Her throat constricted at the familiar sight. It seemed an eternity since she'd been there, adjusting stirrups and talking to Paso. Pain rolled over her as though it had been only yesterday. *Paso... I'm so sorry.*

Jamie took her hand, his expression one of genuine compassion. "You all right?"

She blinked back the tears crowding against her eyelids. "Yes, let's go. I need to do this."

As the wheelchair moved from the bright sunlight into the dim shadows of the barn, her heart lurched painfully. At the threshold of the world she loved, the smells and sounds assaulted her senses, bringing vivid memories crashing into her consciousness. She closed her eyes and inhaled deeply, sure there was no more delightful scent than the inside of a clean horse barn–an odor combined of fresh hay, leather, saddle soap, grain, and warm horseflesh. Familiar joy replaced her fear as the place welcomed her home.

The temperature inside the building felt much cooler than outside, and a gentle breeze flowed through the aisle from the open doors at either end. Once her eyes adjusted to the softer light, she looked around, noting that everything seemed to be in good shape, clean and tidy.

"Oh, Miz Webb! Mistuh James. I didn't know you wuz comin' down."

An old black man snatched off his cap and politely ducked his head toward her, looking apologetic. "I coulda kep' the horses in if I'da known."

"No, no, Cozy. It's okay. This was a spur of the moment idea.

I've really missed being here."

The sun-baked face crinkled into a half-toothless smile. "We miss you, too, Ma'am. Oh, yes."

She moved away from the two men, and guided her chair slowly past the bank of empty stalls, freshly picked and bedded, ready for the return of the occupants that evening. As she neared the end of the aisle, her heartbeat quickened. Paso had lived in the last stall–the room with a view. The pleasant location had been her concession for a sport horse that had often spent more time in a stall than outdoors. From his quarters, Paso had been able to look through the barn door and keep track of his stable-mates in the pasture.

The men's voices murmured in the background, the evening feed routine hadn't started yet, and Beth was alone with her thoughts and her pain. She rolled to a stop directly in front of the empty stall. A worn black ribbon draped across the brass plate engraved with Paso's name. Cozy had respectfully paid honor to the magnificent horse that had once lived there. The anguish of her loss swelled, the tears started, and she finally let go, allowing herself to grieve completely.

Ten

Five days of rain brought all work to a halt. Hal called to describe the mess.

"It's a regular mud-hole down here. The men were sloggin' around in it, up to their ankles."

Beth closed her eyes. It seemed as though Highover Gate was doomed to stay behind schedule—not good news for her investors.

"I suppose the horses are stir-crazy from being kept in?"

He chuckled. "They'll survive."

After hanging up, she thought about her visit to the barn. After the initial shock and pain, she'd relaxed and let the place infuse her with longing and enthusiasm. It was definitely where she belonged, and she wanted to go back.

Connor's office called to reschedule her appointment for Monday, and disappointment seeped into her head. She'd been looking forward to seeing him again. Perhaps, too much. Restless, she flicked on the television, but found nothing of interest. She moved out to the terrace and watched the sky change, heavy black clouds rolling ominously across the horizon. Earlier, the air had been thick and still, but now the wind sprang up, whipping the tops of the giant Beeches that lined each side of the driveway. Beth shivered in the cool breeze.

"Nuts!"

She'd been on the verge of asking Jamie to take her to the barn again. The sky darkened, and she retreated from the terrace. A minute later, she stared in disbelief at the radar image on the weather channel. A massive storm was moving quickly through the region, with heavy rain and hail expected within the hour.

She snapped off the television and exhaled sharply, then glanced through the doors again, clutched by a brief stab of anxiety at the profound change in the sky. The cloud ceiling had dropped, making it as dark as evening, rather than midday.

Heavy thunder rattled the windowpanes and she quickly rolled over to shut the French doors. As she reached for the doorknob, the chilling wail of the tornado warning system sounded in the distance. Heart pounding, she latched the doors and wheeled back into the study. What should she do? Jean was off for the day, and Jamie had left for his own barn early that morning. Tornadoes were common in the region, but she'd never faced one while trapped in a wheelchair.

The huge old house had a storm cellar, but she had no way to get down the stairs. She urged the chair quickly down the hall toward her bedroom, searching for a room with no outside walls, one that would accommodate the damned wheelchair. She spotted the door to a large linen closet. A loud crack echoed through the house and she snatched open the door. She wouldn't be able to get the chair in there, but she didn't dare spend any more time in a vulnerable position.

A pitiful mew caught her attention. Felix's eyes were round and dark with fright, and he jumped with each clap of thunder. Beth braced herself, rose from the chair, then dived into a crumpled heap in the bottom of the closet. She pulled the cat into her arms and shrank deep into the dark corner.

The closet walls hummed with the battering wind. A low rumble vibrated the floor beneath her legs and she closed her eyes tightly, ready to join Dorothy and Toto. Like a jumbo jet flying twenty feet overhead, the rumble grew to a roar. Stacks of towels and bedding rained down on her as she struggled to keep her grip on Felix. She heard the sound of breaking glass, closed her eyes, and prepared to die.

As suddenly as it had come, the roar disappeared and all was still. She exhaled slowly, waiting for her heartbeat to level out. Felix jumped from her grasp and disappeared through the door. With one crisis past, Beth now faced another–how to get back into her wheelchair. Remembering her first attempts to get off the floor by herself, she sank back into the piles of bedding to wait for help.

Twenty minutes later, Jamie's frantic voice echoed in the hallway.

"Beth! Where are you?"

She called out and, within seconds, he kneeled beside her, his dark eyes searching her face.

"Jeez, are you okay?"

"I think so. Was there much damage?"

"A couple of your Beeches came down. That's all I noticed, but I was in a hurry."

"Get me back into my chair. I need to call Cozy."

Minutes later, she stared through the French doors while she waited for someone to answer the barn phone. A large tree limb lay on the terrace, its smaller branches sticking through the broken door-panes. A shiver raced across her shoulders–she'd been sitting in that exact spot just before the storm hit. Peering through the branches to the driveway, she saw the fallen Beech trees–their massive trunks snapped in half like matchsticks.

"Cozy? Is everything all right down there? Are the horses okay?" She closed her eyes and let out a long, slow breath. "Thank God."

An instant later, her insides turned to lead. "I'll be right down."

Jamie's voice dropped to a stage whisper. "What happened?"

"The twister hit the new dressage barn."

Jamie stopped the car at the end of the lane, and Beth stared forlornly at the jumble of lumber that, hours earlier, had been the almost completed stabling barn. A quarter of the arena roof had been peeled back like a sardine can. A dark path of torn-up earth traced the storm's wrath, a straight line between the dressage complex and the jump course. The new stabling barn had been directly in the center of the swath.

Jamie touched her arm. "Do you want to get out?"

"No, I've seen all I can stand for now." A cold pool formed in the pit of her stomach. "I need to call the insurance company. Thank God, Timmy's out of town."

Jamie remained silent as he started the car, then drove it back up the lane toward the house. Beth chewed her lip as she tried to calculate how the disaster would impact her deadlines–and her investors.

A few minutes later, Jamie walked to the French doors and examined the damage.

"I'll cut those branches away, and see about putting something over these broken windows. It might be a couple of days before you can get someone out here."

She flicked on the television, which was still tuned to the weather station. According to the report, the freak tornado had only touched down briefly, then moved due-north, spinning itself out over the Ohio River. Her thoughts were not on tree damage.

"Jamie, I need some time to think...I'll see you in the morning, okay?"

His voice held strained nonchalance. "Right-O. Goodnight."

When he'd gone, she telephoned her aunt and uncle to make sure they were all right.

"Bethey, I've been calling for an hour. Are you okay?"

"Yes, I'm fine. I think the power was out briefly...my answering machine lights are flashing. I've been down at the barn."

"Well, thank goodness there wasn't any damage. The TV said the storm wasn't a bad one."

Beth bit her lip, unwilling to get into a long conversation about her problem.

"Okay, well, I need to call Hal, so I'll let you go. Love to Uncle Earl."

Hal answered on the first ring.

"Beth, I've been trying to get hold of ye. Is everythin' all right?"

Her throat tightened to the point she could barely speak. "No, it's not. We lost the new barn."

"Ah, Lass! I'm so sorry. What can I do?"

"I need you to come over and take some pictures. I'm calling the insurance agent, but he might not be able to get here for a couple of days and I need to be prepared with some answers when the first board member calls."

"I'm on my way."

He rang off, and she dialed the insurance office, praying her agent would be in. He wasn't. She left her name and number, stated she had an emergency, then hung up. The sun broke through the clouds, draping the dripping trees with twinkle lights. She gazed across the hills, despair closing tightly around her chest. Even if the adjuster came tomorrow, it could be weeks before the claim would be paid–weeks she didn't have. The barn had to be rebuilt immediately, and it looked as though that expense would come out of her own, almost-empty pocket.

An hour later, the phone rang and she snatched it up, hoping to hear the agent's voice.

"Bethany? Tim Trent. I understand we have a problem."

A queasy feeling rolled up inside her. How had he found out about the damage so soon? He was supposedly in Indianapolis, attending a land developers' convention.

She inhaled slowly, composing her response.

"And what might that be?"

"Ken Barker was up here at the meeting last night, telling everyone the Highover Gate project is a screwed-up mess. Why didn't you tell me the work is on hold?"

Barker again. What a pain in the butt.

"He's full of it, Tim. Nothing's on hold."

"According to Barker, a piece of equipment went down and CCC wasted a full day trying to get a local replacement. Sounds like a problem to me."

"Well, apparently Mr. Barker conveniently left out the fact that they asked *him*, and he refused. Another one was delivered from Ohio that night. At worst, they lost a few hours' work time."

The line was silent for a moment, then Tim's tone changed. "Did you get any storm damage?"

There was no point in hedging. "Yes, the dressage barn came down and part of the arena roof, but I have the insurance adjuster on it already."

"This project certainly seems to have a dark cloud hanging over it."

Yes, and you're a big part of it.

"We're on schedule, Tim. Don't worry your pretty little head about it."

She said goodbye and stared into space while she replayed the brief conversation. It seemed as though Tim *was* positioning himself for a power play. She thought back to a similar situation, years earlier in LA, where nothing but sheer guts had gotten her through it. Now, locked in her own little prison on wheels, she felt ineffective and helpless, and Tim Trent would use every advantage he could to keep her that way.

A noise on the terrace interrupted her thoughts. Jamie was moving the crumpled patio furniture out of the way, his jaw set in a hard line as he cleared a work area, his solemn expression was something she'd seldom seen. He'd always been a clown, the happy-go-lucky companion who could make her laugh, even under the worst circumstances. Had she offended him when she'd dismissed him so brusquely in the immediate aftermath of the storm? The wheels of her chair crunched through broken glass on the terrazzo floor as she moved toward the doors.

He picked up a handsaw and positioned it above a large branch.

Keeping her voice light, she called out, "Hey, when you're done there, come on in and we'll have a nip."

He turned and considered her for a moment. His eyes did not twinkle, nor did he smile.

"I'll have to pass. I'm meeting someone for dinner."

He turned back to his chore and began sawing through the limb. Stunned by the rebuff, she backed the chair away from the door, but continued to watch him work. Concern squeezed her chest. Lately, everything she touched had disintegrated...projects, relationships. Only the visible aspects of her strong, resilient personality remained. Her true grit seemed to have disappeared.

Eleven

Connor shrugged into a crisp white lab coat, then checked the pocket for his patient notebook. The intercom on the desk crackled, and the receptionist's business-like voice came through. "Mr. Hall, Mrs. Beghley on line one." The day had begun.

After patiently answering Mrs. Beghley's questions, Connor exhaled and leaned back in his chair, rubbing his eyes. He hadn't slept very well the past couple of nights, and coming to work that morning had been an effort, but Beth Webb was scheduled for therapy that afternoon. Weary or not, he wanted to see her again, and *that* disturbed him more than he wanted to admit.

Though he'd worked out a determined plan to keep his distance from her, she'd muscled into his thoughts more and more. None of the women he'd met in the past few years had been as fresh and exciting as the elegant horsewoman. He'd found himself daydreaming about sharing long, leisurely trail-rides with her through the quiet green countryside. The pipe dreams always ended abruptly when he remembered that she might never ride again and, ironically, *he* was the person who'd be responsible for helping her try.

The old nightmare had returned, contributing to the past week's fitful sleep. The dream hadn't intruded on his life for a couple of years, but now it affected him as deeply as ever.

The dream always started with Connor as a little boy, wandering through the wild hills of Harlan County where, hundreds of feet below the surface, the earth is a honeycomb of mining tunnels. In the deserted foothills, he'd hear a voice desperately crying for help, and follow the sound to come upon an old abandoned mineshaft. In the dark hole, his mother lay at the bottom, staring up at him with a look of pure disgust on her pain-ravaged face.

"Aw, you! Go git'cher sister to hep me git outta here!"

He'd run as fast as his eleven-year-old-legs would carry him, arriving breathless at the door to the shack he called home. By that point in the dream, Connor had become a teenager. His older sister would look up from her ironing board, irritated by the interruption. He'd be so frightened that he couldn't talk, or explain what had happened. His sister would return to her ironing, and he'd back away from the door, intending to return to the mineshaft. Suddenly, his mother would be standing beside him, raw anger sharpening her strong features. Connor would then realize he'd become a grown-up, as his mother's words knifed through his fitful sleep. *"You ain't worth nuthin'. Ya cain't even git'cher sister in uh uhmergency. Yer a sorry excuse fer a man."*

Lost in the dream, he stared at the appointment book, trying to shake off the painful recollection. Beth's name leaped off the page and, for one instant, Connor doubted himself again. *Do I have what it takes to help her? Or will I fail miserably at this, too?*

Beth gazed out the car window at the magnificent horse farms lining each side of the highway into town. Normandy, Gainesway, Stoneleigh, Royston Stud—names that echoed with tradition, the very foundation of Kentucky's bluegrass heritage. A horse-lover's heaven.

Jamie touched her arm. "You okay?"

She nodded, but said nothing, her brain ablaze with the chaos of the last few days, but mostly with the recurring image of being on the floor, unable to get up by herself. *I can't ever remember feeling so helpless. I will not live my life like this.*

Connor had wormed his way into her thoughts that morning, and she pondered what his mood might be after his unfortunate day at the Champagne Run. Though she sensed he might be personally interested in her, there'd been a hint of "arms-length" just before he'd left her house on Friday. *He's probably not very comfortable that I'm his patient.* She frowned. *Am I comfortable with it?*

Jamie's voice broke into her mental gymnastics.

"How are the exercises coming along? You haven't mentioned them at all."

She shrugged. "Okay, I guess. I can't figure out how they could help. The movements aren't very hard."

"Maybe they're just so you'll feel involved in your therapy."

"You're probably right–I'll ask Connor."

Beth pushed her chair into Connor's office, and he looked up from his desk and smiled.

"Hi, Beth. Good to see you. I'll just be a minute."

His manner was strictly professional, without any hint of friendship or interest, and her earlier excitement disappeared like a rabbit down a hole. *Maybe I imagined it...No, he was definitely interested. I could feel it.*

Pushing the confusing thoughts from her head, she composed herself and waited. A minute later, Connor rose and came around the desk. He wore a pleasant expression, but his trim body moved with purpose, his mien aloof and professional. Her insides tightened into a hard lump.

Trying to keep the disappointment from her tone, she attempted to steer the conversation to a more personal plane.

"What a shame you had to scratch the jumping on Sunday. Is your horse all right?"

Connor snorted, his features curling with disgust. "Yeah, he'll be fine. That damned water hazard the day before caught us both off guard...I gather you watched?"

She nodded, unable to think of anything else to say, realizing it had been a stupid move to remind him of the disaster, then tell him she'd witnessed the whole thing.

He pulled up a chair, sat down, and leaned forward, elbows on his knees.

"So, how was the week? Any problems? Did you do your exercises regularly?"

His face revealed no trace of anything other than professional interest, and she felt deflated.

Her voice wavered slightly. "I started the exercises on Saturday, but they seem so simple, I can't imagine how they'll help."

He sat back and crossed his legs. "The stress of the repetition keeps the muscles limber so you'll be able to do the real work when you come here. Anything else I need to know?"

She'd decided against telling him about her mishap in the bedroom.

"I've been having episodes with my right leg that worry me."

Concern flashed into his cool demeanor and his eyebrows knitted together, emphasizing his interest.

He leaned forward and took her hand.

"What kind of episodes?"

"My right leg suddenly starts jerking and twitching all by itself, and I can't make it stop. It doesn't hurt, but it frightens me."

A smile lit up the wonderful face. "That's terrific. Your nerves are rebuilding themselves, and telling the muscles to pay attention. Under normal conditions, when you use a limb, your brain stimulates the nerves and, in turn, they command the muscles. But right now, the damaged nerves are sending erratic messages, so the muscles don't know quite what to do."

His encouragement coursed through her head. *Maybe I will recover, after all.* His eyes had softened with compassion, and her confidence grew. She could place herself, and her future, into his capable hands. She looked down at those hands, warm against her own, wanting to preserve the moment.

He sat back. "I read how close that tornado was to you. How did you weather the storm?"

"I lost a brand new barn."

"Oh, Beth, that's too bad. What does that do to your work schedule?

His empathy flipped the lid on her carefully boxed control.

"Screws it up completely." She blinked and looked away. "At this rate, my vision for the future will evaporate into thin air."

His tone was emphatic. "No, I think no matter *when* Highover Gate opens, it will be the best thing this region has seen in a long time."

A sharp edge knifed into her words. "I wish my investors felt the same way. Right now, the board has no confidence in me. I feel like I'm losing control."

He regarded her for a minute, then cleared his throat. "Anger is part of the healing process, Beth, but at some point, you have to direct that negative energy into positive channels. As long as you *feel* vulnerable, you'll *be* vulnerable." He paused. "I think it would be wise for you to spend some time with a psychotherapist to help you regain your self-confidence. You have more at risk here than just your future in the saddle."

She snapped her head up to look him squarely in the eye. "I am *not* going to a shrink!"

He didn't respond, but scribbled a note on her chart.

She pressed. "Do you think I'll ever ride again?"

He glanced up at her, his expression unreadable. "It's too early for me to make that determination."

The therapy session lasted longer than the usual forty minutes and, by the time they'd finished, Beth was exhausted. However, Connor's appreciation of her growing strength and flexibility thrilled her so much she didn't care.

As he pushed her chair toward the waiting room, his teasing voice danced behind her.

"When you can get out of the chair by yourself and walk three steps without me, I'll treat you to dinner at the Seelbach Hotel."

The vision of a romantic evening alone with him was very appealing. "It's a deal."

Jamie rose from his seat and gave Connor the once-over as they came through the door. Beth shifted uneasily in her seat. *Uh-oh, I don't like that look.* She introduced the two men, and they stiffly shook hands. An uneasy atmosphere pervaded the moment and the awkward silence thickened. She dropped her gaze and smiled to herself. *The Testosterone Wars.*

Connor's voice melted the chill in the air. "Next week, same time. See ya."

He patted her shoulder, then sauntered back down the hall toward his office.

Jamie remained silent while the car moved through the streets toward the downtown district.

When he finally broke the silence, his tone was quasi-accusing. "You didn't tell me that your physical therapist was Gorgeous George."

She immediately felt defensive. "Why would I? What does it matter what he looks like? If he can help me walk and ride again, he can look like Austin Powers, for all I care."

Jamie opened his eyes wide with utter disbelief. "Oooh, touchy, touchy! I guess he's manipulated more than your muscles."

She turned away and stared out the window. She didn't like having her emotions on display, even to Jamie.

Connor exhaled sharply. His determination to maintain a professional distance had disintegrated almost immediately after Beth had entered the office. As he'd maneuvered through the emotional mine field between them, he'd wanted to gather her up in his arms and hold her, tell her everything would be all right–that he would fix it. But he couldn't promise any of those things, no matter how much he wanted to.

Twelve

Pale dawn light draped across the opulent green hillside and twinkled through the branches of the ancient sweet gum tree that held court over the back garden. A doe and her two fawns nibbled at the leaves of the forsythia hedge. Beth inhaled deeply, absorbing the heady scent of wild honeysuckle that had overtaken the fence along the back, then turned her thoughts to her last therapy session.

Connor had been Dr. Jekyll and Mr. Hyde, one minute seeming attracted to her, and the next, all business. Then, he'd dangled dinner in front of her. She frowned. Why had she lost the nerve to tell him about her fall in the bedroom? What would his reaction have been? Concern? Anger? Why was she worrying about what he thought? The possibility of life as an invalid terrified her, and if *he* couldn't make things happen, then she *would*. She'd handled things by herself for years, why should this be any different?

The passage from early dawn to outright morning happened quickly, and the terrace now glowed in warm sunshine. The deer had evaporated into the dark safety of the woods, and the rumble of construction equipment rolled through the still air. She gazed across the garden for one more minute, then turned and pushed her chair into the study. Her muscles twanged with pain from the unaccustomed workout they'd had the day before. That morning, she planned to start a new regime: exercise twice a day through the next week, then three times a day, thereafter. She had a life to resurrect.

Jamie appeared in the doorway. "Got a minute?"

The set of his shoulders implied he had something important to say. He strode to the couch and sat down.

"I've been thinking about the situation with this Hall guy, and I don't like it."

Beth's skin crawled with irritation. She did *not* need Jamie's interference. She opened her mouth to respond, but he held up his hand.

"No, let me talk. He's supposed to be helping you get better, but his attitude is totally unprofessional–almost possessive. I can't believe you'd put up with it."

His accusing stare further annoyed her.

"Jamie, you met him for one minute–how does that make you an authority on his attitude?"

He snorted. "Jeez, you came out of there looking like you'd just had sex instead of physical therapy! What else am I supposed to think?"

She looked away, unable to answer that one, then cooled her tone. "Think what you like. It's none of your business."

The ensuing silence crackled with hostility.

Finally, he exhaled sharply. "You're right, but somewhere along the line, you've changed into someone I don't even know anymore."

"Being in this chair hasn't exactly given me a lot of options. You can't possibly understand–"

"Your options are what you make of them, Beth. You've never let anything stand in the way of what you wanted. Why is the wheelchair suddenly the culprit?"

Her bristly facade crumbled and shame crept into her thoughts. Did everyone see her in a similar light? As using her disability for a crutch to rationalize her poor attitude?

Her cell phone went off, and she groaned, seeing Tim Trent's number on the display. "Dammit! Why can't he just leave me alone?" She lifted the phone to her ear.

"Beth, I'm at the site. I can't believe what a shambles this is... The guys are telling me the tornado set them back at least three weeks, maybe four."

Obscenities leaped to mind, but she controlled herself. "There's nothing we can do about that, Tim. The company has assured me they'll put in some overtime, and bring in some extra men."

"They can't go ahead until the insurance claim is paid."

Her restraint teetered on the edge. "I'm putting up the money to keep the project on track."

"The board didn't vote on that."

"It's my property. I'm calling it a loan."

"I still don't think–"

"Tim, I'm in the middle of something. I have to go."

She pressed the disconnect button and glowered at the fading display, holding back the urge to hurl the phone across the room, then looked up at Jamie. His earlier rigid expression had softened with commiseration.

"I take it that was Brother-Dear?"

She sighed. "Yes. He's driving me crazy, and I don't know why."

He chortled. "Because you got the jump on him and he's ticked off."

"What on earth are you talking about?"

"Last year, he was deep in discussions with some of the local hotshots and the Horse Park about collaborating on another facility. Then, you announced the investment prospectus for Highover Gate, and pulled the rug out from under him. Being who he is, he *had* to get involved, but you know he hates playing second fiddle." Jamie's expression sobered. "He's in your camp right now, but don't kid yourself–he hasn't folded his tent."

In the seclusion of her bedroom, Beth considered Jamie's frank assessment of her attitude. It had startled her, but she knew he was right. She *had* changed, and she didn't like the person she'd become. If she could just compartmentalize the events and people bombarding her from all sides, she'd be able to get back on track.

She picked up the exercise instructions and started stretching and lifting her reluctant legs, her thoughts returning to Jamie's astonishing revelation about his brother's interference. Tim must have kept a very low profile while he made his plans, otherwise, she would have heard about it. She loved being on top, keeping her finger on the industry's pulse, beating out the competition–and she was very good at it. Highover Gate would be the springboard to bigger and better things. When the facility was completed, investors would beat down her door to be involved in the next project. She gazed at the floor, immersed in dreams. Maybe Maryland. Or upstate New York. Over three million people were involved in some form of showing horses, and state-of-the-art show facilities were few and far between. She intended to change *that*.

The situation with Tim had gotten out of hand. She needed to find a way to neutralize his impact on the project, but she'd have to tread carefully. Money and power were synonymous, and she didn't need any serious trouble from the renegade investor. It was time to use some of her own influence.

After lunch, she rolled out into the sunshine to join Jamie on the terrace.

"I'd like to go back to the barn today. I can't believe how much I miss being down there."

He gave her a thumbs-up sign. "That's a great idea. It'll be good for you, get your mind off your...well, you know..."

"No, the point is to keep my mind *on* my 'you know'. I'm done feeling sorry for myself, Jamie. I've started a rigorous exercise program, I need to be involved with the second phase of construction, and I want to keep my brain focused on riding a horse again. *Soon.*"

"Any plans for dealing with Tim?"

She gave him a curious look. "Why do you ask? I thought you didn't want to be involved."

He looked sheepish. "Well, I know he's a nuisance. I might be able to talk to him, you know...be a buffer between you two."

"Frankly, I don't think anything will help. Someone's giving him information on things, almost as they happen. He seems determined to see me fail, and *I'm* the only one who can keep that from happening."

Something in Jamie's eyes sent an uncomfortable feeling through her chest. "You wouldn't, by any chance, know who's keeping him informed, would you?"

He looked away. "No. I told you, I hardly ever see him." He rose and headed for the French doors. "I'm going home for about an hour, then I'll be back to take you to the barn."

Beth stayed on the terrace, thinking about the conversation. She'd actually startled herself with the idea of a spy in camp, but it made sense. Tim was on the phone too quickly after the tornado. The construction crew had gone home early, and no one had been in the barn. Who could have called him in Indiana? Her skin crawled with a chilling thought. *Oh God, please–not Jamie.*

Furious with herself for the disloyal thought, she grabbed her cell phone and dialed the clinic.

"This is Bethany Webb. May I speak to Connor Hall?"

The receptionist said he was out of town until the following Wednesday, and disappointment filled Beth's head. "May I speak to his assistant?"

A few moments later, she felt a little foolish, but pursued the information she wanted.

"Hi, this is Bethany Webb. I'm trying to get in touch with Mr. Hall. I have a question about my exercises."

Listening closely, she tried to separate the words in the young man's reply.

"Oh, hi y'all. SeeBee's at a horse show somewhere in Indiana, but I might be able to hep ya."

After a simple question about leg lifts, she thanked him and hung up, slipped the phone into her pocket, and reached for the television control. *Horse show in Indiana. At Connor's riding level, it'll surely be a big one, and probably televised.*

A few minutes later, she located the event just as the cameraman panned over the riders milling about in the starting paddock. Connor appeared on a small chestnut horse, and Beth settled down to watch. She followed the event for the first hour, evaluating the competition and considering the odds. *The riders in this event aren't anywhere near as good as Connor. Why would he enter such a low-key event? And what horse is he riding?*

She watched him maneuver his horse to the starting post, and a warm feeling crept into her chest. Just the sight of his athletic body and perfect posture sent tingles across her shoulders, and interesting images into her head. The camera zoomed up close, treating her to his fine profile, his angular jaw set firmly, his deep-set eyes focused straight ahead as he waited for the starting gun.

He flew over fences, ditches, and water hazards as though his horse had wings. He was a top-notch rider, proven by his score at the end of the ride, beating the best time by over forty seconds. She exhaled slowly, unaware she'd been holding her breath while she'd followed the performance.

Flicking off the set, she sat quietly for a few minutes. Clearly, Connor Hall had worked his way into her life in more ways than one. The question was: Where did she want him?

Thirteen

That afternoon, Hal met Beth at the barn door. "Sammy Ferra wants to talk to ye. He's definitely gonna come in after the Cargill Grand Prix."

"Keep up the good work, Hal. I won't rest until we've signed every top rider in the country–including Stephen Wegner."

Hal chortled. "Aye, and if frogs had wings–"

"No joke, Hal. This is my life we're talking about."

He patted her shoulder. "I know, but everything takes time. Be patient."

She bit back a sarcastic reply. Lately, she seemed to have a knack for antagonizing everyone–including Jamie, who'd barely spoken two words while he'd driven her to the barn. His sullen attitude fed her niggling concern about his loyalty.

She waved goodbye to Hal, then guided the chair toward the grooming area. A minute later, Cozy brought up a young mare.

"Yes-sir! Good for ya to be around hosses. Good for the soul."

The old-time groom's enthusiasm made Beth feel almost normal. His sinewy fingers moved deftly as he positioned the horse on the crossties. He smoothed his hand over the sleek chestnut shoulder, tipped his cap, and ambled off.

The stable hummed with the sounds of afternoon chores and country western music crooning softly, somewhere in the background. She sighed with content. *This is where I belong.*

As she worked a soft brush over the mare's forelegs, whisking away the dust, her thoughts moved again to Connor's entry in the Class-B Indiana event. *If Rex hadn't been injured, Connor would have placed high at the Champagne Run, possibly won. Maybe he's just trying to stay in shape 'til Rex heals.*

Leaning back in the wheelchair, she inspected her handiwork. The mare's coat gleamed like a newly minted penny. Beth rolled the chair back a little to take a better look. She'd purchased the horse as a two-year-old sport horse prospect, but during the previous year, she had been so busy with the construction project, she'd only ridden Paso, and hadn't paid much attention to her other horses.

The mare had matured beautifully, filling out in all the right places. With reminiscent touches of Arabian blood showing through her traditional Trakehner characteristics, she was far more elegant than Paso. *What a fabulous dressage horse she'd make. I'll ask Maarka to look at her and tell me what she thinks.*

Maarka Van der Gelden had been a world champion dressage rider in her younger days. Beth had offered a lot of money to entice the woman to come to Highover Gate, but the dressage program *had* to be the best, and Beth didn't regret the investment for even one moment.

Her thoughts churned as she admired the mare. *I can start slowly by riding dressage. Then, when I'm ready to do something more athletic, I can have her trained for jumping.* A hard lump rose in her throat. At that moment, the thought of flying over fences at break-neck speed was frightening. If she recovered completely from her current injuries, and were able to ride again, would she want to take the chance of another jumping mishap? She might not be so lucky a second time. She glanced down at the gleaming chrome surrounding her body. *This is lucky?*

A few minutes later, she handed the mare off to a groom, then guided the chair into the large office where all levels of Highover business were managed. She gazed around at state-of-the-art computers and equipment, walls filled with calendars and schedules–the core of her life. Maneuvering over to her desk, she looked through the stacks of mail and paperwork that had accumulated since her accident. After one brief flash of disbelief at the incredible amount of work she'd missed, she plunged in.

"Good to see ye back at your desk."

Hal's cheerful face beamed at her from the door, and she glanced at the clock on the wall, astonished to see the time.

"My gosh, I've been here for three hours and it only seems like a few minutes." She pushed back from the desk and wheeled around to face him. "Hal, I haven't really thanked you for the marvelous job you've done keeping the place from falling apart."

"Och, it was a pleasure, an' more's the pleasure seein' ye back in the saddle."

His unfortunate choice of words caught her by surprise and she inhaled sharply.

His features crumpled into lines of dismay. "Aw, Lass, I'm so sorry. That was—"

"No, no, it's all right. I'll beat this, I promise you. Being thin-skinned won't help anything at all."

She turned the focus of conversation to several business deadlines that loomed. "I see the NEF has put in for a show date later this summer. Do we have the personnel to do that?"

"Aye, the crew Cozy has now is pretty permanent. D'ye want to go ahead with the event?"

"Absolutely. The more exposure Highover can garner, the better."

After Hal left the office, Beth moved to the viewing window that looked out over the outdoor practice arenas. Maarka stood at the center of the closest one, concentrating on a young woman astride a black bay. The gleaming gelding trotted elegantly along the straight side of the enclosure, his chin perfectly tucked, forming a smooth arch to his neck. The rider lifted gracefully up from the saddle with each forward thrust of the horse's hind legs. Maarka gestured, then moved toward the pair as they halted. Beth watched the trainer point to the horse's hooves, then stamp her own feet. The rider nodded and resumed the trot.

Beth sighed softly at the familiarity of the lesson. Maarka had been demonstrating the cadence required in a good trot, a perfect and even rhythm. The horse collected himself and, even from a distance, Beth could see the two-beat rhythm, and the moment of suspension when all four of the gelding's feet were off the ground. Maarka nodded encouragingly, and Beth's thoughts drifted to visions of Lizzie performing the very same paces, at some point in the distant future.

With one last glance at the continuing lesson, Beth returned to her desk.

That evening, she leafed through the latest issue of a sport horse magazine. Though tired from the long day, her mental outlook had never been better since the accident. Being involved with her business and horses again was exactly the reinforcement she needed to conquer her disability. *She* wanted to be the one under Maarka's direction–and soon.

On a more personal plane, her re-discovery of the magnificent young mare sent her thoughts on a whirlwind tour of the future. If she were able to ride again, that mare would be the one she'd choose. Her gaze drifted back to the glossy pages filled with photographs of the Longines Royal International Horse Show. She idly read the captions, then zeroed in on a fabulous shot of Connor and Rex, flying over a white gate flanked by shrubs. She'd been in the hospital when the famous British event had taken place. She smiled and carefully tore out the page. She wanted to know more about Connor, and it looked as though the only way to find out would be to ask him.

Jamie popped his head in the doorway.

"Hey, how about dinner tomorrow? Big night out."

She cocked her head. "What's the occasion?"

"Celebrate your return to the barn, of course!"

Her newly found enthusiasm for life was like a tonic, and an evening out was just what she needed. "Sounds like a winner. Where shall we go?"

"I was thinking about that new place in town. Everyone at the country club is raving about it."

"Oh, yes, the place decorated like an art gallery. I read about it in the paper."

She smiled at the man she'd known all her life, an individual with facets she'd never noticed. Shame rose in her head for the earlier traitorous thoughts.

"Thank you, Jamie...for everything."

Fourteen

B eth poked through her closet, looking for a black Donna Karan dress she hadn't worn in ages. As she rummaged, she thought about Jamie. He'd seemed like his old self. Had she only imagined something ominous about his recent body language? Jamie, of all people, would never violate her trust. *I have to stop being so paranoid.*

She found the dress and held it up, admiring the designer's hallmark of simplicity. The scoop neckline revealed just enough skin to be interesting, but still conservative, and the black crepe de chine fell in soft folds to a slightly flared skirt that skimmed the knee. A teardrop pearl pendant and matching earrings would complete the look.

Thirty minutes later, the car moved along the highway toward town, and she glanced sideways at Jamie. He wore a pale rust-colored chambray shirt that brought out the color of his eyes, and his wavy brown hair glistened with dampness.

"You look very handsome tonight."

He didn't look at her, but grinned with pleasure.

"You look pretty fabulous, yourself. Your color's coming back—must be that barn air. *Eau de manure.*"

She chuckled, feeling as though she were on a real date, rather than simply having dinner with an old friend.

On the way home, Jamie talked about his recent purchase of an outstanding harness mare with winner's circle bloodlines, but Beth's thoughts wandered. Over cocktails, he'd again broached the subject of his brother's interference, but she'd brushed it aside, wanting nothing to mar her first real night out. She'd also been intrigued by the changes she saw in him. He hadn't worn his clownish personality, instead, showing himself to be an intelligent individual and serious young businessman. Daily, she was discovering new things about familiar people, and the thought that she'd been so oblivious was not a pleasant one.

The car stopped in the driveway, and Jamie picked up her hand, his expression a reminder that he was still in love with her. He started to lean forward, a kiss in his eyes, and she panicked.

"It was a great evening, Jamie. Thanks."

He cocked his head. "How about a night-cap? I have some really excellent Courvoisier in my room."

"I'll take a rain check. I'm really tired."

A trace of disappointment darkened his eyes, but he recovered with his usual pluckiness. "Right-O."

He wheeled her into the house, turned on the lights in the foyer, and closed the door behind them as she hit the message button on the bleating answering machine.

"Hi. Uh, Beth, it's Connor. I guess you're not home." His nervous laugh sputtered through the speaker. *"Well, I just thought I'd call and see how you're doing. Well, anyway, I'll see you on Thursday. I have a great horse story to tell you."* The message ended and the machine clicked off.

The silence thickened and she knew she'd goofed. Minutes earlier, in the car, she'd acknowledged that their dinner date had been very important to Jamie.

His voice sounded dull. "Well, I think I'll turn in. 'Night."

She spun the chair around. "Jamie, wait..."

The heavy door swung shut, leaving her to tussle with new emotions. *I've taken him for granted all these years, letting him do things for me, letting him hope.* The time had come to be as good a friend to him as he'd been to her. She had to make him understand the relationship would never go beyond that.

As she carefully eased back onto the bed, her right leg jerked violently, then quivered and jerked again. Though the spasms startled her, now that she understood their significance, the episodes no longer frightened her. The muscles jerked again, and she instinctively bent her knee and pulled the leg up, squeezing her thigh muscles until the quivering stopped. She stared in astonishment at the position of her leg, the knee bent at almost a twenty-degree angle, her heart leaping as she realized the damaged nerves were repairing themselves at an accelerated rate.

Moonlight danced on the still swirling surface of the pool, and Connor stared into the ripples. The night air was warm, but he shivered a little in his wet swim trunks. *Cold dips instead of cold showers.* Bethany Webb was getting to him, despite his efforts to keep her at arm's length. He'd fully expected her to be home during the evening hours, and had been caught off-guard when her answering machine had picked up. He grinned and shook his head. *What a stupid message–she'll be _real_ impressed now!*

The moon-dance on the water hypnotized him as he thought about the last time he'd seen her on horseback–the day she was injured. He recalled the charming face and compelling eyes, her cool and confident manner as she'd debated whether to tell him her name. He smiled at the recollection, then his thoughts moved from her face to the rest of the package, and he felt a stir, imagining what it would be like to feel her body against his.

Enough of this! He stood and, in one swift movement, shattered the moonlit pattern on the surface of the water.

A robin's morning song floated through the open window, and Beth drifted from sleep to half-wakefulness in the gauzy pre-dawn light. She sighed and stretched, rolling onto her side to slip back into a few more moments of limbo, then her eyes snapped open and she groaned, remembering her decision of the night before.

She swung her legs over the edge of the bed and, for a minute, was tempted to try taking a step or two. Thinking better of it, she grabbed the arms of the wheelchair, and swiveled her hips into the seat. There'd be plenty of time to experiment when she was a little stronger.

She rolled down the hall toward the kitchen, rehearsing what she'd say to Jamie, but nothing sounded right. She could think of no way to keep from trampling his feelings with the truth.

The doorbell rang and his voice echoed in the foyer. "Honey, I'm home!"

She relaxed. He sounded normal. A minute later, he gazed down on her, an affectionate smile warming his eyes.

"I need to talk to you, Hon."

They headed for the study, and anxiety tightened her gut. Jamie pulled the ottoman up in front of her chair and sat down, then reached out and grasped both her hands, his tender expression piercing straight through her chest.

"Bethey, I'm moving back to my place. I'm just underfoot here."

She started to protest, but he shook his head.

"Hear me out. We both know I hoped being close to you would move our relationship to a more personal level. I was naïve. What's more, it's obvious you're doing just fine on your own." He winked. "Other than your one little mishap, of course."

He rose and paced back and forth, apparently trying to gather the courage to continue the difficult conversation. She remained silent, sympathy filling her heart.

He turned and looked directly into her eyes. "I'll always love you–you know that. But the time has come for me to move on and try to find a life for myself that doesn't revolve around hoping you'll be a permanent part of it."

Her eyes burned at the generous gesture to shoulder all the responsibility for their relationship. She looked down at her lap, blinking away the drops that brimmed on her lashes.

He sat down again and put his hand on her knee. "You *are* going to recover. I can feel it. Your friend, Connor, has already strengthened your morale, and your legs will follow. We'll all be there, cheering wildly, when you sail over the courses again."

"Jamie, I'm so sorry," she whispered. "I never meant to hurt you. Really."

He grinned, tilting his head. "Bethey, Bethey, Bethey–I know that. We've been buddies long enough that I know exactly how you think. That's why I'm going home." He reached out and brushed a tear from her cheek. "Now dry up and listen...I have a great idea."

She smiled at his enthusiasm as he described the plan.

"We'll rent another wheelchair to keep at the barn. To get back and forth, you can use that golf cart that's gathering dust in the garage. You'll be able to come and go as you please...what do you think?"

"It's perfect!"

Not only could she continue her barn visits, but the plan was also another step toward her cherished independence.

The room seemed more than empty after Jamie left. The silence closed in around her, and she moved toward the French doors. The sun had slipped behind a cloud, the waning brilliance producing long shadows that crept over the pastures and woods. Paso's gravesite faded into the murky depths of the trees, and her mood darkened again, as though the shadows had moved into the room and swallowed her, as well.

Fifteen

B eth smoothed her hand over the sleek copper-colored shoulder. "Hello, Lizzie."

The elegant mare's ears pricked forward, and she nickered softly.

Beth had looked through the records to refresh her memory about the horse's background. She'd been right–"Miz Liz" had an outstanding pedigree. Now, Beth maneuvered the wheelchair completely around the mare, assessing her conformation points. The more she saw, the better she felt about her decision to put the mare to work with the dressage expert.

Lizzie stood quietly, watching everything Beth did. The very fact that the horse didn't spook at the wheelchair was an excellent sign. Sport horses had to be open to everything. A fine line lay between a high-strung, intelligent mount and one that went crazy at the first strange object it encountered. The danger in jumping was too great to take a chance with an unreliable horse.

Cozy appeared. "Miz Webb. Da phone's for you." He gestured toward the office, then moved on down the aisle.

"This is Beth Webb."

"Hello, Miss Webb. This is Sammy Ferra. Did Hal MacGregor tell you I called?"

She softened her crisp business tone. "Yes, hello! Hal says you're interested in training here."

"Yeah, I need that extra edge. I can't seem to move off 'also-ran' these days."

Beth rolled her eyes. *Third place at Rolex is hardly "also-ran."*

"We'd be delighted to have you here. I'll put you in Hal's charge to settle the arrangements. I'm not fully back in the office yet."

Sammy's voice softened with sympathy. "Oh, yeah. I was sorry to hear about your accident. But I guess it won't keep you from running the place, huh?"

His attempts to be up-beat had the exact opposite effect, and she pursed her lips tightly to keep from snapping his head off.

"No, it probably won't. Hal will call you later about a boarding and training schedule."

After hanging up the phone, she sat at the desk, lost in thought. *Yes, I can still manage the facility if I can't walk or ride again, but that's not enough. It will never be enough.* She thought about the future, then a niggling little voice sneaked into the back of her mind, asking her just what else she wanted in her life besides Highover Gate.

The days had passed quickly since Beth's return to a somewhat normal routine, and on the trek to Louisville the following week, she and Jamie bantered back and forth as usual about their barns. Nothing more had been said about their personal situation.

In the waiting room, she glanced at her watch again and sighed. *My appointment was for fifteen minutes ago. What's the hold-up?* Next to her, Jamie quietly leafed through a magazine he'd pulled from the dull selection on the table.

As though her mental question had traveled to the inner sanctum of the clinic, Connor's assistant poked his head through the door.

"Beth'ny? C'mon back."

She glided into Connor's office and, a few seconds later, heard his distinctive voice in the hall. Her breath caught briefly as he entered the room.

He shot her a friendly, but impersonal look, and set his briefcase on the desk. "Hello, Beth. How are we doing today?"

Cotton filled her mouth and her thoughts tumbled one over the other. She had so much to tell him, but where to start?

"I saw you on television last weekend at the Indiana Invitational."

He leveled an intense gaze on her. "You did? Now how did you happen to be watching *that* joke?"

She looked down at her hands. "I called here to ask you a question, and your assistant told me where you were."

"And you saw the whole thing?"

At that point, she felt ridiculous. "Well, I don't exactly have a lot to do."

His attitude was just a bit condescending, and her irritation over the poor beginning to the meeting scratched away the warm glow she'd felt moments before.

He shrugged. "After Rex hurt himself, I needed something to do."

How can he stay so composed when he has to be really disappointed?

He settled his hip on the edge of the desk. "I need to stay in shape until Rex's tendon heals. A friend of mine couldn't ride that day, but didn't want to lose the entry fees, so I rode his horse."

He rose from the desk and came over to sit down beside her. The brief personal exchange was over, and he wore his professional hat again.

Reaching down, he gently grasped her ankle. "How's this leg coming along? Any muscle soreness?"

She barked out a laugh. "I'm single-handedly keeping the drug companies afloat."

He smiled, but said nothing, and she became more serious.

"The other night, I was sitting on the bed, and my leg started to jerk really hard again. Without realizing it, I brought my right knee up to almost a twenty-degree angle." She watched his face for a positive reaction. "That's good, isn't it?"

He rocked back on his heels, and penciled a note into her chart. "Yes, that certainly means things are on the mend. Anything else?"

She gulped. If she planned to trust herself completely to his care, she'd have to be honest with him.

"Ahhh...a couple of weeks ago, I missed the bed and spent some time on the floor."

Dismay passed briefly across his features and he rose to his feet.

Hurriedly, she added, "I didn't hurt myself. Really." Her voice dropped to almost a whisper. "It frightened me, though. I recognized how much I have to overcome before I can ride again."

His eyebrows came together. "Beth, you must be very careful. Being able to get up by yourself isn't the problem. You could hit your head, or break an arm." His eyes sparked authority. "You must *not* push yourself beyond your capabilities, just to prove something."

He sat down on the stool, his tone softening. "It's good that your muscles are growing stronger, but it takes time. Trust me."

She looked at the face that had recently engaged her thoughts more and more. His concern seemed genuine—more than just professional solicitude—and that made her feel very good, but at the same time wary. Would her growing attraction to him be an obstacle to her recovery?

She pushed away the annoying thought. "I've been doing the exercises three times a day. The work-out has helped me at the barn."

"The barn?"

She grinned at his surprise, then related her morning routine for the past few days. His approving smile filled her heart with delight.

"Now that's *really* good news." He glanced down at his watch, then jumped up and wiggled his eyebrows. "Shall we proceed to the torture chamber, my dear?"

Beth's rigorous daily routine had definitely paid off. The maneuvers she'd found so difficult at her first therapy session were now fairly easy to perform, and her confidence grew, infusing her with a strong sense of hope for the future. As Connor rolled her chair toward the padded platform for the final set of exercises, a veil of disappointment descended over her thoughts. She wouldn't see him again for a week, time that would drag, days and nights all alone. *Stop! You can't think like this!*

She waved him away when he tried to help her out of the chair. "I can do this. I climb into bed every night all by myself."

He moved back one step, but watched her closely as she rose from the chair, then turned to lean back against the platform. As she braced her hands on the edge, without warning, her right leg buckled, and she pitched forward.

Connor caught her in mid-air, his arms circling her body and pulling her tightly to his chest. She could feel his breath against her ear, warm and sweet. A heartbeat thudded between them. Was it hers, or his? She exhaled slowly, then tilted her head back, losing herself in his gaze and seeing the fires burning deep in the green orbs. For a split second, she felt suspended in time, afraid–or unwilling–to leave the intimate cocoon of the embrace.

He broke the spell. "Whoa, *that* was close!"

He lifted her up and onto the platform, then stepped back and turned away to pick up the clipboard he'd dropped when he'd jumped forward to catch her.

A moment later, the color on his cheeks assured her she wasn't the only one who'd been affected by the incident. Suddenly embarrassed, she focused on a chart on the wall, but all she could think about was the way she'd felt in his arms.

The remaining minutes of the session blurred and, soon, she rolled back out to the waiting room, confused and miserable. After the embrace, Connor had withdrawn, his manner polite and professional, and he hadn't looked directly at her again. *How do I handle this? He's just as attracted to me as I am to him.*

That evening, in the quiet tack room, Connor pulled on his paddock boots. He'd been deeply shaken by the sudden intimacy during Beth's session, and the remainder of his day at the office had been a shambles. He stared at the dusty floor, lost in thought. It had been hours ago, but he couldn't rid himself of the excitement of holding her in his arms.

He turned his thoughts to her progress. Reviewing what she'd told him about the spasms in her leg, it was clear she was getting better. Because of his professional help? Or would she have recovered anyway without him? He grinned. *She is awfully independent and stubborn.* Did he think she'd walk again? Yes. Her dreams of riding again were an entirely different matter.

He shook off the question, and moved down the aisle toward Rex's stall.

"Hey, Buddy, how's the boo-boo?"

Rex nickered and bobbed his head. Connor knelt down and

began loosening the bandage on Rex's foreleg, but Beth's face floated into his thoughts again. Since her very first appointment, her look of terror at the prospect of never riding again had haunted him. He gazed affectionately at his horse, an old friend waiting patiently and willingly for whatever might be next. Connor's chest tightened as he tried to imagine a life without riding.

He massaged medicated cream into Rex's injured leg, vowing that Bethany Webb would ride again, regardless of what his own sacrifices might have to be.

◈

Sixteen

More and more, Beth's personal thoughts about Connor made her wonder if her fast-track life had been artificial. She glanced out the office window at the landscape strewn with equipment, building materials, and construction workers. How did one work another human being into a frantically busy life? Was it something she could schedule and manage like any other project? She sighed. Like it or not, he was already there.

Her gaze shifted to the newly constructed grandstand that skirted the jumping arena. Close by, two stonemasons meticulously measured and placed fieldstones for the final stretch of the surrounding wall. Except for the damaged dressage barn, the facility was shaping up nicely.

She turned back to the desk and paged through the scheduling book. Hal had been busy recruiting, and the months ahead were already filling up with training sessions and a few tentative events. She scribbled a note to call the public relations coordinator right after lunch.

A moment later, the phone rang and her spirits rose. Her stockbroker had just sold a quarter of her shares in the LA stadium, giving her more than enough to rebuild the dressage barn.

Dan Cornell stepped into the office. "You wanted to see me?"

"Yes, we need to get the jump on the barn repair. I want you to figure out how long it will take and what materials you'll need. Then get the stuff ordered so we don't lose any time waiting for delivery.

Dan nodded, making a note in his organizer. He shook his head as he glanced up at her. "Sure is a good thing we hadn't hung all those custom doors and hardware."

"Amen."

Beth lay on the bed and gazed at the ceiling, waiting for the twitching leg muscles to quiet. The spasms had become more frequent as her therapy progressed, but she'd found that, by flexing the leg, she could stop the annoying sensation. The episodes occurred most frequently after she exercised, and this day was no different. She'd worked her legs especially hard, and a deep ache murmured along the thigh muscles. Enthusiasm about Lizzie was helping her focus on goals for the future. The mare would require over a year of training before anyone could begin riding dressage with her. A year was exactly the time frame Beth figured she'd need in order to be ready for the day when she could again view the world from her saddle.

Fatigue slipped over her like a shadow and she closed her eyes. Tight muscles relaxed, and her thoughts carried her on another journey, easing into dreams where she rode beside Connor through deep green woods and endless fields, whirled through a dance in his arms, and lay beside him in the dark velvet of night, lost in passion.

Bright and early on Saturday, Beth watched Maarka slowly circle Miz Liz. Maarka's face revealed nothing, and Beth wished she could read the trainer's thoughts.

Finally, the distinct Dutch accent snapped through the air. "I will put her on a lunge line."

In the arena, the beautiful mare painted a captivating picture as she moved fluidly and evenly around the circle, her muscles rippling with strength, her head high, her tail arched lightly.

Fifteen minutes later, dying to ask for an opinion, Beth rolled silently alongside Maarka as she led the horse back to the stall.

"She is very nice, Beth. When do you want to start her?"

"Now! How soon can you take her? How long before she's ready to ride?"

Maarka smiled indulgently. "I can take her any time. As for

how long, that will depend on the mare's abilities. I would say from six to eight weeks."

After Maarka left, Beth stayed with Lizzie, brushing the brilliant chestnut coat until it gleamed.

"I'll really miss you, but we'll soon be together again as a team."

With each day of exercise, Beth's legs grew stronger and more flexible, the pain diminished, and her mental outlook improved. Plans for Lizzie occupied most of her quiet-time thoughts.

One evening, while idly surfing through the sports channels, she stumbled upon a documentary about riding programs for disabled people. Intrigued, she watched riders of all ages move around the perimeter of a large arena. A small woman in a wheelchair appeared in front of the camera, and Beth listened closely to the program narrator as he interviewed the disabled woman who was the instructor for the group of handicapped riders in the background.

The camera closed in on several of the horses and Beth's interest heightened. An aged roan horse patiently plodded along, carrying a small lump of a boy, his flaccid body secured with leather straps to a specially designed saddle. *How could someone with such severe disability remain upright on a moving horse?* The camera zoomed to the child's face, and Beth's heart lurched. Under the helmet that all but obscured his small features, the little boy's eyes glowed with the joy and excitement that his mutinous face muscles could not display.

The scene flicked to another rider, a young man with no obvious disability, but whose features had the vacant look of mental retardation. He suddenly waved at the camera, a gargoyle smile brightening his face.

Beth sat back and exhaled slowly. *If these severely handicapped people can ride, why couldn't I?* Another interview with the instructor interrupted the racing thoughts. The woman had been injured in a tragic steeplechase fall, five years earlier, and was totally paralyzed from the waist down. She would never walk again.

She smiled nervously at the camera. "But I can ride every day. It's the only thing that keeps me sane."

Beth nodded, feeling a bond with the stranger. *My barn chores are the only things that keep me going.* She sat back, suddenly excited. *I wonder if there's a group like that around here. I could begin working on my balance. It would be perfect.* Connor would certainly know about such things.

Though the mare had only been gone a few days, it seemed much longer to Beth. Paso's old stall had been stripped of all evidence that a horse had lived there recently. The black ribbon had disappeared, and the brass nameplate had been moved into the trophy room and placed under a photograph of Beth and Paso accepting a trophy at some show in the past.

Her gaze moved from the stall to the vast pastures beyond the barn. All the resident horses were already grazing in the dim morning light. The ache in her heart was still there, but she had begun to move past the hurdle of her horse's death, and sad thoughts were gradually being replaced by happier images. She turned her attention back to the empty stall.

When Lizzie comes home, this is where she'll live.

Late that afternoon, she rolled into the kitchen to see what Jean had fixed for supper. Felix appeared, ever hopeful he might be fed twice that day. She opened and closed the refrigerator door, looked idly at the shopping list, all painful reminders of the things she couldn't do, and her dependence on others. Her excess mental energy and deep frustration kicked in. *Why am I tormenting myself? I'm the only one who can do anything about it, and if I don't get a move on, I'll be sitting here forever.*

She wheeled the chair out into the long hall, heading toward the study. At the doorway, she stopped and looked down at her legs. With grim determination, she flexed the muscles in the weak right leg, willing them to lift it. She tried again, and it came up a little higher. Relaxing back into the chair, she surveyed the room. *If I stand up, I could probably get to the back of the couch.* She calculated the distance. *Not more than three feet. If I can balance against that, I can probably make it to the end. From there, it's only two steps to the recliner.* Apprehension thundered through her chest, but determination overruled the fear.

She locked the chair wheels, then carefully planted her feet on the floor and slowly pushed herself up, keeping a firm hold on the chair for balance. She waited for her pulse rate to level off. Testing her left leg and satisfied it would hold her, she let go of the chair, and balanced for a few seconds. *All systems go.* She gingerly moved her weak leg forward and waited a second before transferring her full weight, leaning forward slightly so she could grab the couch if she lost her balance. The leg held. She moved the other leg forward. *So far, so good.*

A wave of light-headedness swirled up and her body swayed precariously. She closed her eyes and tried the breathing technique Connor had shown her. The dizziness passed and she opened her eyes. *Still standing. One more step and I'll be at the couch.* Gathering all her concentration, she shuffled the right leg forward, then grabbed the back of the couch.

Exhilaration surged through her.

"Mr. Hall—You owe me dinner!" she crowed.

A violent spasm racked her right thigh.

"No! No! No!"

She leaned heavily against the couch and, within moments, the spasm dwindled and disappeared. She waited to see if the episode was really over, then carefully took two more halting steps along the back of the couch. Sparkling lights spun through her vision as the dizziness suddenly returned, this time stronger. She squeezed her eyes tightly, but couldn't overcome the attack. Her grip slipped from the couch and she reeled sideways, the floor racing toward her. Instinctively, she twisted her body to break the fall. A flash of pain raced through her jaw, and she gasped to recover the breath that had disappeared from her lungs.

Groaning, she rolled onto her back. Her right leg erupted into a demonic dance again, her adrenaline level began to dissipate, and tears of frustration blurred her vision. She looked around for something close enough to pull herself up on. Felix perched on the seat of the wheelchair, grooming himself, his hind leg stuck straight up in the air.

"Bring that chair over here, would you?"

The cat blinked his large yellow eyes, then resumed his bath.

She hoisted herself up onto her elbows, gauging the six feet between her and the chair. Licking her lips, she tasted the sweet,

salty flavor of blood. *Oh, great. That will look attractive.* A giggle
bubbled up at the foolish vanity that had wormed its way into her
precarious predicament.

Fifteen minutes later, she lolled in the wheelchair, gasping from
the exertion of dragging herself across the floor. Her head throbbed,
her swollen lip burned, and her elbows and knees stung with rug
burn. Exhausted, she headed for her bedroom.

The doorbell chimed insistently in the foggy recesses of her
head, dragging her from a light, restless sleep. Every muscle in her
body protested as she struggled to sit up. The bell sounded again
and she eased into the wheelchair, thinking she'd like to shoot
whoever was at the door.

"I'm coming, I'm coming," she muttered.

*She's not home. I should've called first. I really shouldn't even
be here.* Connor exhaled sharply, then looked around the beautifully kept front garden. The scent of some fragrant bloom floated
on the warm evening air, and the sharp sounds of daytime had been
replaced by the quiet murmurs of evening.

The heavy ache of fatigue pressed in on him. The nightmare
had returned twice after the last session with Beth, but the dream
had taken on a new twist. Now, as Connor peered into the familiar gaping hole in the ground, he was no longer a young boy, but
a grown man, staring down into Bethany Webb's pleading eyes.
As always, his fear paralyzed him, while she begged him to help
her. He'd take off, running to find help, but would continue running–running away. Each night, he'd awakened with a start, cold
and clammy, the scene unresolved.

For the past week, his thoughts had yanked him back and forth
between his professional responsibility to help Beth walk again, and
his desire to draw her into his personal space and make her a part
of his life. One precluded the other–a serious problem.

Seventeen

B eth opened the heavy door and her heartbeat skidded to a momentary halt.

Connor smiled sheepishly. "Hi. Sorry I didn't call first. I was in the area."

"That's okay. Come on in."

"I hope it's not too late for visitors."

"No, no. I'm usually up pretty late, since I take a nap in the afternoon. I was just going to brew a cup of tea and sit outside for awhile."

She tried to stay calm, but her brain reeled. The vivid memory of their last encounter danced through her thoughts, sending tingles across her skin. With Connor standing only an arm's length away, she could barely control her wild imagination.

As she filled the teakettle, she hummed with pleasure, happy to have him sitting in her kitchen. She reached across the counter to pick up the cups and saucers, and glanced at him again. The contented feeling froze in her chest. His expression had changed.

His professional personality surfaced, and his tone was cool and clinical.

"What happened to your elbow?"

The air crackled with tension, and she snatched her arm back, pressing it against her body to hide the wound.

"Nothing. I banged it on the counter earlier."

Pinning her with a hard look, he probed. "You didn't fall?"

She shook her head and avoided looking at him, knowing her

fabrication hadn't fooled him. She busied herself arranging the tea tray, trying to ignore the deepening silence between them.

In the next moment, he knelt beside her chair, and gently took her arm. He inspected the elbow, then reached for the other arm. He said nothing as he compared the two wounds, but the fine planes of his face were now etched with anger.

Her chest tightened at his nearness. Each breath turned into a tiny silent gasp as his touch sent electric shocks through her, even in the face of the imminent danger.

He rocked back onto his heels and peered into her face, his eyes locking intently on hers. "Do your knees match?"

She nodded, feeling like a small child caught in a naughty act. She started to explain, but he rose to his feet and strode away, then turned on his heel and glared at her.

"*What* happened?"

Her initial reluctance to tell him quickly changed to irritation and defensiveness.

"Why are you acting like this? So I fell, so what? There'll probably be more tumbles before I conquer this thing."

She turned the wheelchair around and headed out of the kitchen. She'd reached the terrace by the time he caught up with her.

"I'm sorry, Beth. I only..."

She didn't look at him, just stared across the darkened pastures, wishing he would leave. *Maybe I should find a different therapist. This isn't working. He's driving me crazy, and I need to focus on my future. I have too much at stake to be so emotionally screwed up.*

His touch instantly erased the defiant thoughts, his voice caressing her mind as softly as his hands stroked her shoulders.

"I just don't want you to get hurt. Don't you understand?"

She looked up at him earnestly. "Yes, I do. But I also understand that *I* am the only one who can solve my problem. I can't sit around in this chair, *wishing* I could walk, *wishing* I could ride. I have to *do* something, don't *you* understand? For all your professional expertise, *you* can't make it happen. It's *my* job."

Distress crumpled his features, and she reached for his hand.

"Connor, I *will* beat this. I proved it this afternoon." She smiled confidently. "I didn't fall because my legs didn't work, I fell because I got dizzy and lost my balance." She searched his face for a moment. "Even though I have some scrapes and bruises, I'm thrilled."

He nodded silently, and she released his hand, jerking her thumb toward the door. "C'mon. Just let me show you something."

She rolled over to the back of the couch and, as she started to rise, Connor leaped forward.

"Beth, Wait! What are you doing?"

She grinned mischievously. "Calm down. You know as well as I do, if you fall off a horse, you should climb right back on."

Gathering her focus, she repeated her steps of the afternoon, pausing between each movement to make sure the weak leg would hold her. Balancing herself with the back of the couch, she took four slow, measured steps. Briefly, her head felt light and detached from her body, and she closed her eyes, willing away the sensation. It passed and, when she opened her eyes again, Connor stood directly in front of her, his face glowing with approval—and something else she couldn't quite fathom.

Her cheeks warmed with the flush of victory. She met his gaze, and immediately recognized the look in his eyes. The fragile moment hung between them like the fine thread of spider silk.

"Bethany."

His whisper caressed her heart, sending her thoughts on a fantasy flight as he pulled her into his arms. She felt every beat of his heart, and heard each breath he drew. Within the circle of his embrace, she gazed into the depths of his desire, the spark of his electricity igniting her own suppressed longing. She melted against him, feeling his need against her belly, a reminder that she'd crossed the boundary.

His fingers sifted through her hair, tenderly cradling her head as he softly nibbled and kissed her neck. Then, he stopped and searched her face, a question in his eyes. She met his gaze and exhaled softly. *Yes.*

His whisper was ragged with emotion. "Oh, God, Beth. I've thought about you day and night. I've tried to ignore it, but I can't help myself."

She lifted her face and lost herself in the long, deep kiss.

Curled into the warm circle of Connor's arm, Beth nestled

her cheek against his smooth skin. She could feel his heart beating slowly, matched by the steady rise and fall of his chest as he slept. Her thoughts hummed with the delights she'd experienced hours earlier. She didn't want to sleep, *couldn't* sleep, wanting to savor being there beside him, not miss a minute. *This is all I want.* She smiled into the darkness. *It seems so simple, why hasn't it ever happened before?*

When she awoke later, birds twittered cheerily outside the window, and the sound of the shower reminded her she had company. The memory of the night of passion sent a flush of warmth over her skin and she glanced at the clock. *I wonder if he has time for a quick cuddle before he goes.* She giggled, astonished by her wanton thoughts. In all her life, she'd never felt the way Connor made her feel.

"Well, good morning, sleepy head."

His brilliant smile outshone the sunlight pouring through the window. Her gaze moved to his tan chest, glistening with shower drops, then drifted down to the skimpy towel wrapped around his slim torso.

She tilted her head. "Come cuddle for a minute."

He laughed. "Boy, your accident certainly didn't hurt your libido."

He strolled over to the bed and sat down, but made no move to slip between the sheets. She reached over and fingered the towel, tugging gently, hoping it would fall away.

He grabbed her hand and smiled, trying to assume a solemn expression.

"Beth, I have to leave now. I work, you know. And Louisville isn't exactly around the corner."

She pulled an exaggerated pout, pushing her lower lip out as far as she could, and looking up at him through her eyelashes. He rewarded the comical face with an indulgent smile, but his tone remained firm.

"C'mon, rise and shine. I brought your chair in, and I've made some coffee. Do you need any help in the shower?"

He was all business now, and it was clear he'd not be lured back into her bed.

"No, I can manage all right. Coffee sounds good. I'll be out in a few minutes."

Seated on the shower chair, the hot water streaming over her head and shoulders, she thought about their lovemaking. Just the memory of it stirred her. *For someone who hasn't had much of a love life, you're doing okay in the lust department.*

Twenty minutes later, she rolled onto the sun-drenched terrace. Not only had he fixed coffee, he'd found some bread and made toast. *I could definitely get used to this.*

There were so many things she wanted to tell him, and ask him, but she immediately noticed that the atmosphere had changed. His attitude seemed almost impersonal, as though he felt uncomfortable being there.

He set down his coffee cup. "I'd better get going right now. Don't you have a housekeeper due any minute?"

She cocked her head. "Yes. Are you embarrassed?"

"Not really, but you might be."

The sharp edge of the disconnect sliced through her heart, shattering the earlier dreamy mood. She'd imagined a romantic embrace and tender goodbye kiss before he left her.

He knelt down beside her chair, his face drawn. "I hope last night wasn't a mistake."

The uneasiness that had been lurking inside her for the past few minutes sprang up, large and ominous.

"For whom?" she whispered.

Eighteen

The truck slowly rolled to a stop at the bottom of the driveway, and Connor gazed across the road at the perfect squares of pasture dotted with grazing horses. A beautiful scene, the morning fresh and clear, but the image of Beth's hurt expression cast a dark shadow on his view.

What had he done? How could he ever explain to her that he couldn't mix his professional life with his personal desires? She was a truly unique woman, independent and self-confident, but, at the same time, feminine and vulnerable. He'd felt so comfortable sitting in her kitchen while she'd fussed with the tea, a comfort level he'd never known before.

Her isolation in that huge house bothered him. She could hurt herself, maybe lay somewhere for hours before help arrived. His concern bluntly reminded him it wasn't the physical therapist managing the situation, it was the man. To explain his feelings to her would also require revealing his past, something he wasn't yet ready to share with her. Vivid images of their passion overruled his misgivings, images that exceeded his wildest dreams about her. His thoughts quickened. How wonderful she'd felt and tasted. How deeply she'd responded to him, with more passion than he'd ever imagined possible.

He shook his head to clear the stimulating vision, then slipped the truck into gear and glided out onto the road. *Maybe I can eventually find a way to make all the pieces fit, but I just can't deal with it right now.*

Beth sat for a long time, her coffee cold, her toast uneaten. The numbness engulfing her body had left her mind untouched. Repeatedly, she tried to make sense of what had happened. *Why did he come all that way to see me if he didn't want a personal relationship? He didn't even pretend to be here as my therapist.* A hard knot formed in her throat and tears crowded against her lids, burning to be released, while Connor's words echoed in the confines of her head. *I hope this wasn't a mistake...mistake...mistake.*

She thought again about the ecstasy she'd felt in his arms, the surge of life filling her neglected body. And the hope. How could anything so beautiful, so right, be a mistake? Happiness found and lost in the space of a few hours. The tears started and no dam on earth could have held back the flood.

A lifetime of minutes later, exhausted and dulled by her emotions, she turned her back on the beautiful morning, and rolled into the study to her usual spot in front of the television. The screen flickered to life and she lost herself in world news.

A forest fire raged in Colorado. A laid-off factory worker had gone on a shooting spree. A seventy-three-car-pileup littered a California freeway. Beth watched woodenly as the country's problems dwarfed her own.

The cell phone ring was barely audible over the chaos on the screen.

Jamie's voice sounded overly cheerful. "Hi, Doll."

She didn't feel like talking, but tried to be polite. "You're certainly cheerful this morning."

He laughed. "And obviously, *you* are not. What's going on?"

Irritation prickled across her neck and she resisted the urge to snap. "Just watching the news."

A palpable hesitation echoed over the line.

"Bethey, is everything all right? You sound strange."

She closed her eyes. *Please, leave me alone.* "I'm fine, Jamie. I have a headache."

"Ah-ha! Up all night partyin', huh?"

Irritation escalated to full blown ire, fueled by the hard ache in her chest.

"Jamie, I *said* I'm fine. What's the matter with you?"

His voice softened, reaching through the phone, touching her broken heart with tenderness and love that only he could give.

"Bethey, tell me. It's about Connor, isn't it?"

The trigger slammed down on her brain, and she gulped back a sob. Waves of pain rolled over her, stronger than before, and her chest ached with the emotions.

"Honey, do you want me to come up? Sounds like you need someone to talk to."

She nodded silently.

By the time Connor reached the outskirts of Louisville, he'd approached his problem from every conceivable angle, but his thoughts always came around to the same conclusion: make a choice and live with it. Until he reconciled his past into the proper perspective, he couldn't proceed with his life. *Life? Maybe I don't even have a life.* Beth had brought a glow into what he'd thought was the perfect existence. How could he snuff out that light? And for what? To be the best three day eventer in history? To be the leading equestrian-injury physical therapist? To be the loneliest man alive?

By the time Jamie arrived, Beth had regained most of her composure. Her face felt puffy and she knew she looked terrible, but she didn't care. He leaned down and kissed the top of her head, then sat down beside her.

"Connor stayed here last night, didn't he?"

Her first impulse was denial, then she surrendered to reality and her eyes brimmed with fresh tears. "How did you know?"

He looked down at the floor, obviously embarrassed. "I came by earlier to see how you were doing. Connor had just pulled out of the driveway."

She averted her gaze, feeling her cheeks warm. A moment later, she looked up at him again, her voice breaking as she spoke.

"I don't know what to do, Jamie. I'm afraid I'm falling in love with him."

By mid-afternoon, Beth had calmed down and collected her thoughts. Being able to talk to Jamie and admit her feelings was an immense relief. He'd kept any personal opinions to himself, instead offering some male-oriented insight into Connor's reactions, and she had listened intently, her heart willing to grasp at any positive straw.

She worked on the leg exercises and thought about her appointment the next day. *I'll just wait and see what happens, before jumping to any conclusions. Maybe he was just having morning-after remorse.* Wasn't *she* supposed to be the one who felt that way?

Maarka called with a report on Miz Liz's progress. The mare was doing well in the short time she'd been in training. Maarka's optimism was infectious and, by the time Beth hung up the phone, she felt much better. A call to Hal raised her spirits even more. Sammy Ferra had phoned to schedule an appointment to sign boarding contracts for the fall.

Things will sort themselves out—they always do.

Connor's assistant poked his head in the door.

"SeeBee, there's a Mr. Trent here to see you. He don't have an appointment, but he says it's real important."

Connor searched his memory. "Trent? Doesn't sound familiar." He glanced at his watch. He still had a few minutes before the next client. "Okay, send him in."

Seconds later, Connor looked up, recognition and surprise filtering into his thoughts as Jamie stepped into the room and closed the door behind him.

Connor extended his hand, then alarm grabbed him. "Is Beth all right? Has something happened?"

Jamie's stony expression didn't change, and his hands remained at his sides.

"You tell *me*."

Connor's instinct told him trouble had arrived. He cocked his head and assumed a non-aggressive posture, settling one hip on the corner of the desk. As he returned Jamie's unfriendly stare, the hairs on the back of his neck stiffened with anticipation.

"What exactly do you mean?"

Jamie took a step forward, his animosity obvious.

"Don't BS me, Man! You paid Beth a little visit last night, and left her in emotional shambles. Just who do you think you are?"

Connor straightened up, anger and adrenaline scrambling

through his body. "And who do you think *you* are? Her keeper? Did you come here to beat me up?"

In two steps, Jamie closed the gap between them. Connor's eyes narrowed and his muscles tensed. Hostility crackled through the air like Fourth of July sparklers.

Jamie broke the silence. "I just wanted to tell you to stay the hell away from her. She doesn't need you complicating her life with your selfish one-night stands. Good grief, man! Do you have to drive an hour-and-a-half to get laid? Seems to me you could find something closer to home."

Connor's arm snapped back, his fist balled and ready.

Jamie stood his ground. "Go ahead. Hit me. That'll look real good on your *professional* profile."

Connor dropped his arm and turned away, his voice ragged with anger.

"Okay, you can go now. You delivered your message."

The door closed with a snap, and Connor leaned forward on the desk, weak and shaky as his anger faded.

Nineteen

Jamie touched Beth's hand. "Are you sure you don't want me to go in with you?"

She shook her head. "No, I'll be fine. Really."

Fine? I feel like I might throw up any minute. Her stomach bounded about like a ball caught in the surf and, for one instant, she wanted to head back home and forget the whole thing. The panic passed, and she squared her shoulders and lifted her chin. *This is ridiculous. My goal is to ride again. That's why I'm here. I'll be damned if I'll let anything stand in my way, especially a foolish mistake.*

The waiting room door opened, and she followed the assistant down the hall. Connor arrived about five minutes later, head down, his hands full of papers. He closed the door, mumbled a greeting, and strode across the room to his desk, then went through the motions of reading her chart in detail.

Finally, he glanced up, briefly meeting her gaze. "So, how are you doing today?"

She watched his features as he talked. He seemed extremely uncomfortable in her presence, and she wondered if he truly regretted their night together. But wondering wasn't enough–she needed to know.

"Connor, is anything wrong?"

His tan paled a little at the direct question, but Beth forged ahead, giving him no opportunity to respond.

"Do you regret coming to see me?" She swallowed painfully.

"Our love-making?"

He looked away, his tone gruff with dismissal. "No, of course not. I'm just...well, I'm really busy preparing for an event next week."

His movements were wooden and self-conscious as he tried to maneuver out of the personal conversation. Her chest tightened with pain, making each breath difficult. What had changed? Why would he make love to her if he hadn't wanted a relationship? Her thoughts skirted the lurking worry that her passionate journey with Connor might have meant nothing to him.

Connor's emotions churned as he watched Beth struggle with the impact of his distant attitude. He hated himself for hurting her. His head suddenly filled with instant-replay images of their night together–a night he'd thought about all day. *I have to be strong. It's best for her.* His own pain embroiled him in turmoil. *But what about me? Don't I count?*

Her voice broke into his mental muddle. "I want to ask you something."

He braced himself for another barrage of personal questions he was afraid to answer.

Her tone sounded stronger. "The other day, I saw a program about riding for handicapped people. It was incredible, the way they were able stay on their horses."

Though the sudden shift in focus threw him, he relaxed. *This he could talk about.*

He smiled. "Yes, it's pretty amazing, and very beneficial. Some of those riders have been classified as 'maintenance cases,' patients whose condition can't be helped any further." He shook his head with wonder. "Then, they perch on a horse, and do things no one ever dreamed possible." He warmed to the subject, relieved to be off the hot seat. "I'm involved with a small group just outside the city. I volunteer there once a week. It's very rewarding."

Beth's jaw line hardened as she stared at him, and he immediately knew he'd blundered into trouble.

Her accusatory tone confirmed it. "Why didn't you ever say anything? Why couldn't *I* be one of those riders?" Her voice rose with emotion. "Connor, I could be exercising and gaining strength on a horse, instead of messing around with leg lifts and muscle stretches. I can't believe you didn't consider me for the program!"

He was caught off guard. "I did. I just haven't had time yet. I figured we could do that after I return from Ireland. I've already spoken to my group about a spot for you then."

"I'm ready *now*, Connor! I don't want to wait for months while you run all over the world to horse shows."

He regained his composure, quickly retreated behind his professional wall, and met her stony gaze. "Excuse me, Beth, but you seem to forget who's the professional here. *I'm* the one who determines when you're ready to move to the next level."

Her tone was flinty. "And did you also determine that you needed to insert yourself into my personal life? That I needed some extra *T-L-C*?"

She turned the wheelchair away from him, but continued to speak, her voice hard with anger. "I really feel used."

In two long strides, he closed the distance between them, and knelt down in front of her. "Beth, Beth, I'm *so* sorry. I didn't mean to hurt you. I came to see you last night because all I could think about was spending time with you, talking and laughing, like we did once before." He shook his head. "I never dreamed the evening would take the direction it did."

Her face showed no emotion as she stared at some distant point.

He reached for her hand, and tried again. "Beth, I can not cross over the professional line again. It was a mistake for me to do so, but I was being selfish. I wanted the chance to know you as more than a patient. I fooled myself into thinking I could do that, but it won't work."

She snatched her hand away and glared at him, anger coloring her cheeks.

"Professional concern? I don't think so. I think you're just afraid to be saddled with a cripple. Deep down, you don't really believe you can help me ride again, and you don't want to be around to face your failure."

His ears rang with the stinging retort, the word "failure" echoing through the mineshaft of his head. He felt as though he were

tumbling into the darkness, finally succumbing to his own deepest
fears.

The empty office felt suffocating. The lingering scent of Beth's
perfume drifted lightly around him as he stared at the open door,
his brain numbed by her parting words. She'd disappeared down
the hall before he could stop her without making a scene.

*She's right. I am afraid of failure. If I couldn't help her ride
again, I'd live with her misery every day of my life.* A moment
later, he acknowledged that, whether she was a personal part of his
life or a patient, she'd penetrated his protective shell, and he was
hopelessly entangled.

As the day progressed, Beth's anger dissipated, replaced by
determined resolve. She pushed all thoughts of Connor from her
mind and focused, instead, on what she needed to rid her life of
the wheelchair. She doubled her exercises to make up for the lost
therapy session, then spent some time on paperwork for Highover.
After supper, she went down to the barn and, surrounded by the
sounds of contented munching and the sweet scent of fresh hay,
she finally relaxed.

At that hour, the horses and barn cats were her only company.
She rolled through the quiet building toward the office, stopping
for a minute by the trophy room. The door to her past beckoned
and she was irresistibly drawn through it. Gazing around the small
room, a rush of pleasure filled her as she examined the photographs
on one wall, a testament to her skill as a young rider.

She pulled out the top drawer of a small desk in the corner, and
extracted the tack room key from its hiding place.

The door swung open and Beth inhaled deeply. The warm,
pungent smell of leather caressed her senses, instantly conjuring
up images of her days on horseback. She switched on the light and
looked over the array of fine saddlery, the light reflecting softly off
the fine patina of well-kept leather.

She moved along a row of saddle racks, inspecting each saddle
carefully, then lingering to run her hand lovingly over the smooth
finish of her best Stübben saddle. Her fingers stopped on a large
rough spot on the front edge and, on closer examination, she realized

the damage had happened in the fall with Paso. Pain pierced her chest and she blinked away the burn of tears threatening to intrude upon her happier memories.

Rummaging around in the far corner of the room, she found her old hunt saddle, long retired.

She removed the cover and smiled. "This will be perfect."

After locking up, she left the trophy room, and continued down the aisle to the office. Two hours later, she'd signed all the paperwork for the NEF event in August, outlined an agreement for a couple of events to be held later in the fall, and drawn up an agenda for the next investor board meeting.

"Miz Webb. What you doin' here so late? My, my! It almost dark out!"

"Cozy! I didn't hear you come in."

"Sorry. You all right?"

"Yes, I just needed to catch up on my work, that's all."

The old man grinned. "Okay. I seen the barn door open and thought I forgot to close it. Gittin' old, y'know."

Twenty

Connor hadn't visited the cemetery in a long time, carefully maintaining a comfortable distance between his life in Louisville and his years in Harlan County. As he walked toward the farthest corner of Potter's Field, he was sadly aware that the burial grounds hadn't been very well maintained. *Even in death, poor people command no respect.*

Standing in front of his mother's grave, he wished he could summon an emotion other than apathy. Why had he come? She'd had no use for him while she was alive–why would she care if he visited her resting place?

Brushing the leaves and debris away from the simple headstone, he thought back to the day of her death, wondering if things might have been different if he'd acted on his own, paid attention to whatever instincts he might have had. Would his mother still be alive if he'd disobeyed her orders and thought for himself? Probably. His entire life had been affected by it, and he drove himself relentlessly to rise above the desperation of poverty, and leave that life behind him forever. Would his mother be proud of his accomplishments? Or would she feel he'd abandoned his heritage–thought he was better than everyone else?

He walked slowly back to his truck, reviewing the choices he'd made. Did anyone other than himself care what he did with his life? His love affair with horses–and the power they instilled in him–were the driving forces in the path his life had taken. There was never any question in his mind when it came to whether or not he should ride in a competition, or take risks, or strive to be the very best in the sport. When he was being Brett Hall, he was the boss, fully in charge and needing no one to tell him the right thing to do.

The strength drawn from his riding experiences infused his professional life, as well. Once he'd established himself as a top-notch physical therapist, he worked diligently to carve a special niche in sports medicine. Long hours, hard work, unlimited amounts of determination, and no outside distractions were the formula that carried him to his current success.

He thought about Beth's amazing resilience and strength. Her determination to be up on her feet again was stronger than any patient he'd ever treated. *She could probably lick this thing without me.* He grinned wryly. *So why am I agonizing over the profes- sional/personal thing?* He considered her interest in therapeutic riding. His own weekly involvement with the group in Louisville filled him with more satisfaction, in one afternoon, than a week of working with patients at the clinic. The comparison sobered him. *Exactly what am I doing with my life? Playing it safe?*

The sun hadn't yet peeked over the ridge when Beth rolled her wheelchair down the barn aisle.

Cozy's dark eyes twinkled. "You sure the early bird this mawnin'."

"I want you to help me with something."

He looked puzzled, and she motioned him to follow as she headed toward the tack room.

She flicked on the lights. "Pull down that old hunt saddle in the corner, will you?"

The old groom gave her a curious look, then lifted the saddle down from the rack, and carefully wiped it down with the soft cloth he always carried in his back pocket.

She examined the selection of bridles hanging on the opposite wall, then pointed. "I want that bridle, the black one."

She felt the leather and checked the fittings, then nodded. "This one's good. C'mon. Bring the saddle."

She turned and headed back up the aisle, and when she reached the grooming area, she spoke with an authoritative tone. "I want you to bring Stinger to me."

"Lordy, Lordy," Cozy muttered, shaking his head as he started toward the far end of the barn.

She smiled as she watched him return with an elderly bay Hanoverian she'd retired from jumping competition years earlier. Stinger had been her first real event horse, and he had a fine temperament.

He whinnied loudly, and Beth chuckled.

"Hey, ol' boy. Miss me?"

She patted the horse firmly on the shoulder, and was rewarded with another throaty greeting. She looked up at the groom's worried expression.

"Now, Cozy, don't fret. I'm not planning to do anything dangerous, but I want you to help me try something. Okay?"

He stood stiffly, bobbing his head, fear creasing his already wrinkled skin.

"Saddle him up. I just want to sit on him."

"Miz Webb, I don' know if it such a good idea. You could fall."

Time to play boss-lady. "Cozy, just do it. I know what I'm doing, and my therapist says I'm ready."

She swallowed the thump of apprehension in her chest. *He'd skin me alive if he knew.*

The horse stood stone still while the old man positioned the saddle and tightened the girth.

"I'll need something to stand on." She looked around the immediate area, then pointed toward the corner. "There, that wooden crate will do."

He retrieved the box and positioned it next to Stinger, and her heart thundered as she struggled to breathe normally. *All I want is to feel a horse under me again.* She took a deep breath, and slowly rose from her chair, trying to ignore her anxiety over the bold idea.

"Now, you hold on to my arm and grab me if I start to fall."

She stepped onto the crate, concentrating on each movement, leaning heavily on Cozy's arms, and willing away the fright creeping into her chest.

A moment later, she took a deep breath and closed her eyes. "Now, help me balance while I mount. Okay?"

He nodded, his eyes protruding with fright.

Her right leg wobbled. *No! Don't you dare give up on me now!* She clenched her jaw and willed the quivering to stop.

She grabbed the front edge of the saddle, and leaned against Cozy's hands on her waist, then lifted her left foot toward the stirrup.

"One, Two, –"

"Beth!"

She gasped and let go of the saddle, almost losing her balance, and sagging into Cozy's grasp. She looked toward the familiar voice.

Connor raced toward her, his features contorted with fury.

Her right leg began to shake violently and she sank to the ground.

Connor came to a standstill in front of her and she glowered up at him. "What are *you* doing here?"

He threw Cozy a cursory glance, then pinned her with a hard look, his voice bristling with anger.

"I came to apologize for my behavior yesterday–and to explain some things to you but apparently, you have no confidence in my recommendations or respect for my opinions, so I won't waste my breath."

Her attitude softened a little at his admission that an apology was needed, but she also knew the stunt she'd just pulled was a professional slap in the face, and she gave him a guilty look. Her heart lurched at the hard anger lines that marred his face, and the muscle twitching along his jaw line.

She pointed toward her wheelchair, and the two men helped her from the platform. She sank gratefully into the seat, and Cozy stepped back, a wary look in his eyes.

"I jus' get back to work, Miz Webb."

He hurried away toward the office, shaking his head, and Beth looked up at Connor, who stared at the floor. She didn't know how to proceed, so she kept quiet, and finally, he broke the stiff silence, his manner stern and professional.

"I can't believe you were going to try something so dangerous."

She studied the lines of his face, hoping she'd find a more personal emotion buried beneath the controlled exterior. Seeing none, she bristled in self-defense.

"I was just going to sit there. I wasn't going to try to ride."

He erupted. "No! You don't understand! You could fall off onto the concrete. The horse could spook. Any number of things could go wrong, and you don't have any muscle control to help yourself if something happens. Can't you get that through your stubborn head?"

She looked down at her hands, knowing he was right, but determined to go forward. She looked back up and gave him her most engaging smile.

"But you said I was about ready for the riding program and, since you're here now, will you help me up?"

His look of astonishment was truly comical, and she giggled. He threw his head back and laughed loudly.

"Beth, you are the most independent pain-in-the-tail I've ever met!"

She tilted her head and grinned. "Well...will you?"

"Unbelievable."

Shaking his head, he stepped up beside Stinger, checked the girth and stirrup leathers, then wiggled the saddle to see that it was secure. Beth held her breath and watched, her pulse dancing wildly with anticipation.

Her legs behaved themselves as she maneuvered herself next to the horse, and Connor's hands held her waist firmly as she stuck her left foot into the stirrup. Then, with every ounce of strength she could muster, she pulled herself up and dragged her right leg over the horse's back. Dizzy with exertion and excitement, she exhaled sharply, and closed her eyes to savor the victory.

An hour later, Connor glanced at Beth's glowing face as she settled into the seat of the golf cart, her voice drifting like music on the warm breeze.

"Would you like to come up to the house for coffee?"

"I really should get going, but I guess a few more minutes won't make a difference."

The cart putted up the lane toward the house, and he followed in the truck, thinking about the amazing transformation he'd witnessed that morning. Beth was a skilled rider with excellent balance, even with her disability. As he'd walked alongside the horse, his professional assessment had told him she would probably ride again.

Later, settled on the terrace, her eyes sparkled and her brilliant smile accentuated her enthusiasm.

"Connor, I can't believe how wonderful it felt to be up there. I didn't realize how much I've missed riding...Thank you *so* much." She tilted her head, assuming a more serious expression. "You wanted to explain something. What is it?"

He gulped. The speech he'd rehearsed all the way from Louisville had flown from his head when he'd entered the barn. Coming back to it unprepared left him feeling like a fool.

"Oh, nothing, I just thought...well, nothing. It's not important." He remained silent for a moment, then lowered his voice. "I'm really sorry about the scene at the office yesterday. I'm pretty confused right now, and there are some things about my past that make this situation very difficult."

She opened her mouth to respond, and he panicked, quickly gulping down his coffee and leaping to his feet.

"I have to run. I'm leaving for Pennsylvania tonight, and I have a lot to do."

"Oh, that's right. Well, I can have Cozy help me mount Stinger, and walk with me, like you did. If I do that every day–"

"Beth! You are *not* to do this again! Do you understand me? I mean it."

Her exuberant smile faded and her eyes grew dark. "Wait a minute. You just saw that I could do it. Why are you being so obstinate?"

"Me? You're the one who's being..."

He backed away two steps, then pinned her with his I-mean-business-look, measuring his words carefully.

"Let me explain something. Therapeutic riding isn't just climbing up on a horse and wandering around the barn. These programs are carefully controlled. Each rider has *three*–count them–*three* people working with him or her. One person leads the horse, and a side-walker is positioned on each side of the horse to steady the rider. Anything less is a recipe for disaster."

He examined her face to see if he'd made any impression. Her steady look of determination fanned his aggravation.

"If you won't follow my professional advice, then you'll need to find yourself another therapist. I won't be responsible for your actions."

He turned toward the door, and Beth's hard-edged voice echoed behind him.

"Fine. That's exactly what I'll do."

Twenty-One

The sound of the front door echoed through the emptiness, slamming shut on Beth's thoughts. *Why does he have to be so obnoxious? He just can't stand it when I do something for myself, yet he's always preaching that I'm the only one who can beat my disability.* Her irritation grew. *What a control freak. He probably dates needy women who make him feel important and manly.*

Suddenly, her head switched gears, and memories of the glorious night in his arms consumed her. The bittersweet images played through her head, bringing a familiar ache to her chest, the pain bringing her back to reality and the decision she'd just made. She swallowed her misery and blinked the mist from her eyes as she reached for the phone.

As she went through the steps of making an appointment with Jim Reed for the following week, she realized she wouldn't ever see Connor again. Numbing pain filled her chest, but the emotion was brief, quickly replaced by the powerful memory of sitting on Stinger.

This is something I can do on my own. I don't need Connor. Tears sprang up, and her heart lurched.

"Yes, I do," she whispered.

Striding through the dimly lit aisles of the quiet barn, Connor ranted to himself.

"Darn it! Why can't she just take her time, and let me be the judge of what she can or can't do?"

Inquisitive heads popped over stall doors, nickering for treats. Connor looked around and smiled. *Such a hodgepodge of horses.* They'd all been donated to the riding program–big ones, little ones, old ones, pretty ones, and some really homely ones. But then, there was always that gift-horse thing.

He stuck his head through the office door and grinned at a chunky woman seated behind a battered old desk. Her lopsided smile revealed several gold teeth.

"Hi, Connor. What's up?"

"Hey, Charlie, I just stopped by to see if you have space for another rider in one of the next sessions."

She consulted the schedule book, then shook her head. "Doesn't look like it 'til the end of the month. Is this a kid or an adult?"

"Adult." *Some of the time.* "She's an accomplished rider, but had a bad accident last winter. I think she's ready to do this, but I had hoped to postpone it until I return from Ireland."

"That's right, you're headed over there to ride with the blue-bloods. Excited?"

"I guess so. I need to keep after Stephen Wegner."

"Yeah, can't let him keep that crown for too long."

Connor left the stable and climbed into his truck, worrisome thoughts bombarding him–Beth's reckless attempt to mount the horse with no one to help her, but an old man–the terrible conse-quences of another fall–her parting nasty retort. Irritation prickled beneath his collar. *I'll call her as soon as I get back from Penn-sylvania, and see where we stand.* He scowled and threw the truck into gear. *Here I am, headed for an important show, and personal stuff is interfering with my focus. Again.*

Beth found it difficult to concentrate against the background drone of construction equipment, men's voices shouting instructions and macho repartee, and hammers clanging against nails. A dull ache had slipped into the base of her skull and her eyelids burned. She leaned her elbows on the desk and tipped her head into her hands. *I'll have to come back later if I want to get any work done.*

"Miss Webb?"

A young man stepped through the door, his movements smooth and precise, testimony to the excellent fitness of his athlete's body.

"Hello, Sammy. Welcome to Highover Gate."

"Thanks. Hal just took me on a tour of the construction site. This place is fabulous!"

"Glad you think so–tell all your friends." She laughed and reached for a folder on the corner of the desk. "I have your stabling agreement drawn up and ready to sign." She pushed it toward him. "If you plan to train with any of the coaches, you'll have to make separate arrangements with them. They're private contractors, not employees."

He nodded, then pulled a pair of reading glasses from his pocket and grinned sheepishly. "Need my specs."

Beth turned back to her own paperwork, leaving Sammy to read his contract.

A nasal voice drifted from the doorway. "Bethany Webb?"

She rolled her chair back from the desk and cocked her head at the visitor.

"Yes, may I help you?"

A short, balding man entered the room, his officious expression sending a ripple of warning through her head. He stepped to within a foot of her chair, then extended a folded sheet of pink paper.

Without thinking, she took it. "What's this?"

He cleared his throat. "I'm Stanley Ferguson with the Kentucky division of the wetlands commission. We've received a complaint that your construction has compromised a stretch of protected land."

Her voice cracked. "There must be some mistake. Our contractors have followed every guideline to the letter."

Immediately, she noticed that the background noise had stopped. No engines, no voices. A cold slab of fear slid through her chest.

Ferguson stepped back. "Your project is on indefinite hold while we investigate. I'll get back to you."

Stunned, she watched him disappear through the door. It *had* to be a mistake. She'd hired the best architect in the area. He'd secured all the permits and surveys...every detail had been carefully planned.

A polite cough brought her back. "Oh, Sammy–Sorry 'bout that." Her gaze dropped to the stabling agreement, still unsigned.

Apology softened his voice. "I'm sorry, Miss Webb, but I'd really like to hold off on this 'til you get your problem sorted out."

"It's just a mistake. We haven't violated anything."

He smiled gently. "I'm sure you're right, but I'd be more comfortable waiting until it's resolved...you understand?"

She nodded numbly, and he left the room. Anger replaced her dismay. This had Tim Trent written all over it.

A few minutes later, Jake's gravelly voice rumbled through the phone, filling her with a sense of security. He would support her one-hundred-percent.

"Jake, I want to call an emergency board meeting. We have a serious problem. Will you get everyone together as soon as possible? We can meet here."

"Sure. Is this about the wetlands thing?"

"Holy Cow! How did you hear about *that* already?"

He chuckled. "Small town, Beth. The claims analyst at the zoning office is a good friend of my wife's."

"She wouldn't happen to know who filed the complaint, would she?"

"Didn't say, but I'm sure the woman is smart enough to keep the details to herself. She could lose her job."

Beth tried a wheedling tone. "Jake? Would you see if your wife could find out?"

"I can try, but don't hold your breath. I'll get back to you about the meeting."

The following morning, Beth rode with Hal to Maarka's training barn on the west side of Lexington, a long enough ride to catch up on all the news. Word of the work stoppage had spread quickly, and Hal shook his head.

"It's a durn shame, Bethey. These bureaucrats seem to jump at any chance to do an investigation."

"I think Tim Trent set us up."

"Whoa, Lassie! Those are strong words. Be mindful of where ye repeat that, or ye'll be up on defamation charges."

She exhaled sharply and gazed forlornly out the window. "We may have lost Ferra."

Hal patted her hand. "This'll all get straightened out. Ye'll see."

Maarka's usual Dutch reserve took a back seat to her enthusiasm, as she talked about Miz Liz's progress.

"She is wonderful. I think she will do a fine job for you."

Seconds later, Beth gasped with delight when Maarka emerged from a stall, leading Lizzie. The mare was blossoming into a fully mature animal, toned muscles rippling under her glossy coat, and a prance in her step that could only have come from intensive schooling and enthusiasm for her work.

Maarka wheeled the mare around to face Beth. Lizzie's ears pricked forward and she nickered softly as she caught her owner's scent. Beth stroked the velvety muzzle, and her throat tightened with joy. More than ever, she wanted to try mounting a horse again.

At first, the skirmish with Connor had only fueled her determination to pursue a riding program without him. Later, after her common sense had kicked in, she'd realized that being part of such a program would require a specialist's referral. Jim Reed wasn't comfortable with the idea, and she'd killed her chances of getting the go-ahead from Connor.

He's right. It would be foolish to try to ride without proper help. She thought about her options again, but came up with nothing new. *I guess I could eat crow and call him. Ask him to help me.*

During the weekend, trying to keep thoughts of the wetlands mess at bay, she glued her attention to the television. She watched every event of the Pennsylvania Invitational, consumed by the occasional glimpse of Connor and Rex, as they moved through the competition. Connor seemed off his game, racking up faults, and certainly not riding with the skill and precision of the world-class equestrian he was.

Her sympathy for his poor performance curled around her like a damp blanket. *How awful to spend all that time in training, then do so poorly. And Rex still doesn't move like he's completely healed.* She wondered again about the past to which Connor had so mysteriously referred. As usual, simple thoughts of Connor became intimate thoughts, and she ached with the loneliness of their separation.

On Sunday afternoon, Jake telephoned during the show award ceremonies, and Beth muted the sound, turning her back on the screen and listening carefully to his words.

"As usual, Trent's schedule had the rest of us jumping through hoops, but we're all available on Friday. Five o'clock okay?"

"That's the soonest? Well, okay, that's fine...Did you find out anything more from your wife?"

"Nope. That one's a dead-end. Anonymous tip on the hot-line."

Beth pursed her lips. *Trent's no dummy–he's not going to get his tail caught in a wringer.*

Jake's voice brought her back to the conversation. "Do you have an agenda for the meeting?"

"Oh, indeed I do."

Twenty-Two

B eth left Jim Reed's clinic infused with enthusiasm again. He'd been pleased with her progress, and had told her she could begin using a walker whenever she felt ready. Her strength had almost fully returned and, since the blowup with Connor, she'd been working diligently at her exercises, including walking along the back of the couch twice a day, carefully warding off memories of another time in that same place.

Through the car window, she watched the green hills slide by. Today, she planned to ask Maarka to let her sit on Lizzie. The pieces were slowly falling into place.

Jamie's voice broke into her thoughts. "I have some news."

Seeing the happy glow on his face, she lifted her eyebrows and waited.

"I've met someone–someone *really* special."

A brief stab of sorrow flew through her head. *Will I lose Jamie, too?*

She reached out to touch his arm. "That's wonderful! Who is it? How did you meet? Tell me everything."

The tale of his chance meeting and whirlwind courtship of a woman who'd just moved to Lexington consumed the remainder of the trip. He chuckled, relating how he'd almost skipped the black-tie dinner where he'd met Lucy Braxton. She had recently purchased a large farm, not far from Jamie's, and joined the Standardbred Owners Association.

"Bethey, it was destiny. She's a horse lady, she's pretty, she's single, and she *needs* me."

His pleasure in finding someone who would let him be in charge unnerved Beth. *What is it with these guys? Is there anyone out there who likes self-sufficient women?* Irritation crackled across her skin, dampening her enthusiasm for her friend's happiness.

He gave her an apologetic look. "I guess I just like to feel wanted."

She didn't reply, her thoughts moving immediately to her own situation. *Yes, I like to feel wanted, too. Connor made me feel that way, even if it was only for one night.* Remembering the sad look on his face as he'd left her that morning, she wondered if she'd ever again surrender herself to anyone, open herself to the vulnerability and pain that came with needing someone.

Jamie's tone was sympathetic. "Are you going to tell me about it?"

"Nothing to tell," she said sadly. "It just didn't work."

The brilliant afternoon sun dimmed with her melancholy thoughts. Connor had called twice following his return from Pennsylvania, but, torn between her desire to see him again and her uncontrollable drive to do things her own way, she'd screened her calls carefully so she wouldn't accidentally find herself on the phone with him. She rationalized that she could talk to him after she'd gained control of her life again. But, the more time that passed, the more awkward and confused she felt.

At Maarka's the next afternoon, Beth pressed her cheek against Lizzie's smooth, warm shoulder and inhaled deeply, gathering every bit of the distinctive horsy smell. Moving a hand over the mare's shiny coat, her fingers followed the outline of muscling that had developed with conditioning, the promise of a strong athlete. But, try as she might, she couldn't picture herself over fences on this horse. The thought was unsettling, and she dismissed it for at least the tenth time that week.

Maarka's cool smile creased her broad face. "Well, do you want to sit on her?"

Beth grinned brightly. "How long can I be gone?"

The woman's pleasant expression changed to one of concern. "Bethany, I really don't think you are ready to ride her. She is too fresh. You said you only wanted to sit on her."

Beth winked and chuckled wickedly, and Maarka's solemn features relaxed a little.

Lizzie stood quietly while Beth scrambled awkwardly up onto the saddle. Other than flicking an ear back occasionally to monitor what was happening, the mare didn't move a muscle. Beth took up the reins, secured her feet in the stirrups, then looked down at Maarka.

"Would you and Jamie just walk along on either side of me with your hand on the back of the saddle, so you can grab me if I start to wobble?"

Maarka frowned and opened her mouth to speak, but Beth cut her off.

"It's okay. I just want to take a few steps to see how she feels."

The trainer's lips settled into a thin line, and Jamie looked downright frightened, but the two of them moved into the positions Beth had indicated.

Once they were beside her, Beth took a deep breath and squeezed gently with her knees. Lizzie jerked forward, quivering with excitement, fresh and eager to go. Startled, then frightened by the raw power beneath her, she cried "Whoa!" a little too loudly, Lizzie jolted to a halt, and Beth nearly toppled off. Realizing she courted disaster with her foolish ego, she began to tremble.

Her voice shook. "She's wonderful, Maarka. You've done a fabulous job–and you're right. I'm not ready yet."

"Yes, she's extremely strong, Bethany. She'll need *very* firm handling once she gets going."

Beth's legs were a little wobbly after her experiment, not so much from the exertion, but more from the adrenaline soaring through her system. Her body and brain hummed as they walked toward Maarka's small office.

The trainer headed for the coffee pot. "Would you like a cup?"

Maarka's coffee was nationally famous for being strong and bitter, and it was a standing joke at competitions that, if a rider was caught drinking the nerve-jangling brew, they could be disqualified for substance abuse.

"No thanks. I really need to get back to the office."

Jamie sat down beside her, his voice low. "What happened back there?"

She gave him an embarrassed look. "I realize now that Connor really knows what he's talking about. My previous riding skills have no bearing on my current ability."

He nodded thoughtfully, then turned to Maarka.

"How soon could Lizzie return to Highover? Could you continue her training there?"

Maarka raised an eyebrow. "Yes, any time, I suppose." She looked at Beth. "Is that what you want?"

Caught off guard by Jamie's question, Beth didn't respond right away. She hadn't had time to think about when Lizzie might come home, but now, a tremor of excitement rippled through her chest.

"I'd love to have her there with me–to groom and enjoy."

Maarka's features revealed nothing of what she might be thinking. "Okay, but if I release the mare to you, I want your assurance that you won't try to ride her until your doctor says you're strong enough."

"I promise. I don't want to end up back in that wheelchair. Right now, I'm trying to find a therapeutic riding program and, when I'm ready, I'll call you and we'll start my own dressage instruction."

Maarka took a swallow of coffee and leaned against the counter. "What therapeutic program are you looking for? There is one in Louisville."

Beth swallowed hard. "I'm not sure. I haven't really figured out how to proceed. Dr. Kellart has given me the okay, but I also need a referral from a qualified physical therapist."

Jamie chimed in. "Hey, wait a minute. I heard about a new program opening up sometime this winter. Over in Frankfort. Don't know much else about it, but I'll bet Connor would."

On the drive home, Beth apologized for her seeming indifference to Jamie's news about his lady friend.

"I guess I've always had you to myself, and don't like the idea of sharing."

He gave her a shrewd look. "You mean, you dislike the prospect of not having me at your beck and call?"

She gasped. "No! That's not what I meant at all. Boy, I just can't say anything right lately."

He squeezed her hand and smiled. "Don't you worry. I'll still be there for anything you need. I promise."

Connor looked through the lease papers and smiled. *My dream barn.* He scooped out a bare spot in the clutter on his desk. *I need to make a list and get organized, or I'll never get everything done.* As he stacked professional journals and unopened mail out of the way, his gaze fell on the entry form for the Dublin Grand Prix. Picking it up, he looked at it as though he were seeing it for the first time. *If I want Beth in my life, I need to be around to make it happen.* He'd called her a couple of times after returning from Pennsylvania, but she hadn't responded to his polite messages.

He gave the entry form one more cursory glance. *What a waste of time and money.* Without hesitation, he opened his fingers and watched the yellow paper flutter into the wastebasket.

Twenty-Three

B eth could now walk firmly with the aid of the walker, but still tired easily, and impatience stifled her at what she considered very slow progress. Regaining her strength on horseback was the answer, if she could just get connected, but despite her efforts, she couldn't find out anything about the rumored new riding program. Frustrated, she phoned Jamie, but spoke to his answering machine, instead. After her afternoon exercises, she went to her room to rest.

Lizzie erupted over the hedge like a rocket, and Beth held on tightly, knowing her horse was out of control. Gasping raggedly, she struggled to stop the galloping mare. Ahead loomed the woods–and Glen Trail. She frantically tried to turn the plunging animal, but Lizzie forged on. Disaster lay ahead, and no one could help Beth as she disappeared into the dark forest. Her brain spun and bells rang in her ears.

Her eyes flew open. The phone was ringing. Releasing a deep sigh of relief, she reached for the phone. *It was only a dream.*

"Beth? Did I wake you?"

Her clattering pulse escalated. *Connor!*

"Beth? Are you okay?"

Gathering her wits, she tried to sound calm. "Yes, I was having a bad dream."

He didn't respond, and she wished she hadn't answered the phone. She fought off the memories, trying to think what to say.

He retreated to a professional position in the conversation. "I'm disappointed that you didn't come back to the clinic. I thought we could work it out...you were doing so well."

"Connor, I don't want to discuss it. We're obviously not a good match. I mean, clinically..."

Her brain screamed, *You fool! Open up, let him in. Isn't that what you want?*

His tone softened. "Please call me if you change your mind."

She set the phone down, and the pain of the past few weeks flooded over her, slipping into every unprotected part of her mind, and lapping against her heart, searching for a way to penetrate the fortress she'd built. Her chest tightened. Here she was, *completely* in control again–just what she'd wanted. Right? Then, why wasn't she happy about it? Why couldn't she let go? Take a chance with him? The victory felt hollow.

Jamie returned her call about an hour later, and she reiterated her futile efforts to locate information on the riding program.

She pushed him for more details. "How did you hear about it? Where?"

"I think it was just a remark by someone at that dinner I attended."

"Do you remember who it was? Could you call them and ask for more information?"

"I could ask Lucy. She might remember." A hesitation echoed over the line. "Actually, I thought we might come over tonight, if that's all right with you. I really want you to meet her."

"That'll be great. I'll look forward to it, but don't forget to see what you can find out about the riding program."

Lucy Braxton turned out to be a charming young woman with curly red-brown hair, interesting pale blue eyes, and an impish smile. Beth liked her immediately. While Jamie told barn stories, Beth felt as though she'd never really known him. His manner was totally different, obviously the result of Lucy's attentions. Beth felt genuinely happy for her old friend, and deeply moved by his obvious adoration of his new partner. Lucy's eyes followed his every move, making it clear to Beth that the match was perfect.

Lucy turned to Beth. "James tells me you're starting to ride again. That's wonderful."

James? Hmmm. "Well, not really riding, yet, but I've climbed up on a horse twice now, and it was *great*." She turned to Jamie. "Have you found out anything more? About the riding program?"

He shook his head. "Sorry. Neither one of us can remember who mentioned it." He brightened. "But I'm sure it'll be well advertised when it's ready to open."

"James has told me so much about you and your determination. I *know* you'll be able to ride again, I can just feel it. I'd love to come over some afternoon and visit you, and see your horses."

Beth's own pleasure surprised her, and she realized that she'd never even had a girlfriend. Her life had been just one non-stop business meeting.

Beth moved slowly along the barn aisle, concentrating on each step.

"Lassie, ye look wonderful!"

Hal planted a warm kiss on her cheek, then stepped back. "The last time I saw ye, y'had wheels."

She chuckled and looked down at the walker. "Unfortunately, this contraption isn't quite as speedy."

"Didn't I tell ye Connor Hall was the best? See how far ye've come?"

Her chest tightened. A gaping hole lay in her heart, and each reminder kept the wound open and oozing.

She looked away from Hal's inquisitive gaze. "I'm not seeing him now. I'm working with Jim Reed in Lex."

To her relief, Hal changed the subject. "I saw your beautiful mare yesterday. She's a honey. Maarka has people falling all over themselves tryin' to buy the animal."

"But I don't want to sell her–I want to ride her."

Hal chortled. "Aye, and so ye will. I've watched her train and she's comin' along well. She's a natural, loves her work. I'll be looking forward to startin' her over fences."

His enthusiasm acted as a tonic, and Beth longed for the day when she would sit astride the lovely mare, feel the power as Lizzie obeyed subtle leg and rein commands. However, a mounting certainty overshadowed her confidence--she didn't want to return to jumping. Was she simply afraid she'd fall again, or was there something else behind her ambivalence? A niggling thought crept into her head. Perhaps her decision to put the mare into training had been premature.

Hal laid a hand on her shoulder. "Chuck Prentis will be here in a few minutes. Want to come see him work?"

She glanced toward the office door, torn between the call to duty and the pleasure of watching a professional in training. During the past few weeks, she'd reviewed the fast-lane lifestyle she'd settled into over the years. A few casual acquaintances, the occasional therapeutic sexual relationship, no personal time–doing nothing but driving herself to build a career and a name for herself. It all seemed shallow now and, at thirty-two, she stood at a crossroads with no signposts.

She smiled. "Lead the way."

They crossed the lane, and Hal held her elbow while she lowered herself onto the front bench of the grandstand.

She shaded her eyes and looked up at him. "How's he doing? Think he'll make it this time?"

"Oh, Aye. He's well on his way. His leg's almost as sound as before his accident."

A chill ran over Beth's skin, even in the midday sun. Three years ago, Chuck Prentis, an Olympic Team contender, had been badly injured in a pedestrian hit-and-run accident, one month before the final qualification jump-offs. His left leg had been shattered in four places, and the word had spread that he'd never ride again.

A movement by the barn proved the prognosis wrong. A muscular Trakehner stallion moved boldly from the shadows of the barn door into the sun, the rider gathering his reins. A moment later, the horse snuffled Beth's arm, and Chuck's freckled face grinned down at her.

"How are you doing? Good to see you up and around."

Beth smiled at her counterpart, the only difference between their situations being the level of expertise. "Thanks. It's wonderful to see you back at it, too."

He laughed. "I never give up. I'm going to do this, if it kills me."

He reined the horse around and moved into the arena, with Hal right behind him. Chuck's words reverberated in her head as she watched him begin the warm-up. Had he been so confident from the very beginning, or had he experienced the same peaks and valleys as she? How were their goals different? Her gaze followed the pair over the obstacles, her brain absorbing Chuck's focus as he folded forward into each jump. Horse and rider were a perfect working team, and Beth had no doubt that she'd see them succeed next time out. With such an example, she had no excuse to fail in her own quest for recovery.

Soft light from the pewter wall sconces reflected off the gleaming mahogany table in Beth's formal dining room. She took another quick look around to be sure everything was ready for the board meeting. Coffee service and finger sandwiches were arranged on the sideboard, and she'd placed meeting notes at each seat around the table. A brief flutter of apprehension tightened her chest. This meeting could get real messy. Then, determination replaced uncertainty–Trent could either play by the rules or get out of the game, and she was counting on the board to support her.

Twenty minutes later, a hint of tension slithered through the men's conversations, polite laughter punctuating the small talk. Beth glanced at her watch, and Jake snorted.

"It's a game, Beth. Trent likes to feel he's controlling the situation. He's probably parked down the road a ways, just waiting to make his usual late entrance."

The doorbell chimed and Jake winked. "I'll go let Napoleon in."

Tim sauntered into the dining room, all smiles and howdies, taking his time with the social amenities. Beth's skin crawled with annoyance, and she quickly maneuvered to take control of the meeting.

"Let's get started, Tim."

He cast a haughty look her way, poured himself a cup of coffee, and sat down.

Ignoring his condescension, she gazed around the group. "As you all know, as the result of a complaint, work was stopped by the wetlands commission." She carefully avoided looking at Tim. "Apparently, someone thought the plans for the jump arena had been altered from the original. The stream along the property line is classified as wetlands, so naturally, they had to investigate."

One of the men piped up. "How far back does this set the project?"

"I spoke to Agent Ferguson today, and he tells me they haven't found any violations, and will probably release the hold by Monday."

Tim uncrossed his legs and sat forward, his features tense.

"So we've lost a week on Phase Two, plus the dressage building needs to be rebuilt?"

She swallowed the urge to snarl an answer. "Yes, but I've spoken to the site boss, and he assures me they can make up the time, if the weather holds."

A murmur ran through the group, and a couple of them shook their heads. A needle of anxiety stitched its way through Beth's thoughts. Wet stormy weather was the norm in mid-spring, but this year had been anything but normal. The timing on the project had become critical–funds for the third phase of construction were due in three weeks. From the looks on a couple of faces, she might have to do some real selling to keep them on-board and enthusiastic.

Pete Woods, an investor from Richmond, spoke up. "Where did the complaint come from? Who'd want to cause trouble?"

Without thinking, she shot a glance at Tim, and a flush of anger darkened his cheeks.

She addressed Pete directly. "Someone called it in on the hotline."

Tim's condescending tone sliced through the discussion. "How convenient! Blame this mess on an anonymous phone call." He looked directly at her. "Have you made any effort to find out? There *are* ways, you know."

Jake interrupted. "Hold on, you two." He threw her a warning look. "Let's stay on track. Even if we can find out who did it–which I doubt–no law has been broken. The question is: Why? What motive would this person have?"

Beth's thoughts churned. If the project continued to flounder, she'd lose her credibility and Trent could say, "I told you so." Worse, he'd make sure the world heard about it, further stifling her grand plans.

Jake's serious tone brought her back. "What about a grudge?

Someone out there pissed off about something?"

Beth nodded slowly. "Ken Barker was pretty unhappy."

Jake turned back to Tim. "You know anything about that?"

Tim narrowed his eyes at the burly board member. "I get the distinct feeling I'm under suspicion."

"No one's accusing you of anything, but you *are* pretty tuned in to the community buzz. And, I will say that we've all been concerned about your constant nit-picking and interference in the continuity of the project."

"Bethany?" Tim's ice-blue gaze pierced her like an arrow. "Do you think I'm responsible for this latest debacle?"

Caught off guard, she stammered, then flushed.

He jumped up from the table, sending papers flying everywhere. "Just because you're incapable of managing this thing, you want to blame your shortcomings on someone else, anything to keep yourself untainted."

Jake rose and grabbed Tim's arm. "Hey! Calm down."

Tim jerked his arm away and scowled around the table. "You guys can have this damned project! I'm out!"

He strode toward the door, turning briefly to pin Beth with the wickedest stare she'd ever seen, his voice menacingly low.

"I hope you go down in flames."

Hours later, Beth closed her eyes against the darkness, listening to thunder boom somewhere in the distance. More bad weather on the way. Her weary body relaxed into the mattress, but her head buzzed with flashbacks to the meeting.

Tim's hotheaded exit didn't worry her–he wouldn't really pull out of the project–but his open hostility in front of the board disturbed her a great deal. Embarrassed her, actually, making her feel as though she needed to justify her actions. Even Jake's reassurances hadn't dispelled the grim promise of a rocky road ahead.

Twenty-Four

Beth uncurled beneath the sheets, enjoying the first fuzzy feelings of waking-up. Soft rays of sun slanted through the window, and Felix crawled out from under the covers, stretching and yawning. His loud motor rumbled to life, and he butted his head against her shoulder.

Sleep had softened the hard edges of her memory of the meeting. She stroked the cat's plush fur, and sighed. She'd dealt with equally obnoxious investors in the past. She could do it again.

"Okay, Mr. Felix. I'm up."

She swung her legs over the edge of the bed, feeling a dull ache along the top of her thighs. The therapist had told her to expect some muscular discomfort as she increased her activity, but, apparently, she'd overdone it the past couple of days.

The phone rang.

"Beth, it's Jake. Trent's been in an accident."

"No! What happened?"

"Wrapped his car around a tree down on Ironworks, near Franklin Stud. He's been flown to Louisville...It's bad."

The black cloud that had been hovering over Highover Gate, and her own life, billowed to inordinate proportions. When would it all end?

"Will he...?"

"I don't know, they don't talk to outsiders. Since you're friends with his brother, I thought you'd want to know."

Self-serving thoughts flew out the window and her chest caved in. "Oh, God, I'd better call him."

A few minutes later, wrapped in her robe, Beth slowly pushed the walker down the hall toward the study, where her cell phone lay on the coffee table.

Jamie's voice cracked when he answered. "Bethey?"

"Honey, I just heard. How is he?"

A long, agonizing silence thrummed over the line before he was able to answer.

"In a coma. Unresponsive." A deep sob. "They're not sure he'll make it."

"I'll be there as soon as I can."

She stared out the French doors at the beautiful morning. Birds chirped and flitted about the trees, the sound of a tractor drifted on the still air. How could life just trudge on in the face of disaster? In an instant, everything had changed again, just as her own life had taken a different course, one rainy morning in the woods.

Twenty minutes later, fully dressed, she stared at the shiny yellow sports car, then swallowed her apprehension.

"Why not? I'll have to try this sooner or later."

She eased into the soft leather seat and tested the brake pedal to see how the pressure affected her leg. *Seems all right, a little shaky, but that's probably just my nerves.* She carefully backed the car out of the garage and swung around to face the driveway.

Smiling with newly found freedom, she idled the car down to the bottom of the drive and stopped, exhilaration briefly eclipsing her reason for the experiment. She pulled onto the road, and headed west.

By the time Beth pulled into the visitor parking lot of University Hospital, her arms ached and a dull throb rumbled through the base of her skull. She turned the key off and leaned her head back, feeling the tension sing through her muscles. *This was probably a little ambitious for my first time out.* Her gaze settled on the huge brick building across the street and a wave of anxiety ran through her chest. In there, somewhere, Tim Trent's life hung in limbo, and her best friend struggled with the possible outcome.

Automatic doors whooshed open, blasting her with the sharp antiseptic hallmark odor of hospitals. The olfactory reminder of her own sojourn in this same facility sent a jolt through her pulse, and she closed her eyes.

"Miss, are you all right?"

Concern narrowed the wrinkled face of an elderly man wearing a shirt with the hospital logo on the pocket.

"Yes, I'm fine. Thank you. Where is Intensive Care?"

He gave her directions, pointing toward the elevators. The silent ride to the fifth floor gave her time to wrestle with her emotions and, when she emerged into the softly lit corridor, her only thoughts were for Jamie.

A long night without sleep had transformed his handsome face into features lined with fatigue and sorrow, and his usually twinkling eyes were dark with emotion. A blue-black shadow wrapped his jaw, and his curly hair stuck out in every direction. Sympathy rolled through her heart and she stepped away from the walker, and into his arms. His hard body quivered, and he hugged her so tightly she could barely breathe.

She hugged him back. "How is he?"

Jamie's voice was dull and lifeless. "No change." He stepped back, still grasping her shoulders. "Did Hal bring you?"

She grinned sheepishly. "No, I drove myself."

His face crumpled and his voice broke. "Oh, Beth! You shouldn't have taken such a chance. What if you'd had an accident, or—"

"Hush. I'm fine. Let's talk about you."

"Nothing to talk about. My brother's in critical condition, and we don't even know how it happened."

A hollow feeling moved through her chest. Indirectly, *she* was to blame. What could she say to him? One look at his devastated face moved her from indecision.

"Let's sit down. I can tell you."

Puzzlement furrowed his forehead, but he said nothing as she settled herself into a straight-backed chair against the corridor wall.

She took a deep breath. "We had a board meeting last night. At my place. The—"

"Jamie! Oh, Honey, I got here as soon as I heard!"

Lucy swooped down and enveloped Jamie into her arms, cradling him against her breast like a child, smoothing his hair down, kissing the top of his head. A shaft of heartache seared through Beth's soul. No one had ever loved her that way. Her throat tightened and her eyes burned. *That's what I've missed in my quest for prestige and money.* Connor's face immediately appeared in her head. *Could I still have it?*

Connor hooked another bale of hay and heaved it off the truck and into the corner. Almost a month had passed since his last conversation with Beth, and he'd been stung by her seeming indifference, but not surprised. *What did you expect, Dummy? You've played so hard-to-get, she'd be a damned fool to take a chance on you.* He flung another bale across the feed-room floor.

"Hey! Quit throwin' 'em so hard!"

He turned in time to see his young helper scramble back to his feet, frowning as he dusted himself off.

"Sorry."

His thoughts returned to Beth. He needed a plan, but had no clue where to start.

When the last of the hay had been unloaded, he walked down the main aisle of the barn, gazing proudly at the rough oak walls and stall doors. A solid, comfortable feeling settled into his chest. *Ol' Rex will love living here.*

A voice interrupted his thoughts.

"Mr. Hall? The grading's done. Do you want to look at it before I leave?"

Connor stopped at the entrance to the indoor arena. The soft brown dirt had been expertly moved and sifted and smoothed. The smell of freshly turned earth filled the air, and dust danced in a band of afternoon sunlight streaming through the windows. *The stage for the future.*

Before leaving, he located the woman he'd hired to look after things.

"Katie, the horses will start arriving tomorrow. Be sure you get someone over here to help us. I have to run up to Lexington right now. I'm not sure when I'll be back today."

"Just be back in time for the television crew."

"Oh, Jeez! I completely forgot! Yes, I'll be here."

As he cruised along the winding highway toward town, his

thoughts raced. *I can't believe I'm finally doing it.* He'd wasted the past six years dreaming about starting his own therapeutic riding center, but now the dream was becoming a reality. He'd spent his adult life making things happen. If he'd wanted it, he'd found a way to have it, and this ambitious project wasn't any different.

He gulped, thinking about the huge steps he'd taken to fulfill the vision. *I hope I can keep things afloat until the center is self-sustaining or sponsored. Taking all this time off from my practice isn't helping my bank account much.*

He parked the truck, and smiled with self-satisfaction at the modern building that would house his new therapy offices. He'd be busy, running back and forth between three places, but it would be worth it. *Besides, I'll be closer to Beth.* Breaking through her icy reserve would be a challenge, but he was determined to try.

The answering machine light blinked from the hall table, but Beth ignored it. Her legs felt so wobbly she could barely remain standing. She'd taxed herself to the limit and she would pay for it. Slumping into the wheelchair, she exhaled sharply.

A few minutes later, she located the Dublin Grand Prix being televised by satellite from Ireland. Why was she doing this to herself? She'd made the decision to eliminate him from her life, and now could do nothing but watch from the sidelines. The screen flickered with the brilliant pageantry of opening ceremonies for the prestigious horse event. Felix appeared, loudly proclaiming he was lonely, and Beth absent-mindedly stroked his soft fur while she watched the riders parade into the arena to rousing music and the noise of an enthusiastic crowd. The cameras panned over the audience, briefly stopping to focus on this celebrity, or that member of the royal family. Unseen event announcers discussed the horses and riders in conversational tones.

The memory of Lucy and Jamie replaced the television images, and Beth again considered her reasons for avoiding Connor. He'd looked so right, sitting at her kitchen table, and she'd felt so right in his arms. She had no good reason for her actions, other than sheer terror of being vulnerable. Pride wouldn't bring him back–she'd have to make the first move.

Her throat tightened painfully at the memory of their last

conversation. Why had she cut him off? *Because you're afraid. Because Connor Hall has a power over you that you can't control, and you know how much you like to be in control.* She smiled sadly, recognizing her own guilt of the very thing she'd accused *him.* She wanted to talk to him, see if she could repair the damage, find out more about him than he'd revealed. How had everything become so complicated? Through her own pig-headed determination, she'd pushed him away, and now could think of no way to reverse it. She could only wait, and hope he would call again when he returned.

She turned her attention back to the television, watching for a glimpse of the man who consumed her thoughts. An hour passed without any sign of him. The day caught up with her and she flicked off the program, wondering if her life would ever return to normal.

Twenty-Five

Beth pulled up to the barn door and sat quietly for a moment, keenly aware of the beauty around her, the fresh morning air nurturing a new feeling of optimism inside her. *I won't give up trying to find out about that program. I know riding will be the best way for me to continue my recovery.*

Because of the large size of the building, she still used the wheelchair for her morning rounds and grooming. She rolled down the aisle, calling out to Cozy as he emerged from the feed room.

"Lizzie's coming home this week. I want you to set up Paso's old stall for her."

The words were hard to say, but as time had passed, memories of the good times together were slowly replacing the terrible images of the accident.

The more recent tragedy of Tim's accident gripped her. The front page of the morning paper had outlined his distinguished career in real estate and land development, detailing his involvement in the Highover Gate Equestrian Center project, but making no mention of any previous collaboration with the Horse Park. Tim had truly kept his secret under wraps to everyone, except Jamie.

As she'd read the article, the old irritation had brushed aside her concern. For his own selfish reasons, Tim had been willing to make her look incompetent, screw up her chances for taking the Highover Gate concept to the equestrian industry throughout the country. Then, her annoyance quickly dissolved into shame–the man might not even live. She had no business keeping her grudge alive.

She rolled into the office and called the hospital.

"I'm calling about Timothy Trent. How is he doing?"

"Are you a member of the family?"

"No, but I'm a close friend."

"I'm sorry. We can't give out patient information."

Beth punched the disconnect button, then dialed Jamie's cell phone and left a message on his voice mail.

Through the huge window of the high-rise condo, the hard lines of downtown Louisville glowed with the last rays of sun. Connor stretched his aching shoulders and yawned. Wrestling ten nervous horses into their new stalls, meeting with the electricians in Lexington, and painting his new clinic office had consumed the entire weekend. *And Beth didn't return my call. Big surprise.*

He pushed away the minor irritation and flicked off the television. The news people had done a good job with his interview, and showcasing the new riding facility. Exposure would be the key to getting Hope Ranch on the map. He grinned. *Hope Ranch. Name's startin' to grow on me.* He sobered. *Just like someone else.*

After his visit to the cemetery, he'd contemplated his last disastrous love affair with Betsy Cooke, a charming, intelligent young woman from an old-line Lexington Thoroughbred family. Though they'd shared an interest in horses, their conflicting backgrounds had generated a yawning gap between them. When Betsy had insisted he give up his "silly chasing after that Wegner-person," Connor had balked. Betsy hadn't understood his unrelenting drive and, in turn, he'd been strangled by her vapid society lifestyle. More disgusted than hurt by the breakup, he'd thrown himself into his sports therapy career, and the pursuit of Wegner's crown.

Once he'd managed to literally climb out of the pits, his poor beginnings in the heart of coal country fed a deep desire for independence. Emotional entanglements hadn't been part of his plans, but now, the plans had changed, based solely on his real dreams. If Beth wouldn't pick up the phone, then she'd find him on her doorstep.

The phone rang as Beth scrunched down under the soft goosedown quilt.

"Tim's vital signs have stabilized." Jamie's voice broke. "He's not going to die."

Beth had a vivid flashback of Lucy's comfort. "Thank God. Jamie, are you okay? Do you want to come over, talk about it?"

"Not tonight, I'm exhausted. I have to meet the attorney in the morning. I'll come by afterward."

"Good. I'll fix us some lunch."

"Beth? You said you knew what happened to Tim...."

"Not tonight, Hon. We'll talk tomorrow."

A moment later, she stared thoughtfully at the phone. Reason had kicked in that day, convincing her that she really wasn't responsible for Tim's accident. Jamie needed to know the sequence of events, and she'd tell him, but she did not intend to accept blame for the tragedy. What she needed now was some input on how it would affect Highover's investment plan.

Business thoughts stormed through her brain and she climbed out of bed. If an investor left the group or, in this case, became incapable of participating, what were the consequences? Would she have to hold off beginning the third phase until another investor was found? She groaned. That would throw off the construction crew's completion deadlines, possibly violate some union code, and most definitely stir up the current shareholders.

She clenched her jaw. Through an unfortunate and unintentional set of circumstances, Tim Trent had succeeded in screwing her up royally.

The doorbell chimed at noon as Beth was slicing tuna sandwiches. She wiped her hands and grabbed hold of the walker as Jamie appeared in the kitchen doorway.

Less tired-looking, but still gaunt with tension, his grim smile reflected the emotions that had ruled his life for the past seventy-two hours.

"Ah, the gourmet cook exceeds herself again."

She lifted her cheek for a kiss. "Shut up."

He carried the plates to the terrace, and Beth followed behind, trying to get her thoughts in order. She'd taken one bite when Jamie opened the conversation.

"You have something to tell me?"

She carefully laid the sandwich down, arranging it neatly on the plate, swallowing the bite in her mouth, wishing she could disappear.

"The board meeting on Friday did not go well. Somewhere in the middle, Tim got the idea that I thought he was responsible for the work shutdown."

Jamie's eyebrow lifted. "Work shutdown?"

"I never had a chance to tell you about it. I never see you anymore since you found Lucy."

He ignored the jab. "So tell me about it now."

"You remember my comment about a saboteur on the project? Well, someone made an anonymous complaint on the zoning commission hotline, implied we were violating the wetlands act, changing plans from the blueprints, some darn endangered snake, et cetera."

He watched her thoughtfully, nodding throughout the account of the situation.

She pushed her plate away. "I don't know how the meeting fell apart so fast, or exactly what set Tim off, but even Jake Biggs had to sit on him." She threw Jamie an apologetic look. "You know Tim–he won't let stuff go. He blew up and stormed out..."

She dropped her voice to almost a whisper. "I guess we know the rest of the story." Jamie's silence unnerved her. "I'm so sorry. Who would've expected something like this?"

"What, exactly, did Tim say before he left the meeting?"

Caution slipped into her head. "Um, that he hoped we'd all go down in flames."

"Anything about his own business involvement?"

Could she get away with a lie? No, Tim's words were part of the meeting minutes. *Where is Jamie headed with this?*

He answered her silent question. "I've been named his temporary guardian. If he doesn't regain consciousness..." Jamie's voice cracked and he looked away, his Adams-apple quivering with his struggle to maintain control.

She remained quiet, giving him the time he needed.

Finally, he cleared his throat. "If he doesn't regain consciousness in a week, my guardianship will be court-appointed, and permanent." Apology edged his features. "I'll have to manage his involvement with Highover Gate, so I need to know what his plans were before he left the meeting."

She shook her head with disbelief at what a mess she had on her hands. "He said he wanted out, but I know he was just angry. He's too money-oriented to walk away from a sweet deal."

"I can't be sure of that, Beth. I *did* tell you he'd had similar plans of his own. Maybe he was ready to head in a new direction."

Uneasiness trickled into her thoughts. "What are you saying?"

"I'm not sure yet. Right now, I need to think about what's best for Tim."

The trip down the barn lane gave Beth time to mull over Jamie's position. His legal obligation would be to protect Tim's interest, but perhaps his long-time devotion to *her* would influence his decisions. A tiny prickle of shame intruded at the selfish thoughts, then righteous justification took over. *I have a lot of money tied up in this project. I have to protect myself, and the other investors, too.* Clearly, a call to Jake Biggs should be first on her agenda.

The welcome sounds of earth-moving equipment and shouting men sent a shot of optimism into her thoughts. *Get back on track, stay there, and start putting out fires before they start.*

"Miz Webb, Mistuh MacGregor called. He's bringin' the mare home tomorrow."

The news excited her, instantly restoring her mental energy. She'd so looked forward to having Lizzie back in her own barn. She recalled Maarka's serious expression as she'd extracted the promise not to try riding the mare, but Beth's growing strength filled her with courage, making her feel as though she could ride anything. Immediately, she remembered her fear as Lizzie's strength and energy had sizzled beneath the saddle. Common sense returned. *I'll just have to wait until I'm stronger.*

Twenty-Six

E arly the next morning, Hal's truck pulled up in front of the
barn, and Lizzie whinnied as she caught the scent of her herd-
mates. Beth made her way to the barn door and watched eagerly as
the beautiful up-headed mare walked off the trailer, ears pricked,
nostrils flared, absorbing the sights, sounds, and smells of home.
Beth stepped out into the yard, and Lizzie let out a heart-warming
nicker.

Hal handed over the lead rope and grinned. "She's all yours,
Bethey."

She gazed at the gorgeous horse standing quietly in front of
her. "Hal, I can barely stand it, she's so beautiful. I'm going to work
very hard so I can ride her soon."

Another voice filled the air, and her heart skipped a beat.

"You'll outshine the mare, Beth."

She spun around and her gaze snapped like a magnet to the
green eyes sparkling back at her.

"Connor! What–? I thought you were in...." Her voice trailed
off while her brain tried to grasp the situation.

"Dublin? Nope, I canceled my entry."

She could hardly breathe. He was right there, close, accessible.
All she had to do was bridge the chasm she'd allowed to separate
them. Her thoughts reeled as she struggled for the right thing to
say.

Hal cleared his throat, breaking the awkward silence.

"Well, I needs be gettin' back." He winked at Beth, then turned
to Connor. "I'll be seein' ye next week."

Connor saw Beth's confusion and swallowed hard. *Uh-oh, this is not a good start.* Playing for time, he ran his hand over Lizzie's sleek neck.

"This is a fantastic mare. Did you just buy her?"

Beth shook her head. "No. I've had her for a long time. She's been in training with Maarka Van der Gelden." She narrowed her eyes. "Why did you cancel the Grand Prix? What are you doing here?"

He explored her lovely features, now tight with apprehension, seeing the defensive barriers she'd thrown up to stave off any pain that might be headed her way. How to tell her about all the changes that had occurred inside him? All the decisions he'd made? About what he wanted more than anything in the world?

He touched her arm softly, hesitated for a moment as he tried to control his breathing, then dived in.

"I've spent the last month reassessing my life. For years, I've directed all my energy into striving to be the best. The best therapist, the best rider, the best whatever else I thought I wanted."

He stopped and searched her face for a sign that she cared about what he had to say. *Tell her now. Tell her how you feel about her.*

He swallowed hard and continued. "I've driven myself to be a high achiever for so long, that I never knew what it meant to be needed."

She snatched her arm from his grasp and glared at him. The sharp edge to her voice cut through his train of thought, bringing him up short.

"And being needed by a cripple made you feel better?"

He was dumbfounded. In his profession, disabled patients feared pity more than anything else, but his emotional involvement with her had blinded him to the reality of her situation. *You fool! No wonder she's on the run!*

She'd turned away and started toward Lizzie's stall, the mare following quietly amid the tension crackling in the air.

"Beth! That isn't what I meant. Please, stop! You haven't even heard what I came to tell you."

He started after her, wishing he could begin again, but knowing he'd just have to muddle through, or give up.

Beth led Lizzie into the stall. Her hands trembled as she un-
snapped the lead rope. Her eyes burned with humiliation. Connor
only felt sorry for her. How could she have missed that? Been so
stupid to think he cared about her as a woman? She glanced through
the wrought iron bars of the stall door and her heart lurched, seeing
the confusion and concern on his face. Her mental tirade stopped
briefly. Had she judged him too quickly? Keeping her eyes lowered,
she came out of the stall and latched the door behind her. *Calm
down and hear him out.*

"I'm listening."

"I'm opening a therapeutic riding center. In Frankfort."

She fixed him with a cold stare, her earlier anger resurfacing
with the impact of his words. He'd lied to her, knowing of his plans
all along and never saying a word, letting her babble about it like
a fool.

"And you're here because you need students? Is that it?"

She started toward the office, but he reached out and grabbed
her arm.

"No! Just listen to me. I thought you'd want to be a part of it.
You were so enthus–"

She shook off his hand, hostility raging through her head like
a wildfire. "If you think I'm going to be one of your guinea pigs,
you have another think coming. Now, please leave my barn."

She slipped into her office and shut the door.

The golf cart inched up the driveway toward the house, a blurry
wash of green and white shimmered through her tears. By the time
she reached her room, a mounting wave of emotion had overtaken
her. Burying her face in the satin pillows, she wept until she drifted
into a troubled sleep.

An hour later, the telephone woke her and she stared at it
warily. *What if it's Connor? What will I say?* Taking a deep breath,
she picked it up. Jake's rumbling voice filled her with surprising
disappointment that it *wasn't* Connor.

"Hi, Beth. I see the work crews are at it again. Are we back
on track?"

She heard her own disillusionment echo through the words,
but she couldn't help it. "If nothing else goes wrong."

"Where do we stand for Phase Three?"

"That's what I wanted to talk to you about, Jake. Tim's brother has been appointed guardian. Unless Tim regains consciousness soon, we'll be dealing with Jamie." She hesitated, not wanting to stir up any rumors. "Right now, I don't know what he plans to do with Tim's part of the contract."

"We'd better get a contingency plan in the works, find someone who'd step in and fill the shareholder void. Any ideas who we might approach?"

A dull ache started behind her eyes, and she massaged her forehead. What was the likelihood of finding someone to cough up three-hundred-thousand-dollars on short notice?

"I'm thinking maybe we should all assume an equal portion of Tim's projected share. It would be easier than finding someone new."

Jake was silent and she guessed he didn't think much of the idea. When he finally spoke, he was brisk.

"Let's get everyone together and put it to a vote. I wouldn't hold my breath, though. We're talking about a significant amount of extra money."

Beth eventually recovered from the shock of her scrap with Connor that morning, but she felt detached and lonely for the rest of the day. Jean had taken the afternoon off to visit her sister in Cincinnati, and Beth rattled around the empty house, unable to settle down. On top of it, the day had been cold, hinting at an early winter, which did nothing to improve her mood. She slipped into a fleece vest and left the house.

In the murky dusk, the partially rebuilt dressage barn gave silent testimony to her mood. She looked around the area, reassuring herself that most of the project was in the final stages. Whether ground for the driving course would be broken on schedule was a situation that had been taken out of her hands. She could only hope her long friendship with Jamie would count for something.

The huge sliding door quietly rolled aside to admit the golf cart to the dark, quiet barn. The staff had left hours ago, and she had the place to herself. A few curious snorts and some shuffling inside the stalls were the only sounds on the still air.

Lizzie dozed in the corner of her stall, hip cocked and ears flopped. Beth didn't make a sound, just watched, hoping her dreams for the future would include the mare. She walked back to the trophy room, feeling the need for some quiet introspection.

She flicked the light switch for the lamps by the couch, then pulled her legs up under her for warmth, and settled into the soft cushions. On the table beside her, scrapbooks filled with her life on horseback and a career in the limelight of success, drew her into the past.

She paged through the albums, reading each article, scrutinizing each photograph, and feeling the warm glow of personal achievement. She'd loved riding, loved her horses, and had done well as a youth equestrienne. But, her financial ventures had been the most exciting part of her life, filling her days and nights with scheming and anticipation, bargaining and concession, tightrope walking and tap-dancing. By no fluke had she become the darling of the entrepreneurial world.

However, the best chronicle of her achievement lay in two full albums marking the progress of her dreams for Highover Gate. The entire history was there, from the first spark of the idea for a world-class training facility, through the latest wins and honors for those athletes who already called Highover their training home.

She stared at the pages. *This is my mark on society. Would anybody miss this great contribution?* The morbid thought surprised her, and the unpleasant truth seeped in—she'd built herself a life that had effectively kept out any intimate challenges. *All business—that's me.* Her thoughts turned to the past months during which she'd been under Connor's spell. She'd felt so different since meeting him. No longer had her thoughts only been filled with the business of Highover, or her own riding ambitions. Consuming a larger and larger portion of her innermost thoughts was a man who'd made her feel desirable as a woman, for the first time in her life. Bitter recriminations crawled through her mind. *My poor judgment.*

A small noise caught her attention, followed by a throaty chuckle from one of the stalls. She held her breath and listened. Cozy had probably seen the light and come to investigate. Though she appreciated his sense of responsibility for her barn, the intrusion annoyed her a little. She listened intently, but heard nothing more. Then, a horse whinnied, and she sat up straight. Someone was in the barn, and it wasn't Cozy–the horses wouldn't pay much attention to *him*.

Frightened, she glanced around the room, feeling compelled to defend herself and her property. She spied a shotgun that Cozy kept for running off coyotes and wild dogs. Grabbing her cane, she moved silently to the wall and lifted the gun down, then turned to face the door.

The scrape of a boot on the concrete floor just outside the door made her heart hammer so hard she feared the intruder would hear it. She lifted the gun and pointed it as a dark figure appeared in the doorway.

Twenty-Seven

Connor moved into the light, his eyes widening in horror at the sight of the gun, his hands leaping into the air.

"Jeez! Beth, it's me. Put that thing down!"

She nearly fainted as her heart slammed against her ribs and adrenaline ripped through her body like a rocket. A wave of nausea billowed up, then subsided and she closed her eyes, leaning against the wall to steady herself, catching her breath, willing her heart to stop pounding.

"Beth, please put the gun down."

Confused, she opened her eyes and looked down at the shotgun still leveled at his chest. She lowered it, exhaled slowly, then sank into a chair.

He dropped his hands and let out a ragged breath.

"Beth, I'm really sorry. I didn't mean to scare you. I probably should have called out when I came into the barn." He grinned foolishly. "Next time, I'll remember you pack a shotgun."

She shook her head weakly. "It's not loaded."

When the tension finally dissipated, Connor cleared his throat nervously.

"Beth, I came back here because I need to start over. I bungled this morning, and you deserve better. There's so much I want to tell you."

His expression emphasized his sincerity, and her heart fluttered at the prospect of a fresh start.

He moved to the couch and picked up a scrapbook. He idly

turned a couple of pages, and his face warmed with admiration.

"Pretty impressive stuff."

"I never rode in the Rolex, or any international shows."

He put the album aside. "Riding over fences isn't the ultimate goal in life, believe me."

She met his gaze. Had she been wrong about him? Was he also looking for something more in life?

He took a deep breath. "That's why I decided to reduce my time at the clinic, and start my own therapeutic riding center. It's been a long-time dream. My life needs some purpose, other than serving my own ego. Everything started making sense to me after our...night together."

A crimson flush moved across his cheeks as he continued.

"When I was eleven years old, I was responsible for my mother's death."

"Oh, my God! What happened?"

He didn't look at her, but rose from the couch and paced the floor while he talked.

"My mother was a hard woman. She had to be. My father was killed in a mine accident when I was three, and she raised my older sister and me, all by herself in a tiny three-room shack provided by the mining company. She worked long hours in the town laundry, and barely got by. Both she and my sister bullied me constantly for being a wimp. I was afraid of my own shadow, the kids at school harassed me unmercifully. I just did what I was told, without question."

Beth watched him walk restlessly back and forth. *He is anything but a wimp.*

His soft drawl curled around his words. "We lived in Harlan County, the heart of coal country, one of the poverty pockets of Kentucky. The hills are peppered with mine shafts, many of them abandoned. One day, Mother and I were out picking mushrooms, and she fell into one of the abandoned half-shafts. It was about twenty feet deep and I just stood at the edge of the hole and cried—I didn't know what to do. She hollered at me and cursed, told me to go for help.

"So, I ran home and told my sister what had happened. She screamed obscenities at me, then ran down to the mine office to get the rescue team. By the time they pulled Mother out of the shaft, she'd bled to death. My sister blamed me. *I* blamed me."

Beth hadn't moved a muscle during the entire desperate story, and now she exhaled softly. Her heart ached for the boy/man standing forlornly in front of her.

"But, Connor, you were only a little boy. How could anyone blame you? It wasn't your fault."

His voice broke. "I know that *now*. But the problem was that I didn't think for myself. I just went home so someone could tell me what to do. Even though I didn't cause her death directly, I've felt responsible all my life. That guilt drove me to crawl up out of the squalor that threatened to suck me in with all the rest of the sorry souls in that area. Getting out is almost impossible. A vicious circle controls the poor. No money–no skills–no job–no money. I stayed in high school, let my sister take care of me, but a plan to escape was always in the back of my mind."

He returned to the couch, pale and quiet, drained of his darkest secrets.

Beth leaned forward in the chair. "What did you do?"

"My escape from home came in the form of a grooming job at a Thoroughbred farm in Callaway. I walked twelve miles every morning and every night, just for the chance to be somewhere else with real people–folks who weren't in desperate straits. The owner liked me, and gave me an old beat-up dirt bike to ride back and forth to work.

"I discovered I really loved working around horses, and it wasn't too long before the owner let me ride some of them. I guess I made a pretty good impression, 'cause he encouraged me to think seriously about my life, consider college–thoughts that had never entered my mind. Where would someone like *me* find the money for college?"

He smiled at the memory, then a wry look changed his face. "Believe it or not, the old man *gave* me the money to get started. I chose physical therapy 'cause it was easy to break into, and there was a big need for practitioners in most of the larger towns, assuring me of a job when I graduated. I eventually got my certification and settled into practice. I discovered I had a knack for treating horse-related injuries, so I began developing that niche. The rest is history, as they say."

The temperature in the room had dropped considerably, and Beth heard the wind whistling outside.

She spoke softly, almost shyly. "Would you like to go back up to the house? It's getting cold down here."

He rose and moved toward the door. "I really should leave. I think I've done enough damage here for one day."

She rose and walked haltingly toward the man who'd opened his wounds for her. She gazed into his sorrowful eyes, resisting the urge to run her fingertips over his face.

"Connor, I'm really sorry about the things I said this morning. I was so hurt that you hadn't told me what you were doing, especially when you knew how desperately I wanted to get into a riding program."

He smiled down at her. "I wanted to surprise you. Actually, I was sure you'd see the television interview before I had a chance to tell you myself." He grinned. "Then, this morning, Hal's comment complicated my plans, and, well...you know the rest."

She studied his lips while he talked and her pulse quickened, whisking away any sense of the cold. His gaze dropped to her mouth and, without thinking, she licked her lips. In an instant, his arms snaked around her, pulling her close. His face drew closer, a question in his eyes. Their lips met, softly at first, then more intensely as their mutual desire burst into flames.

His mouth caressed her neck, his breath hot and sweet, while his arms tightened their grip. Her body sang, responding to her growing passion. His hand slipped to her waist, then moved under her sweater to caress her bare skin, his touch setting off a volley of fireworks in her head, followed by a surge of panic.

Breaking the embrace, she gasped, "No! Connor, please. I can't."

Cold air swirled between their bodies when she pulled away. His face registered surprise, his eyes searching hers.

"Honey, what's the matter?"

The term of endearment caught her off guard, diffusing her fear, and she stepped back into his arms and laid her cheek against his chest. Closing her eyes tightly, she memorized the firm security of his strong embrace. *I want this. I need this.*

He stroked her hair and held her gently, waiting for an explanation. She sighed and stepped back again, looking down at her hands.

"I'm afraid. I...well, the last time we–"

He pulled her back to him and hugged her fiercely. "Oh, Bethany," he whispered, "I was such a jerk. *I* was the one who was afraid that morning. Afraid to let you depend on me. Afraid I wouldn't be able to help *you* out of the mine shaft."

Her leg began trembling violently and she slumped against him. Without hesitation, he scooped her up, carried her to the couch, and sat down to cradle her on his lap. Hot tears lurked just beyond her control, but tenderness softened his finely chiseled features as he lifted her chin.

"Beth, I didn't come here to seduce you. I came to see if I could mend the fence between us."

Connor slid open the barn door and watched Beth climb into the golf cart, his chest thumping at the possibility that his dreams of a life with Beth might come true.

"See you back at the ranch," she said, her breath curling into the cold night air.

A few minutes later, the golf cart moved slowly up the slight incline of the driveway. He idled the truck along behind her, shaking his head at her determined independence. She parked the cart, and he hurried toward her.

"Woman, why are you so stubborn?"

"Because, for now, this is the way I get back and forth to the barn, and I don't want to be stranded up here without it."

Holding her arm, he steadied her on the steps, his skin humming with her nearness. At the door, she turned and looked up at him. A clear and sincere invitation glowed on her face–she wanted him to stay. A small warning wiggled through his thoughts. *Don't get carried away. Take it nice and slow, or you'll be in trouble again.*

He smiled. "I'd like to show you the new facility tomorrow. Do you have some time in the morning?"

She smiled up at him. "I'll make time."

The softness in her eyes almost unraveled his resolve. "I'll be here about nine."

"I'll be ready."

He pulled her into his arms again and kissed her, struggling to quell his rising desire. He whispered goodnight, then headed for his truck. Halfway there, he turned around for one last look. His shadow stretched out across the gas-lit pavement, reaching for Beth.

Her voice tinkled like bells in the cold night air.

"Good-night."

Beth could not fall asleep. Connor's sad story echoed through the confines of her head, adding a whole new dimension to their relationship. She gazed at the brocaded ceiling, following the swirls and loops of the elaborate designs. He'd shown her the chink in his armor, opened himself to attack–all because he cared for her. He hadn't voiced it, but his actions spoke for themselves.

Could *she* open up, too? She'd never cleared time or space in her life for a committed relationship, but it appeared the time had come to do some personal project management.

Twenty-Eight

B y the next morning, the frosty night air had transformed the
woodlands into a fiery artist's palette of reds, golds, and greens.
Beth stood by the French doors and gazed at the brilliant panorama,
her focus moving, as always, to the corner where Paso lay buried.
Brilliant colors dressed the landmark trees, painting the spot into
the surrounding background, pushing it farther back into another
world and another time.

Connor arrived at the stroke of nine, looking incredibly handsome in a red plaid lumberjack shirt. His features looked relaxed,
and he grinned as he stepped through the door.

"Ready for your big adventure?"

She averted her eyes so he wouldn't see the telltale desire
smoldering there. Having him within arm's length sent all sorts of
exciting thoughts through her head.

"I most certainly am. And then some."

The property lay on the outskirts of Frankfort, just off the main
highway. Fenced pasture skirted three sides of the building. Unlike
the traditional New England barns at Highover, Connor's rust-colored California-style stable had everything on one level.

He stopped the truck partway up the road leading to the barn,
then pointed, directing Beth's gaze to the gently sloping, tree-cov-
ered hills on the far side of the building.

"There's a nice trail that runs from the back of the barn, up
through there. It's a really great ride." He reached over and squeezed

her hand. "We'll go trail riding there next spring."

She caught the excitement in his voice and knew she was seeing a whole new side of him, a view she liked. *He would be so easy to love.*

Connor parked the truck next to the building, then pulled the wheelchair out of the back. He'd wanted to bring it along, in case she became tired.

As he helped her out of the truck, holding her firmly as she stepped onto the ground, he began talking about the riding program.

Enthusiasm sparkled through his words. "We plan to open in December, and already have six students signed up. Enough for a class."

She glanced up at his face as he walked beside her. *He's a totally different person. This is obviously very important to him.*

Inside the barn, he nudged her arm. "Welcome to Hope Ranch. What do you think—pretty nice, huh?"

She looked around, appreciating the functional style of the building, well suited for a public facility. She inhaled, enjoying the familiar barn odors drifting on the cool air.

"Yes, it's perfect. You couldn't have picked a better place."

His features glowed with the compliment and he flashed her one of his breath-taking smiles. "Well, come on and see the rest of it."

She smiled, slipping her arm through his as they walked down the aisle. Several inquisitive faces peered through black iron bars.

"How many horses do you have here?"

He stopped at a stall where a large gray horse watched them with interest. "About ten, so far. All donations."

A soft, throaty nicker drifted from inside the stall, and the horse moved closer to the bars. Connor reached through and scratched the horse's chin.

"Meet Rex. He lives here now so I can enjoy him more often."

Beth stepped up closer. "You know, the first time I saw you on this horse, I was a little taken aback. Not many professionals ride Irish Draughts."

Connor chuckled. "I know, and you should have heard the

guffaws and ribbing I received in the beginning. Had the nickname 'farmer boy' for a while." He turned and winked. "No one's laughing now."

Beth gazed at Rex's gentle face and kind eye. "I don't know much about the breed."

"First and foremost, they have fantastic temperaments, and they can jump absolutely anything." His voice softened as he stroked the smooth gray jaw. "I love this horse."

An hour later, Beth's legs protested, and Connor helped her into the equipment room, where she sat on a tack trunk while he retrieved the wheelchair. She gazed around the room, absorbing every detail. Most of the equipment looked new, and the room smelled of saddle soap and leather oil. Her perusal stopped on a peculiar-looking saddle. The customized seat was fitted with several straps and an iron handle, similar to those she'd seen on the television documentary.

"That puppy cost me almost a thousand bucks." Connor pulled a woeful face, but his pride showed through. "In the beginning, we'll use it to assess balance for riders, before we let them sit on a horse. Eventually, we'll need to buy a couple more for the really severe cases."

His tone softened and his eyes shone while he talked about the children he'd worked with in the past.

"Beth, you can't believe how good it feels, watching these kids perform the simplest tasks. For them, to be in control of *anything* is an accomplishment."

He stopped talking and gazed at some distant point, then shook his head sadly. "I'm just sorry I wasted all those years chasing after my own ego."

His manner had changed so much from the arrogant, impudent male she'd met on horseback that spring. His pseudo-professional facade had fallen away, revealing a gentle and caring man, ready to pay back a life-saving favor by helping others.

She stood up and touched his arm. "I think what you're doing is wonderful. Seen from this side of the wheelchair, I can appreciate how important this program will be to those who are part of it." She stared at the floor, sadness briefly chilling her heart. "I wish *I* had something more to contribute to the good of humanity besides a fancy facility...My accident certainly provided me with plenty of time to think about my life, and what I *haven't* done with it."

She fell silent, and he slipped his arms around her.

"Honey, you have a whole lifetime ahead of you, time enough to mold your life into whatever you want *now*."

A few minutes later, they moved down the aisle and stopped in front of a bright red door with a small "Office" sign. Connor fumbled through a ring of keys, then opened the door, and swept his arm through the air like a tour guide.

"And here we have Central Ops, deep in the bowels of the organization."

Two gray metal desks occupied the large room. One desktop was clear, the other was piled high with papers, books, newspapers, a computer, adding machine, and a riding helmet.

She threw him an amused look. His cheeks colored and he began shifting a couple of piles around on the desktop.

"I haven't had time to organize myself and put stuff away."

She pointed at the other desk. "What neat and tidy person sits here?"

"That's for the facility manager. I haven't hired anyone yet. We should have our non-profit status by the end of this month. I've invested in a short lease for the building and buying some equipment, but the goal is to have the program self-sustaining, or one hundred-percent-sponsored, as soon as possible." He rolled his eyes. "*Really* as soon as possible. My bank account is dwindling quickly, now that I'm only seeing patients part-time–which is only temporary. Things will be tight until the Lexington office opens and this place is operational, so I'll keep the paid staff to a minimum until I have some experience under my belt."

She felt the small shift in his optimism. He'd taken a huge leap, and now feared it wouldn't work. Her own worries about keeping Highover Gate on track made her sharply sympathetic to his anxiety. She rose from the wheelchair and stepped close to him. Reaching up to brush her fingers across his cheek, her chest ached with the intensity of emotion in her heart, and she wondered how her life could have gone on so long without it.

"It *will* work, Connor. You're doing something wonderful and, before you know it, you'll have plenty of money and lots of employees to handle the work load."

His face brightened at the encouragement, and he chuckled nervously. "Yeah, I know. Just...well, sometimes I get nervous about heading over unknown fences. I'll probably be less jittery once I move in down here."

"You're actually moving from the city to way out here in the boonies? Are you sure you'll be happy?"

He laughed. "My dear, you forget that I am originally from the grandfather of all boonies–mining country."

His expression sobered. "I'm looking forward to it more than you could know. The fast pace and superficiality of the city were wearing thin on this ol' country boy. I'm ready to return to the earth."

His optimism sent visions of the future flashing through her head. Where were they headed? Would there really be a future together? Despite her years in Southern California, she'd longed to return to her home in the rolling hills, and Highover Gate had been her ticket back. Would she be willing to relinquish any part of that for Connor? Apprehension crackled through her chest, and she glanced at him as they wended their way through the dim barn.

His smile briefly soothed her turmoil. "C'mon, I'll show you the house."

As they left the barn, her thoughts reeled again with the obstacles ahead for both of them, if they were to be together. The demands of Highover Gate required all of *her* time, and Connor would be immersed in establishing the success of the riding center. When would they ever find enough time to nurture a love affair?

A small ranch-style house with red shutters sat a few hundred yards from the back entrance.

He slashed the air with karate chops. "The shutters have to go."

"Oh, I don't know...they sort of...well, yeah, you're right. They're pretty tacky."

While they moved through the house, he talked about what he'd like to do to make it more livable.

She gazed around as she followed him. "It's not a bad little place, it just needs some TLC."

He shrugged. "I guess I'll have to live with the chaos, but I don't care. I can't wait to get away from the city."

They stood silently, side-by-side in the small living room, gazing at the panorama of gentle hills framed by the large picture window. Several deer moved out of the woods and into full view.

Connor took her hand, emotion deepening the color of his eyes. "This is how I want to live."

She met his gaze and nodded, fully in tune with her emotions. He gathered her into his arms and she melted against him, molding to every curve and surface, her heartbeat matching tempo with his.

Parked in front of the big house, Connor watched Beth collect her gloves and cane.

"You've made fantastic progress, Honey. I just wish I'd been responsible."

She shook her head, looking a little shamefaced. "I'm sorry, Connor. I'm so stubborn when it comes to wanting what I want, when I want it." She gazed at her hands for a minute. "I built my fame and fortune on my hard-headed nature."

He softened his tone. "I've been following your drama in the newspaper. How are things shaping up?"

"Things have become fluid, actually. At this moment, I have no idea what will happen next."

His interest apparently released her frustration, and she began to talk.

"My friend, Jamie, seems to be on the fence about his brother's involvement in the project."

"You know these men pretty well, huh?"

"Sometimes, I think *too* well. When we were kids, Tim was always a bully–he's *still* a bully." She frowned. "He and Jamie had more than one fistfight in those days."

Connor grinned. *I suspect the fistfights weren't over horses, my dear.*

"As soon as he graduated, Timmy left town to make his fortune. He planned to show us all that he was an entrepreneurial genius."

"From what I've seen, he does quite well."

She glowered. "Of course he does, he's a shark in a fish bowl!"

She stared at her hands for a moment, then sighed. "If he doesn't regain consciousness by Monday, the court will permanently appoint Jamie as guardian and executor of Tim's assets–and that includes stock in Highover."

"Surely there are other business people who'd jump at the chance to be involved. That seems the most logical solution, doesn't it?"

"It's an option that's already been broached. Personally, at this late stage, I'd rather divide Tim's share amongst the current investors, than bring in an unknown."

Connor hesitated before responding, wondering if he was overstepping his bounds.

"Are you sure this isn't a personal control thing, rather than straight business? I mean, your history with Tim being what it is?"

Anger flashed through her beautiful eyes, then disappeared. "No, I'm *not* sure." She looked away. "God, Connor, I'm so tired of struggling with this thing...sometimes I just want it to go away. Let me ride horses, have a life."

His heart ached with her misery. *If I can be any part of that life, just sign me up.*

Twenty-Nine

B eth brushed the tangles from her hair and studied her reflection in the bedroom mirror. The woman gazing back at her
had changed drastically in just one day. Thinking back over her
life, she recognized the joys she'd missed without even knowing it.
How could I have lived this long without finding my soul mate? An
inner voice immediately took up the argument. *Buried your head
in your work and never looked up long enough to give anyone a
chance–that's how. Always unwilling to give up control of any part
of your life.*

Was she ready to give up that control now? Exactly what would
be required if she wanted Connor as a permanent part of her life?

The doorbell rang and she took a deep breath, casting one last
look at the stranger in the mirror. Male voices echoed in the foyer
as she started down the hall, her thoughts already refocused on the
emergency board meeting.

Jake smiled broadly as she entered the dining room. "Afternoon, Beth. My, looks like you've almost got it licked."

She glanced down at the cane and nodded. "Pretty much." She
looked around at the others. "Where's Pete?"

"He couldn't make it, but I talked to him for quite awhile. I
know where he stands."

Jake more or less took over the meeting. His strong financial
background made him well suited for analyzing the complicated
situation, but more important to Beth, having his support was para-
mount. Besides that, she was tired of playing the heavy.

After a brief glance at his notes, Jake cleared his throat. "As it stands, the contract gives us several options." He looked directly at her. "You said the court will step in if Tim hasn't regained consciousness in seven days?"

She nodded. "Yes, but I'm sure Jamie–"

He held up a hand. "Beth, we all need to understand the wording in the contract. Right now, James Trent is not an investor–he's an instrument for Tim's participation. Until there's a permanent power of attorney, James has no say in what we decide."

A mix of anger and trepidation trickled into her thoughts, but Jake's firm rebuff kept her from arguing. She listened closely to his summary of the choices available.

"Best scenario would be if Tim regains consciousness and can tell us what he wants to do." A crease deepened across Jake's forehead. "Unfortunately, it doesn't sound like that will happen, so the next best thing would be for the temporary guardian to act on Tim's behalf, and invest in the final phase." He threw an apologetic grin at the attorney in the group. "But, lawyers being what they are, I'd bet money he'll be advised not to do that. He's not a mind-reader."

A chill moved across her shoulders. She was sure that Jamie would support her, prevent the derailment of Highover, but, apparently, the others didn't share her confidence.

"Beth has suggested that we all absorb equal portions of Trent's participation to keep this thing moving forward. Anyone want to discuss that option?"

Disgruntled murmurs drifted around the table, then the accountant leaned forward in his chair.

"We're talking about a helluva lot of money, Jake." He glanced ruefully at Beth. "I don't have it to spare. If I can't come up with it, does that mean I'd have to withdraw from the whole project?"

The lawyer shook his head. "Under the circumstances, we could write an emergency addendum to the contract to override the requirement of full participation."

Beth finally spoke up. "Why don't we just wait and see what happens with Tim? And Jamie's guardianship? I think you're blowing this all out of proportion."

Jake held up his hand. "Since we don't know what James will decide, the easiest and most obvious solution is to get busy and start looking for another investor who'd be willing to step in, if it comes to that." He frowned. "Your friend James needs to let us know right now where his inclinations lie. Once the judge's gavel comes down on the decision, we have to be ready to move quickly, if we're going to meet our deadlines."

Beth said nothing. It looked as though the future of Highover Gate might become someone else's responsibility.

Jake rose from his chair. "I suggest you all spend the weekend talking to your wealthy friends and relatives, or even business contacts." He turned to her. "Did James give you *any* indication of when he might make a decision?"

She shook her head. "No, but I'll talk to him tonight and–"

"Beth, in view of your personal involvement with him, it would be better if I talked to him about this. When we're finished here, I'll give him a call."

Jamie called early the next morning.

"Jake Biggs left a message on my machine. You know anything about it?"

"Yes, the investors met last night to discuss the situation with Tim. How *is* he?"

Jamie's voice was tight. "No change. I'm here with him now. You were saying...?"

"Naturally, everyone is concerned about Tim's recovery, *and* his status as a member of the project. We talked about possible options if Tim doesn't...er, can't..." She closed her eyes tightly. This was *so* hard! "Jamie, I know you're hurting right now, but, do you have *any* idea what you're going to do?"

He sounded offended. "Why did Jake call me? Why not you?"

"They think I'm too personally involved with you to be effective in this, that I can't think or act in the best interests of the project."

Silence hummed over the line, then he exhaled heavily. "Okay, I understand. I'll call him back later this morning. Tim's scheduled for a brain scan, then I'll head home."

"Jamie? Do you–?"

"Beth, I just can't make any decisions right now. I'm sorry."

"Ouch!"

Connor swore softly under his breath and shook his hand, glaring at the stubborn pipe joint that had just bitten his fingers. A minute later, he again wrestled with the assembly, his thoughts drifting to Beth, thoughts that had filled every waking moment since the night they'd opened up to each other.

For all his determination to win her, he still felt cautious. He'd need to take things slowly. She'd been "in charge" her entire life, and changes wouldn't come easily to someone so independent. *What changes are we talking about? Marriage?* Another thought popped into his head and he closed his eyes. *Where would Highover Gate fit into this picture?* He hadn't given that one any consideration. A permanent relationship would definitely entail more than just mutual love.

He rocked back on his heels to survey the assembled contraption before him.

A telephone lineman stuck his head in the door. "Phones 'er workin'."

Connor moved to his new desk, and dialed Beth's number. *I'll just put this number into auto-dial—I plan to call it a lot.*

Beth spent the rest of the day in the barn office, working on marketing plans for the coming year, and trying to keep from second-guessing what Jamie would eventually decide. She glanced at the calendar, then out the window to the grounds. Would it be the end of the world if the third phase were delayed? Or didn't happen at all? She sucked in a deep breath, stunned by the uncharacteristic thoughts. Highover's success had been carefully planned as a stepping-stone to a second career, one that revolved around her passion for horses and riding, a way to be successful *and* have the life she wanted. When had that changed?

"H'lo Miss Webb. Are ya busy?"

Sammy Ferra's smile twinkled from the doorway.

"No, no, I need a break. Come on in."

"I understand everything's back on track, and I'd like to sign that contract, if you'll still have me."

She laughed. "I'm not sure which track we're on, but I'll certainly sign you up for the ride."

A few minutes later, he pushed the papers back across the desk. "I was wonderin' if you might have a spot for my little brother."

"He rides, too?"

Sammy's cheeks reddened and he shook head. "Oh, no, I mean a job. He's still in high school. I'm from Richmond. My family's still there. Tip, my little brother...well, he's been worryin' me a lot lately."

Beth listened to the tale unfold. The Ferras were an old family whose wealth had sprung from the discovery of oil and gas in turn-of-the-century coal-rich Kentucky. Apparently, with too much money and too little parental attention, young Tip had headed down the wrong path, spending his time with a group of unsavory acquaintances, skipping school, and thumbing his nose at the world.

Sammy's disappointment shadowed his face. "He's really a good kid, I think he's just frustrated by the situation."

She nodded, giving him the time he needed. He shifted in the chair, obviously feeling guilty about his disclosure.

"Our folks stay pretty busy with their social life and all. We sorta raised ourselves—just us two and the nanny. I've taken him with me on some of my show trips, and he seemed to like it. He does like horses."

While Sammy reviewed his brother's problems, Beth thought briefly about Connor's childhood of despair. Excitement buzzed through her head. *Here's a chance for me to do a good deed for another human being. Maybe I can provide this boy with a chance to do something worthwhile on his own, something money can't buy, something that'll show the world he's a real person—not just a spoiled rich kid.*

Her own enthusiasm startled her. She hadn't spent much time worrying about other people's problems. What had changed?

She smiled. "I'd be happy to help out."

Relief and gratitude washed over Sammy's features. "Thank you, Miss Webb! Y'all won't regret it, I promise. I'll keep him in line while he's here—Oh, I mean, I don't think he'll be any trouble, but just in case, I'll be around."

She laughed, hoping to ease his discomfiture. "Don't worry—unless he's doing something illegal, as far as I'm concerned, he can just be a teenager while he does his chores." She winked. "I don't think it'll be a problem. We work hard enough around here to stay out of trouble–we're all too tired."

After several sincere thank-you's, he left, and her thoughts returned to Connor's story. *This is almost the same, but at the other side of the pendulum.* She picked up the phone and dialed the riding center. She couldn't wait to tell him.

The answering machine picked up, and his rich voice said to leave a message. *Nope, I want to tell you in person.* Thinking about the past few days, and how quickly her life had changed in so many ways, a sense of purpose filtered through. Whatever obstacles lay ahead, she would overcome them, regardless of what she might have to do.

She'd just eased her tired body into the golf cart when Cozy stuck his head out the barn door.

"Miz Webb, the phone's fer you."

"Tell them I'll call back tomorrow. I'm going home."

The cart moved up the lane, and she gazed around at the magnificent landscape. The thin tinkle of her cell phone broke the crisp silence, and Connor's soft voice sang through the tiny instrument. She braked the cart and nestled the phone closer to her cheek, remembering how wonderful it felt to be in his arms, the thought stirring the desire simmering deep inside her.

She smiled. "I called your barn earlier. They said you were in Lex. How's the office coming along?"

"All set. I can open for business as soon as I transfer all my files and papers–probably another week. You busy tonight?"

"No, in fact, the reason I called was to see if you'd like to come over. I have some exciting news."

"How 'bout I bring a pizza? You supply the beer."

She giggled as she pocketed the phone. *Beer and pizza...classy dinner date.* Romantic scenes poured into her thoughts and, by the time she'd reached the porch, her skin tingled with the anticipation of being with him again.

Feeling like a kid, she grinned mischievously and affected a shrill soprano voice. "Who is it?"

"Pizza delivery."

Connor pulled a comical face and exaggerated his drawl. "Y'all order twenny-five pizzas?"

He stepped into the entry, and planted a firm kiss on her forehead. "Where's the beer? I'm starving."

Thirty minutes later, they sat at the kitchen table, surrounded by the debris of carryout. Half listening, Beth watched Connor's movements and expressions as he talked about the new office. Suddenly, she realized he'd asked her a question.

"What?" she stammered.

He set his beer mug down. "I said, what's your news? You had something exciting to tell me."

She leaned forward, elbows on the table, and related Sammy Ferra's story. When she finished, she sat back.

"I think it would be very good for the boy, don't you?"

He nodded emphatically. "I do. I believe that if you can keep even one youngster from starting off on the wrong foot, you've done a service to humanity. Imagine how great the world would be if every single person took responsibility for just one kid."

She gazed at the man who knew, better than anyone, how important that could be. She met his gaze and saw frank admiration. Her heartbeat quickened and vivid intimate images stormed into her thoughts.

He reached across the table and caressed her fingers. "I know you've sometimes felt as though your life has been self-serving, but believe me, something good will come of your dedication."

Without a word, she rose and moved to his side. She leaned down and kissed the top of his head, closing her eyes as his arms encircled her hips. He pulled her close and laid his face against her belly as she sifted her fingers through his silky hair, succumbing to the feelings that raged through her.

He rose and pulled her into his arms, his soft lips moving down her throat toward the tender flesh peeking from the open collar of her shirt. She pulled his head into the soft cleft between her breasts, her skin on fire from his touch. At the bold invitation, he moaned and fumbled with her shirt buttons.

Drawing back gently, she gazed into his eyes, letting him see her longing. Then, without a word, she took his hand and led him down the hall to the bedroom. ▨

Thirty

B eth's gaze swept across the ambitious project that had been the focal point of her life for the past two years, her thoughts on the intimate breakfast she'd shared with Connor, mere hours ago. Warmth eased through her chest and curled around her heart. She'd awakened at dawn and watched him sleep beside her, resisting the urge to run her fingers across his cheek. Instead, she'd slipped out of bed and headed for the kitchen to fix breakfast for her lover–for the first time in her life.

She closed her eyes and listened to the muted sounds of morning in the barn. Her warm fuzzy feelings faded, and she sighed. Why had she suddenly frozen up as they'd said their goodbyes? *Life just isn't fair. Now that I know he cares, I should be able to relax and enjoy this new part of my life. Why does it frighten me so much? I've almost conquered my disability. I should be able to pick up the pieces of my life and fit them all back together neatly.* Problem was, she now had an extra piece. Where did Connor fit?

She stared at the phone, her thoughts prodding her to pick it up and call Connor, try to apologize for her panic attack. The electronic tones danced through the receiver, then a woman's monotone recited, "You have reached the Lexington offices of Connor Hall. The office isn't open now, but if you'd like to leave a message..."

Beth's shoulders sagged, and she turned to face the pile of work on her desk.

Cozy stopped by to look over the next month's schedule, and she told him about Tip Ferra.

The old man smiled and nodded. "That's good, Miz Webb. Boys need sumpin' to keep 'em busy. They gits in trouble without it."

She wrote Tip's name on the work roster, idly wondering if the boy would stick with it when he realized the hard work involved in maintaining a large horse barn.

"When Sammy calls, tell him Tip will work afternoons, then arrange for us to meet the boy before he starts. I'd like to get a feel for young Tip's interest in the job."

Cozy disappeared and Beth checked her watch. Lucy would be arriving in about an hour, and Beth looked forward to a relaxing lunch, and afternoon of company. She'd originally planned to ask Lucy how meeting Jamie had changed her life, and what effect those changes had made on her, personally and emotionally. But now, Beth had doubts—she barely knew the woman.

Lucy sat back in her chair and let out a long contented sigh. "That was delicious, Beth. I'm stuffed." She glanced around the elegant dining room. "You have such a gorgeous house. I bought my own place because of the fabulous barns, but the house isn't much." She brightened, her voice bubbling. "But it works for me. Oh, that reminds me—I'm having a party in three weeks, sort of a house-warming thing. Will you come? Do you need James to pick you up?"

"No, my therapist gave me the go-ahead to start driving again, but I haven't practiced much."

Lucy's face reflected curiosity. "Is this the therapist James mentioned?"

Beth grinned. "Which one? I've used up two so far."

Lucy looked embarrassed. "Oh, well, he said you were working with a therapist who also rides horses."

"That was quite a while ago. I've been with Jim Reed in Lexington for the last few weeks."

The awkward silence grew, and Beth tried to think of a graceful way to change the subject without explanation.

Lucy leaned forward, a warm glow brightening her face. "If you'd like to bring someone to my party, please do."

"Thanks, I might just do that." Her cheeks warmed. "Lucy, may I ask you something personal?"

Blue eyes twinkled with mischief. "Mmm, I don't know. *How* personal?"

Beth faltered for a second, then jumped in. "When you met Jamie and the two of you got together, did you have to give anything up? I mean, anything important? How much has your life changed?"

Lucy laughed with delight and leaned back in her chair. "Do you have a couple of days?"

For the next hour, Beth listened to Lucy's day-by-day description of Jamie's courtship. Her love for him was obvious, and her voice sparkled as she related the story of the weeks she'd spent sparring with Jamie's wit, and dancing around the strong attraction that had quickly grown between them.

"I kept telling myself the timing was all wrong, that I needed to be settled in my new surroundings, put my barn in order, blah, blah, blah..."

Beth grinned, recalling all the similar thoughts she'd been having.

Lucy continued. "Then, one day, I looked back over my life and realized I'd been given a chance for a new start. So, I just turned my back on what I thought I should be doing, and let myself be swept up in the joys of the romantic learning curve."

Beth followed every word for the next hour, relating keenly to Lucy's story. Strong independence had cemented Lucy's success in the Standardbred industry, but that same strong will had almost been her undoing with Jamie. Her situation paralleled Beth's, and the comparison clarified Beth's vision of the future. If she wanted Connor, she'd better be ready to throw caution to the wind and let it happen.

Lucy's voice cut into her thoughts.

"I've only recently returned to a somewhat normal routine at my barn." She set down her empty coffee mug, grinning impishly. "And you know what? The place was still there, hadn't suffered even slightly by my absence."

Beth smiled ruefully. "Yes, I know that feeling. Business here continued pretty much as usual while I was recovering from my accident. It kind of brings you up short to realize just how dispensable you are."

Lucy's tone turned serious. "I'm so grateful to be able to be with James right now. I think he needs my support, and I'll do whatever it takes to help him weather this tragedy." She hesitated, her sweet face reflecting sincerity and friendship. "I don't know anything about your personal life, but he did mention that you were having an emotional roller-coaster ride with someone. If you ever need some girl talk, or want a shoulder to cry on, I'm just a phone call away."

Hot tears sprang up behind Beth's lids, and she blinked them back.

"Thanks, Lucy. That might happen sooner, than later."

Twenty minutes later, Beth guided the golf cart down the driveway. Beside her, Lucy chattered pleasantly.

"So, tell me about your plans for Highover Gate. James says the place is *huge*."

"Yes, it is. The full estate is about three thousand acres. When the facility is finished, it will be the only one of its kind in the country, other than the Horse Park, of course." She smiled proudly. "We already have two Olympic hopefuls signed up to train here."

Lucy's face registered genuine awe. "Wow! That's really neat. Will any of them be around today?"

"I never know. Besides, like you, I've been away and my staff has been running the place." She shook her head solemnly. "Quite well, I might add."

Lucy reached over and touched her arm.

"Just *remember* that, as you struggle to make choices in your personal life."

Thirty-One

The afternoon light had faded and the barn office was almost dark. Connor flicked on the lamp and stared at the papers in front of him. No matter how hard he tried to concentrate on the new volunteer schedule, his thoughts kept returning to Beth's chameleon act that morning.

Why is our relationship such a yo-yo? First, I can't make a decision, and now she's on the run. I know she cares–she can't hide it, but what's driving her fear? He'd been over the scenario several times already, and still couldn't come up with an answer. After a glorious night together and a warm, intimate breakfast in the sun, her strained goodbye had been unsettling.

He leaned back and rubbed his eyes, then stretched the tension from his shoulders. Heaving a discouraged sigh, he turned off the light and headed across the aisle toward Rex's stall. As he slid the door back, a rich throaty chuckle greeted him, and he smoothed his fingers over his best friend's glossy coat, while again reviewing the uncomfortable parting. *I shouldn't have let it go. I should have challenged her to tell me what's bothering her...Hah! Easier said than done.* When provoked, Beth had the power to send him scuttling for cover.

The telephone echoed across the aisle and he tuned it out, while he scratched Rex's chin. "We're not here. Right, Buddy?"

Beth's voice echoed on the speaker, and Connor dashed toward the office door.

Snatching up the phone, he gasped, "Hey! I'm here!"

Her giggle caressed his ear. "How far did you have to run to catch the phone?"

"I was across the aisle, visiting Rex."

A large gray head peered curiously into the office, and Connor laughed out loud.

"Hold on a minute. I forgot to close his stall door, and now he's over here looking for a job."

When he picked up the phone again, he winced at her serious tone.

"Connor, I'm sorry about this morning. I've been so confused and–"

"Beth, we really need to talk. I want to know what's going on in your head. Why do you send me such conflicting signals?"

"Could you come over for awhile? Maybe I can explain."

He closed his eyes tightly and frowned. "I can't tonight. I have a meeting in Louisville at seven. How about first thing in the morning?"

Disappointment shaded her voice, but she assured him that the next day would be fine. After hanging up the phone, he wondered briefly if he should have dropped everything and driven over. *No, I have a life, too. Much as I want to find out what makes her tick, I have too much invested in this place and the new office to put everything on hold for my personal life.*

The newspaper settled into Beth's lap and she gazed out the French doors at the barren landscape, pale in the winter dusk. The view didn't help her mood. Most of the snow had melted, uncovering the dismal stark brown hills and bare trees. After Lucy's visit, Beth had been so infused with optimism, she'd fully expected Connor to come running when she called. *I guess I shouldn't try to fit him into the mold I use for everyone else. I definitely have a lot to learn about personal relationships.*

His firm tone had let her know, in no uncertain terms, that he wanted some serious answers. But, before she could give him any, she'd need to face her own fears and put them into perspective. Her chest tightened at the possibility her waffling might have already endangered their budding love affair.

Trying to shake off the unsettling thoughts, she looked out

the window again, casting about for something else to occupy her mind. *This might be a good time to practice my driving skills. I'll go down to the barn and visit Lizzie.*

A few minutes later, she climbed behind the wheel of the Miata for the second time since her accident. She smoothed her fingers over the soft leather and smiled. She'd missed driving the charming little car that whizzed around like a bumblebee.

Gliding through the dim light of dusk, she turned onto the driveway leading to the barn. Feeling frisky, she punched the gas pedal and shot down the lane, her spirits soaring, pushing away the dark cloud that had hovered over her day.

A flash of brown moved into her peripheral vision and, horrified, she stared at a large buck standing directly in front of the car. Her weak leg jerked violently as she called on reserves that weren't ready. The brakes locked and the back end of the car fishtailed, the wheels connecting with soft mud on the shoulder of the road. The deer disappeared from her line of vision, replaced by trees spinning around her. The motion stopped, and she stared at a darkening sky.

The back of the car lay in the ditch, and the hood pointed up at a crazy angle.

"Oh, no, how will I ever get out of here?"

She reached for the cell phone, then closed her eyes as she pictured the phone where she'd left it on the coffee table, next to the television remote.

She tried to think what to do. She wasn't close enough to the barn for anyone to see her, even if someone was still around. She'd just have to climb out of the car, if she could, and walk down to the barn to call a tow truck. She tried the door, but it was jammed firmly against the embankment. Eyeing the passenger door, she wondered if she could climb over to it in the cramped space of the tiny car.

Leaning her head back against the seat, she closed her eyes. Her head ached, she'd started to shiver, and nausea churned through her stomach. *I just need to sit here and rest a minute. I guess I'm more shook up than I thought.* She exhaled slowly, fighting the darkness closing in around her.

Thirty-Two

That's Beth's car!" Connor's heart hammered in his throat as he leaped from the truck and ran toward the yellow sports car in the ditch.

The vehicle was wedged into the soggy ground, front wheels up in the air. He could see a small figure behind the steering wheel. He jumped down into the ditch, and peered into the car. His heart thudded to a stop. Beth lay slumped against the door, her eyes closed.

For one instant, he felt as though his world had ended. She'd sneaked in and stolen his heart—he couldn't lose her now.

"Beth! Bethany!"

He grabbed the door handle and pulled hard, but it didn't budge. He looked inside again and saw that her eyes had opened. She stared out the windshield. He ran around to the passenger side.

"Beth! Honey!" he hollered, pounding on the window.

A hard yank on the door, and it opened. She looked at him, a dazed expression on her face. Blood oozed into her left eyebrow from a small cut.

Her voice was thin. "Looks like I've really done it now."

He crawled into the car, and grabbed her hand. "Are you all right? Beth, you scared me half to death."

She closed her eyes again, and leaned her head back against the seat. "My head hurts."

"Okay, let's get you out of here. I'll be right back."

Beth watched through a hazy brain-fog while Connor clambered up the embankment, and trotted over to his truck. *My knight in shining armor has come to rescue me.* It was a foolish thought, but fitting–she was thrilled that he was there with her.

In moments, he returned with a shovel, and started digging the mud away from the car door.

When he'd finally pried it open, he leaned into the car, his face just inches from hers. "Do you hurt anywhere else? Can you move? Maybe I should call an ambulance."

"No, I'm okay. Get me out of here." She smiled weakly. "Please?"

She moved her legs and arms to reassure him. Dizziness rushed in and she closed her eyes again, as Connor slipped his arms under her legs and around her shoulders, then lifted her out of the car. She nestled into his neck as he cradled her against his body. His wonderful scent filled her senses, and she felt safe and secure in the warm strength of his arms.

When the truck pulled up in front of the house, he turned to her, his faced lined with concern. "Do you think you can walk?"

She hesitated, remembering how good his arms felt, then shook her head.

"I think I'm a little too wobbly right now, and my cane's still in the car."

"Okay, I'll carry you into the house, then go back for it. I need to pull the car out of the ditch, anyway."

Firmly wrapped in his arms again, she savored the short trip through the door and into the study. As he lowered her carefully onto the couch, his face was only inches from hers. Shivers of pleasure rippled down her neck, and the urge to kiss him was almost unbearable.

He stroked her cheek. "I'll be back in a few minutes. You sure you're all right?"

She nodded. "I'm sure."

He brushed her forehead with a kiss, then left the room. Watching after him, her thoughts ran wild. *I'm so all right I can't believe it. It's time to stop playing hide and seek, and go after what I want.*

Connor opened the car door and Beth's tantalizing perfume met him head-on. He closed his eyes, reliving his terror at the thought of losing her. She'd felt so small and vulnerable in his arms, and he'd been keenly aware of her face burrowing warmly into his neck while he'd carried her to the truck. All the emotions felt so right. Today, he felt more like a man than ever before in his life. Today, he'd been there for someone who needed him and, this time, he'd made the right decisions. Today, he knew he could believe in a future with Beth.

When Beth opened her eyes again, Connor was kneeling beside the couch.

"I must have drifted off."

"Are you sure your head is all right? You could have a concussion. Maybe I should take you to the hospital."

She waved away the suggestion, and struggled to sit up. "No, I'm fine, really. My head has actually stopped aching already, but I think I'd better use the chair for awhile, 'til I'm over the wobbles."

He smiled and squeezed her hand. "Okay, if you're sure. I pulled your car out and drove it down to the barn. No one was around, so I just left it." He nodded toward the front entry. "I put your keys on the table by the door."

She loved this facet of him, so caring and protective. His beautiful green eyes looked as though he could see directly into her thoughts, and a rush of contentment filled her.

"So, do you plan to tell me about this latest adventure, or do I have to use my own imagination?"

He sat beside her on the couch while she recounted the unexpected meeting with the deer.

"I felt so good, and figured I was safe on the barn lane, so I gave 'er a good shot of gas, and it was downhill from then on."

Connor watched her features, letting his gaze linger on her beautiful mouth, and resisting the urge to grab her. She suddenly pinned him with a puzzled look.

"I thought you had a meeting tonight."

He blinked. In the confusion, he'd completely forgotten his reasons for coming there. Again, he'd been sidetracked, and now the moment didn't seem right. Glancing away, he improvised.

"I skipped it. Not that important."

This is ridiculous. Don't be such a wimp. Get on with it and get some answers. He looked at her again, gauging her expression. Instead of hostility or curiosity, tenderness softened her features. He met her gaze and drew on the strength of that look.

"Beth, I need to know why you're so frightened. I want this to work for us. What do I need to do?"

"No, Connor. It's what *I* need to do."

The evening closed around them as they talked. At first, Beth could barely find the words to tell him what she'd been feeling. Too new to romance, she had no idea how her thoughts and actions might be perceived.

Her voice wavered. "Connor, I just don't know how to act. You haven't done anything wrong." She smiled shyly. "Actually, everything you've done has been very, very *right*."

His professional skill for being a good listener, never interrupting her tangled train of thought, encouraged her. Looking down at her hands, she thought about the consequences of not explaining herself adequately, then swallowed the lump in her throat and dived in.

"I've never had to think about anyone but myself. Whatever I've wanted, I've gone after it, and carefully positioned it where I wanted it." She sneaked a look at him to measure the impact of her words, then continued. "While I was your patient, I was torn between wanting you to help me ride again, and...and just plain *wanting* you."

He nodded his understanding.

Before she could lose momentum, she continued. "When we are together, nothing else matters. Then, when I'm alone, all the obstacles and worries about how everything in my complicated life will work out come crashing in around me, and I panic. I'm afraid of losing you, but I'm also afraid of losing the life I've worked so hard to build."

Her heart had been thudding wildly while she talked, but now that the hardest part was over, the rhythm slowed and smoothed out. A wave of relief soared through her head, and she closed her eyes. When she opened them again, Connor's eyes were filled with compassion.

"Beth, I *know*. I know because I've been going through the same thing. Then I just decided that nothing was more important than being near you. Nothing."

He took her face in his hands and kissed her cheeks. "You don't have to give up *anything*, or lose any part of the life you've built. Just let me be a part of it somehow—and you be a part of mine."

She leaned against him, letting his reassurances smother her fears, and feeling as though there was nothing she couldn't do.

He stroked her hair. "You look really wiped out, and I have a lot to do tomorrow. Anything I can do before I go?"

"I...would you like to go to a party with me?"

His face crinkled into a brilliant smile. "I'd love to!"

Driving through the darkness toward Frankfort, Connor thought about Beth's deep-seated fears. Being in charge for so long had conditioned her to be afraid to relax and let nature take its course, be willing to take a chance. *It would certainly explain the ups and downs.* Then, he laughed out loud. *And how are you so different, Buddy-Boy?*

In the dim light of the barn office, he spread a sleeping bag over the sofa, and punched the pillow into shape. Minutes later, lying awake in the dark, he began to form a plan that would prove to her they *could* have a bright future together. Whatever Beth wanted, she could have—he'd see to *that*.

Thirty-Three

Beth awoke to Hal's voice on the phone, thick with concern. "Lassie! Cozy says your wee car's been parked down here all night. Are ye all right?"

She assured him that everything was fine, and explained the circumstances of the abandoned car. She set the phone back into the cradle and smiled wryly. Now everyone would know that Connor had been there again.

"So what?"

She stretched, then eased out of bed, her muscles proclaiming that her little escapade had staked more than a minor claim on her body. *At least the headache is gone–I have a million things to do today.*

She moved slowly down the hall toward the kitchen. Suddenly, a painful twinge ran through her lower back and she gasped. She leaned against the wall and, instantly, another stab of pain sent a wave of fear coursing through her head. *No! Please, no...* She closed her eyes and breathed deeply, trying to relax, keenly aware of the vague burning sensation across her hip. After a few minutes, she gingerly straightened up and continued down the hall without incident.

She poured a cup of coffee, then eased into one of the kitchen chairs. Her right leg quivered, even as she sat still. As she reached for the sugar, another jolt of pain ran through her hip and down the back of her leg. Spidery tingling started at the top of her thigh, moving over the surface of the skin like tiny needles dancing a pattern toward her knee. *Something must have happened to my leg last night in the car.* She envisioned agonizing months as an invalid again, and the thought crushed her. She sat quietly, breathing evenly, determined to out-wait the episode. Fifteen minutes later, the leg felt as normal as it had the day before. Seizing the chance, she rose, collected her cane, and headed toward the study to watch the morning news.

She sank into her favorite chair and breathed a sigh of relief. As the world's woes flickered across the television screen, a nagging worry grew in the back of her mind. *I should probably call Dr. Kellart tomorrow, or maybe Jim Reed.* The possibility of being placed under house arrest again was a strong deterrent to making either call, and she channeled her thoughts to the week ahead. She'd be setting up the event schedule with Hal that afternoon, meeting with Dan Cornell on Monday for the final project report on the jumping stadium, plus finalizing the specifications for the driving concourse. And Tim's guardianship hearing was first thing the next morning. She didn't have time to worry about her aches and pains.

The phone rang, and Jamie's voice rippled across the lines. "Good Morning. Just checking in. I'll be in Louisville all afternoon."

Beth's heartbeat hammered in her ears and she swallowed hard. "How is...?"

"Tim's stable. The doctor says he has a good chance of regaining consciousness, but it could be a month, or it could be tomorrow. Listen, Bethey, I just wanted to let you know that I'll do all I can to help you out. I've talked to my folks, and they'll go along with whatever I decide. I'll call you after the hearing tomorrow."

She exhaled slowly. She'd been right–Jamie would support her. Problem solved.

The phone rang again, and Connor's rich voice flooded her heart with happiness.

"Morning, Beth. How are you feeling?"

A delectable vision appeared in her thoughts, one of spending an entire day with him, making love. Her thighs tingled again, but this time with excitement.

"Pretty good. The headache's gone, but I'm a little stiff."

His tone changed quickly to one of concern, and she knew his professional ear had heard what she hadn't told him.

"Beth? What is it?"

Unprepared for the swift change in direction of the conversation, she stammered, "Oh...nothing...I just had little twinge this morning."

"Tell me exactly what happened. What kind of twinge?"

His tone frightened her. *It's almost like he knows what happened.* Swallowing the urge to try to control the situation, she relented and told him the sequence of events.

He was quiet for a moment before he spoke. "I was afraid something like this might've happened. You'd been tossed around quite a bit by the time the car finally stopped. You may have re-injured the nerve that was damaged in your riding accident. You need to call Dr. Kellart immediately–and, Beth?"

Determination steeled his tone, sending chills of apprehension through her chest.

"You must *not* move around or do anything until you've talked to him. Do you understand?"

"But, I have a meeting–"

"Beth! How many times do we have to go through this *control* thing? Your meeting can wait."

She couldn't speak, stung by his sharp outburst. When he spoke again, his tone was softer, and somewhat apologetic.

"Honey, if you damage the nerve again, you could end up back in the wheelchair. And the next time, you might never leave it."

Too many thoughts vied for Beth's attention, filling her with a sense of uncertainty. After calling Hal to reschedule her meetings, she stared at the dark television screen as she waited for Dr. Kellart to return her call. Connor's words reverberated in her head. The prospect of the rest of her life in a wheelchair pushed all other thoughts aside, including the future of Highover.

She quickly dialed Jamie's number. "Oh, good--you haven't left yet. Would you take me over to the emergency room?"

"What happened?"

"I got frisky yesterday and drove my car into the ditch. I may have pinched a nerve. It's probably nothing, but Dr. Kellart wants to see me."

"I'll be there right away."

Sitting bare-legged in the overly air-conditioned examining room, Beth shivered, partly from the cold and partly from her apprehension. Behind the curtain separating the cubicles, a child bawled non-stop while the mother tried to comfort it. The hall echoed with incessant pages for this doctor, or that orderly, and Beth's anxiety grew.

The curtain whisked aside and Dr. Kellart smiled brightly. "Been into mischief again, I see." He pulled up a stool and nodded. "Okay, tell me again what happened."

His expression gave no clue to his thoughts as he listened to her story. When she'd finished, he reached for the phone.

"We'll run some tests to help me figure out what's going on."

Her anxiety deepened while she listened to him order procedures with frightening names. She glanced down at her legs, now behaving themselves. Earlier, however, as she'd dressed for the trip to town, she'd experienced two more episodes of intense pain that had literally taken her breath away–pain accompanied by a heavy weakness in her right leg.

"The nurse will be right in to wheel you over to x-ray. The tests shouldn't take long. The results will be available by this evening, and I'll call you." He rose from the stool and closed her chart. "I suspect you've just pinched a nerve, but I want to be positive before I give you any medication, just in case something else is going on here."

She nodded numbly. As the nurse wheeled Beth out of the room and down the hall, a sense of impending doom settled into her bones.

Three hours later, Jamie jumped up from his chair in the waiting room. "All done?"

His ever-ready smile sent a flush appreciation through Beth's heart.

"Yes, now I just go home and wait."

He squatted down beside the wheelchair. "Bethey, it'll be all right. Think positive and try not to get yourself worked up until you know for sure. Okay?"

He stroked her arm, and she fought the impulse to let go and cry her eyes out. *I wish I could talk to Connor.* She sighed, blinked away her tears, and managed a feeble smile.

"You're right, let's go."

As she spoke, her cell phone chimed, and she heard the voice she'd just wished for.

"Hi, your housekeeper told me where you went. I hope you don't mind me chasing you down, but I've been worried."

She told him about the appointment, and promised to call him that evening after she'd heard from the doctor.

Slowly placing the phone back into her pocket, she beamed up at Jamie. "That was Connor."

"Oh, *really*? I couldn't have guessed."

She settled into the car, and gave Jamie time to merge onto the highway before she pounced.

"Do you have a plan? About Highover?"

He glanced over, his face expressionless. "I'm considering a couple of options."

A crawly sensation moved across her shoulders. "Like what?"

"Could we discuss this later? After the hearing, and when I've had time to organize my thoughts?"

"Don't take too long. Jake will be breathing down my neck before the end of the day tomorrow. This investment group doesn't plan to wait around and twiddle their thumbs. They're actively looking for Tim's replacement."

"I'll call you tomorrow night, okay?"

She stared out the window at the bleak countryside, wondering how she could have known Jamie for a lifetime, yet not be able to predict what he'd do now.

He changed the subject. "Are you bringing Connor to the party?"

"Yes. That is, if I'm able, now that I've messed up my leg again."

Jamie's voice took on a speculative tone. "You know, I was very worried about you and him, and I'm still not sure he's right for you. Be very careful, Beth."

Anger snapped through her chest, then she realized she hadn't really talked to Jamie for quite a while, and he wasn't aware of the major changes in her relationship with Connor.

"Jamie, you can't *imagine* how right he is for me. He's not at all like you think."

For the remainder of the drive home, she filled him in on everything that had happened, including Connor's amazing transformation because of his involvement with therapeutic riding.

The car came to a stop in front of her house and Jamie switched off the engine, then turned to her with an affectionate smile, his eyes betraying a touch of sadness.

"I'm really glad, Bethey. I want you to be happy." His voice warmed. "By the way, I'm thinking of asking Lucy to marry me."

"Married! You mean, like, forever?"

He hooted. "Of course, forever! Isn't that what it's all about? Beth, you're a nut-case."

She flinched at the sarcasm, realizing how ridiculous she must have sounded. For her, the thought of "forever" was mind-boggling, but Jamie didn't seem to be concerned about such a commitment. The jumble of obstacles and challenges in her life roiled through her mind. *Will I ever be able to move forward into "forever"?* The thought stunned her. Why was she worrying about it? She hadn't even been asked. In fact, she'd artfully dodged any opportunities for serious conversations about permanency.

Thirty-Four

B eth eased into her wheelchair, then pressed the "play" button on the answering machine. Lucy's voice bubbled through the speaker, thanking Beth for lunch, and reminding her about the up-coming party. Worn out from the tension of a long day, Beth rolled down the hall to her room, the gravity of her situation pressing in on her. Everything she'd struggled for in the past–and her vision for the future–hinged on one phone call from Dr. Kellart. Grim thoughts of life in a wheelchair reeled again through her head, and frightening questions echoed through her thoughts. Would Connor still care for her? Could he stand to deal with her angry dependence? Would her life be bearable *without* him?

The phone rang and her heartbeat skittered as she reached for what she prayed would be good news.

"Beth, Doctor Kellart. The test results came back, and it's just as I suspected. You've pinched a nerve, but it's not the one you injured last winter. So, that's very good news."

She'd been holding her breath, and she let out a long sigh of relief, then listened closely to the doctor.

"The nerve is inflamed, which causes swelling, and *that* causes pressure, which, in turn, causes pain and tingling. We need to re-duce the inflammation in order to eliminate the pain. I've called in a prescription to your pharmacy. You need to start taking it right away."

"Do you know how long it'll be before I'm better?"

"That will depend entirely upon you. I know how driven you

are to stay involved in everything around you, but you'll have to take it easy while this situation corrects itself. Once a nerve becomes sensitized, it tends to flare up occasionally, so it's very possible this could happen again. Don't lift anything, don't do any strenuous bending, climbing...*you* know. Let's give it some time. I'd like to be sure it won't become a chronic problem."

She replaced the phone in its cradle, her fear of life as an invalid fading, her thoughts immediately consumed with the restrictions the doctor had set in place. She began to rationalize that she had important commitments to Highover, issues that couldn't be left to chance, or the whims of others. As her thoughts accelerated, making mental lists, Lucy's advice about personal choices intruded. To have the life she now wanted, Beth would have to make some major changes in the priority of her goals.

The phone rang again, and Connor's voice wrapped around her like a security blanket.

"Hi, me again, being a pest. Any word?"

She shoved all the other problems out of reach, and told him about the test results.

Relief washed through his tone. "I'm so glad it wasn't your original injury. Listen, I'll be over your way in a little while. Want me to pick up your prescription?"

She smiled. As far as *she* was concerned, the man on the other end of the phone was the only medicine she needed.

The doorbell chimed as Beth rolled down the hallway toward the kitchen, and Connor's voice rang out. "Hello, it's me."

Heart thumping with anticipation, she continued past the kitchen door and into the entry hall. Connor's twinkling green eyes arrowed to the center of her heart, sending erotic messages to command central.

His voice sounded husky. "You certainly look bright this evening."

He leaned down to kiss her forehead, and his touch sent more tingles across her skin.

She smiled seductively. "Why wouldn't I? *You* were coming to visit."

He gently lifted her up into his arms, and held her close.

Everything went into limbo for a few moments, while she savored the comfort of the embrace.

He carefully extricated his arms from around her and helped her settle back into the chair.

"I should know better. I'm sure Kellart said you were supposed to take it easy for a while."

"Yes, I'm under strict orders. No strenuous activity." She threw him a sly look. "I wonder just *how* strenuous he meant."

Connor laughed wickedly. "You *are* a temptress, but I'm not staying. I just came to deliver your medicine and see for myself that you're all right."

He pulled a small white package from his jacket pocket, and headed for the kitchen. "I'll bring you a glass of water, then I'm outta here."

Five minutes later, he kissed her forehead. "You get some rest. I'm going home."

He disappeared through the door and her thoughts went with him. *As soon as I'm able, I'm going to start spending some time with you on your own turf.*

Thirty-Five

In the bright light of morning, Beth immediately remembered it was Monday, and a brief chill of anxiety ruffled the hair on her arms. She glanced at the clock, seeing only a long stretch of time in which to wait for some answers, and some clarification of her direction with Highover. The phone rang and she tried to swallow her fear.

Jamie's tone held a hint of relief. "It's a done deal. I'm Tim's official guardian."

His calm tone alleviated some of her tension. "So, where do we go from here?"

He released an audible sigh. "In view of Tim's previous secret investment plans with the Horse Park, his explosive exit from the Highover board meeting may have been legitimate. I believe he really meant to withdraw from the group."

"But, he couldn't without losing–"

"Let me finish. Whatever his real plans were, we can only speculate about them until he tells us himself."

A hollow pause sent dread racing through her thoughts.

"Morally, as his brother, I don't feel comfortable going against what appears to be his last plan. Legally, as his guardian, I can do anything I deem reasonable."

Every muscle in her body sank with dread at Jamie's apologetic tone.

"Bethey, I simply cannot reinvest Tim's money, but–"

"Dammit, Jamie! How can you do this to me?" Anger and

tears threatened to choke off her words. "Doesn't our history mean *anything* to you?"

A long silence ensued before he responded. "More than you know. Give Jake Biggs a call–he'll tell you."

The soft click of a disconnect faded into the hum of dial tone.

Shaken, she stared at the instrument. *What's going on?* A few minutes later, reality charged back into her life, and she dialed Jake's home number.

At Noon, Connor called, his voice soothing her unsettled emotions.

"How are you feeling today?"

"Like one of those cork floats caught in the surf."

His tone sharpened with concern. "How so?"

"Tim Trent's guardianship hearing was this morning, and Jamie called to tell me he couldn't invest his brother's money. I exploded."

"Jeez, *now* what are you going to do?"

"There's more. I talked to Jake Biggs just a while ago. Jamie has offered to invest his own money in the project, and Jake accepted." She exhaled sharply. "I feel like such a jerk. I never even let Jamie tell me himself, and I know he's doing this just to help *me* out."

Connor's tone was firm. "You need to call him back, let him know how you feel. He is truly a devoted friend."

"I know," she whispered. "But I'm sure not worthy."

"Yes, you are, but you don't realize that your healing process isn't finished. Disability does something to a person's mind that can sometimes linger, even after the physical problem is resolved. Try to take your life one day at a time–it's easier to manage that way."

Beth's courage waned, but she steeled herself for Jamie's hurt anger. He answered on the second ring.

"Jamie Trent here."

"Hi, it's me, carrying a big tray of crow."

He chuckled. "Would you like me to cut it up for you?"

"Listen, I'm really sorry about this morning. I guess yesterday kind of lowered my level of tolerance. Jake told me about your plans."

"Seems like the best way to go. When Tim gets back on his feet, if he wants to continue with Highover, I can sell him my shares, and nothing's been lost."

"Jamie, I don't know what to say, except, thank you from the bottom of my heart."

"You just concentrate on getting well."

After saying goodbye, she sifted through the mail, sorting the bills and tossing the junk mail. A small cream-colored envelope embellished with delicate handwriting caught her attention. *Lucy's party invitation.*

"Semi-formal. Oh, Gee–I'll have to go shopping. I haven't a thing to wear."

Her light-hearted thoughts changed to thoughts of a future with Connor. She considered their two vastly separate worlds and wondered, again, how they could manage to share a life without one of them giving something up. As she struggled with possible scenarios, the short distance between Lexington and Frankfort seemed to lengthen by the minute.

Where would we live? She couldn't imagine living anywhere but Highover House. *The little house behind Connor's barn?* She wasn't ready to make *that* much of a sacrifice. The thought stunned her. *What am I willing to do to have him be a part of my life?*

Mentally exhausted and drowsy from the medication, she headed for the bedroom to lose herself in blessed sleep for awhile. As she maneuvered onto the bed, a stab of pain shot down her leg–a sharp reminder that she still was not in control of *anything.*

Connor stood by the picture window in the living room of the little house, watching a herd of small brown deer forage in the dry brush. His thoughts drifted from the rustic view to a house in Lexington. *We do have a chance for a life together, if we want it badly enough to work for it.*

Then, thoughts of everything he still had to finalize before opening his office in Lexington crowded in with those of starting the riding program in December. *When will there be time for romance? What do I give up? What will she give up?* He stared through the window with unseeing eyes, struggling with what seemed to be insurmountable obstacles. A few minutes later, he squared his shoulders and addressed the walls.

"We'll just find a way to make it work."

Beth's week passed slowly, and as the medication worked its miracle, she felt better. With the exception of one brief episode of pain on the day after her doctor appointment, she'd been comfortable. Connor called every day with a progress report on both Hope Ranch and his new offices, and Beth began to settle into a comfortable frame of mind.

Jake came by on Thursday with Jamie's signed contract and a check for three hundred thousand dollars. After a brief friendly conversation about the project, he left and Beth heaved a sigh of relief. *Bullet dodged. All systems go.*

That afternoon, she called Dan Cornell and asked him to come up to the house to go over the project. When he arrived an hour later, they spread the paperwork over the dining room table.

"Dan, I want to tell you how much I appreciate your diligence in the face of one disaster after another."

The ruddy face reddened even more. "I'm used to it. Most projects have their problems." He grinned. "This one, more than others, though." He looked at her curiously. "What did you do to tick-off Ken Barker, anyway?"

"He didn't get the bid. Why do you ask?"

Cornell hesitated before answering. "Oh, well, it just seems like he overreacted. Hell, in the construction business, you win some, you lose some."

Something in his manner told Beth she was on to something important. "What do you mean by overreacted?"

"Aww, I shouldn't say anything more. I–"

"Dan, *please* tell me what you know."

He shuffled some papers around on the table before answering. "Barker got tanked up one night at the Horseshoe Bar, and was bragging to some guy about sending the environmental guys after you." He glanced up nervously. "That's how the work stoppage happened. *Jerk.*"

"How did you hear about this?"

He grinned. "My brother-in-law was sitting at the same bar. He told my sister, who called my wife...well, you know how it is in a small town."

Do I ever. A shift in the man's body language caught her attention.

"Is there something else?"

He considered her for a moment, then cleared his throat.

"He was pretty thick with one of your investors a while back."

"Tim Trent, by any chance?"

Cornell bobbed his head. "Yeah, that's the one."

"Dan, thank you for telling me. Listen, has CCC put in a bid on the next phase?"

"I think so, heard something about it last week."

"Good, I hope so. You guys have done a great job. I'll see that the board hears about it."

When he'd gone, Beth stared out the French doors at the quickly diminishing daylight. So many things were clarifying themselves. Cornell's revelations at least reassured her that she *hadn't* been paranoid. She'd actually been the target of a nasty plan, but there wasn't much she could do about it, but keep moving forward.

The doctor had finally given Beth the go-ahead to return to the office for three hours a day, and she was eager to get back into the mainstream of her life. As she slipped into her favorite cords and buttoned the waistband, she thought about her imminent meeting with Sammy and Tip Ferra. A minute later, she caught a glimpse of the gorgeous Vera Wang gown peeking from her closet. A shiver of delight ran across her shoulders and through her mind. In the store, she'd been stunned by how wonderful the dress had looked on her, but her practical nature had kicked in, telling her the strapless creation was far too fancy for her. When she'd emerged from the dressing room, her aunt had gasped with delight. *"Bethey, that is the most beautiful dress I've ever seen."* The saleslady had agreed: *"No one who's tried on that gown has looked as good in it as you do."* The glowing compliments had sent Beth's practical nature packing, and she'd written a check.

"Hal, are they ever going to leave me alone?" Beth frowned as she handed the newspaper to him. "I hope the press will give us as much good publicity as they've given us bad."

"Ah, Lass. It's part of the business. At least folks will remember hearing the name a lot."

"I guess I'd better think about some kind of media tour, or grand pre-opening. I need to dispel some of the speculation about our problems."

He grinned and saluted. "You're the expert on that. I'm going back to the horses."

Two hours later, she'd set her irritation aside and reduced a large stack of papers to two or three items that could be handled later. Relaxing back in her chair, she thought how good it felt to be back at work. Gingerly stretching her right leg and flexing her ankle, she waited to see what might happen. Guarded relief passed through her thoughts–the medication seemed to be doing its job. In a few days, she'd be dancing the night away.

Giving a last cursory glance at the newspaper article, she stepped out of the office and gazed around at her world. The background sounds of a busy working barn soothed her tired brain as she started down the aisle toward Lizzie's stall. She hadn't paid much attention to the mare lately and, remembering her ambitious plans for the fine animal, a pang of guilt saddened her. The subtle decision not to jump again had sent her mindset scurrying off in another direction, away from the deep disappointment of the changes affecting her life. She'd abandoned Lizzie, and now wondered if she'd ever ride horses again in any capacity.

An animated nicker drifted from the mare's stall and she poked her nose through the bars, nostrils opening to catch every scent. Stroking the velvety muzzle and murmuring little words of love, Beth suddenly felt as though the real meaning in her life had ended. Her throat tightened with self-pity and she shook her head angrily at the lapse. *Don't start this. Life has many other options and all I have to do is choose one. Riding isn't the only thing in the world.* Connor's face appeared in her thoughts and she smiled. Of all her options, he was definitely the most delightful one in her new life.

The sound of a car door caught her attention, and she turned as Sammy entered the barn, followed by a tall, slim young man. Hal appeared from the other end of the barn and moved purposefully toward the visitors. Beth couldn't see the boy's face from where she stood, but the kid's unmistakable body language said he was bored and didn't want to be there. She sighed and left Lizzie's stall, heading across the aisle to greet her soon-to-be new employee.

Sammy's face brightened when he saw her. "Hi, Miss Webb. How are ya?" He gestured toward the teenager. "This is my brother, Tip."

She smiled and extended her hand to the boy.

His smooth cheeks creased only slightly into a polite smile, as he limply shook her hand. "Hi."

Oh, great, Mister Personality. Her manner became brisk. "I understand you're interested in horses. We have some outstanding ones here at Highover Gate."

Tip shifted his weight and glanced at his brother. "Yeah, well, Sammy's the one who's interested in me being interested in horses."

Annoyed at the obnoxious tone of voice, she cocked her head and narrowed her eyes. "Then why are you here? We're a very busy facility, and if you're not serious about being here, then please don't waste my time."

She turned on her heel and started toward the office. Angry mumbles drifted after her, then the boy's voice rang out.

"Sorry, Miss Webb. I *am* interested in being here."

She turned around, but didn't return to the group. "Fine. Hal will give you the tour, and set up a work schedule."

With that, she continued on to her office, and closed the door with a snap.

Arrogant little twerp. He won't last a week. She picked up the newspaper article again, feeling her irritation grow. The years and sacrifices she'd expended in planning and developing Highover Gate had left little time or resources to squander. She'd surrounded herself by people with positive attitudes and similar work ethics, and she didn't appreciate having her dreams taken lightly. The final phase of Highover, and planning for the events to follow, would require a great deal of her time, and lots of hard work.

She abruptly stopped the mental rant and stared out the window at the hills, now bathed in soft early winter light. Yesterday's resolve to find time for a real life echoed in her head and she exhaled slowly. Obviously, it would demand a great deal of self-discipline to keep from falling back into her old habits.

Half an hour later, Hal knocked and stepped into the office. "They've gone. Quite the rascal, eh?"

"Rascal, my foot! He's a snotty rich kid who has no desire to work. I wonder how Sammy managed to convince him to come."

Hal laughed. "Well, the lad seemed to warm up to the place once we got going. Maybe he'll turn out okay."

"*I'm* not laying any money on it."

After Beth returned to the house, she felt strangely isolated. The quiet atmosphere she'd always loved now felt hollow and solemn. She stirred through the empty rooms, at a loss for what to do with herself for the long, solitary evening ahead. Her thoughts wandered through the maze of her perfect past life. She'd lived alone for years and had never felt lonely, but now she longed for company.

Felix meowed, as though reminding her she wasn't really alone. She scooped him up and settled into her favorite chair. As she reflected on the changes in her attitude, she also wondered if Connor had the same thoughts. Was he lonely for company, too? What did he do with his evenings? Her thoughts spun forward to contemplate what it might be like to have him around all the time. *How would we spend our time? Reading? Watching television? Making love?–What do couples do?* She had no clue.

The cell phone rang, and Connor's soft drawl warmed her heart.

"Hi, whatcha doin'?"

She laughed out loud. "You'd never in a million years believe me if I told you."

"Try me."

"No, I think some things are better left unsaid. What are *you* doing?"

"Just rambling around this place, wondering what to do with myself. I spent the day finalizing stuff at the office, and I'm too tired to work on the house."

She smiled. *We're both doing the same thing, but in different places.*

He interrupted the thought. "Have you eaten yet? I thought maybe we could grab a bite in town."

"I can be ready in an hour."

Pocketing the phone, she giggled with delight. Tonight would be the beginning of her journey to a new life.

Beth popped a French fry into her mouth, savoring the crispy texture and sharp, salty flavor. "Mmm. Just what my hips need." She turned sideways in the seat and leaned against the truck door. "I haven't been to this drive-in since I was in high school. The kids used to cruise through here on Saturday night, seeing who was out, and *being* seen."

Connor chuckled. "Trolling for girls. I remember it well."

He stirred a fry through a gob of catsup, a far-away look softening his features.

"Did you catch any?"

He glanced up, looking embarrassed. "Never had time. I was too busy avoiding the clutches of Harlan County."

Beth felt awkward. His attitude about his past seemed to change his personality, almost as though talking about it opened up the possibility that he might fall prey to it again.

He cleared his throat. "Enough about me. I notice you're in the papers again."

"Can you believe it? They've followed every snag since Day One." She sighed. "I hope the negative coverage doesn't affect our ability to attract clients."

His eyes sparkled. "*I'd* sign up in a heartbeat."

A warm murmur ran through her belly, and she touched his arm. "Then I'd *never* get any work done."

He leaned across the seat and kissed her on the nose. "You wouldn't hear *me* complain." He sat back and cocked his head. "You know, I might be able to help you recruit customers."

Intrigued, she listened to his strategic plan and, as he talked about what amounted to a team effort, she realized her solitary life had ended. The delicious morsel of time spent with Connor was a tantalizing taste of things to come.

The next morning, Connor exercised the lesson horses and, as he worked, reviewed his evening with Beth. The air around her had positively hummed with excitement. He grinned foolishly. Never

Toni Leland

in his life had he been so focused on a woman, or had such a desire to be part of someone else's life. He'd even surprised himself with his bold plan to help her. The evening had passed in conversation about the things in their lives that had molded each of them into the individuals they'd become, and he now fully accepted that his life would have no real meaning without her.

While he showered, he thought about the last time they'd made love, and the fear it had kindled in both of them. Visions of her willing body stirred his desire and, as the water streamed over his naked torso, he replayed each caress and every kiss. He stepped quickly out of the shower and exhaled sharply, breathless from the sexual energy storming through his body, but resolute about his future. *No more fears. We were meant for each other.*

Thirty-Six

B eth woke up earlier than usual the following Saturday morning, her thoughts buzzing with anticipation. She had some things to do in the office, and wanted to be finished early enough to have a nap and a leisurely afternoon to primp for Lucy's party.

A few minutes later, she carried her coffee into the barn office and settled down in front of Connor's notes, the bold scrawl a reminder of his enthusiasm as he'd outlined his idea. Repeatedly, she'd considered their relationship and the positive direction it had taken. It could work—of that, she was certain. Her biggest challenge would still be corralling her own independent streak, and channeling that energy into building a strong foundation with him.

A rap on the door interrupted her thoughts, and Sammy Ferra stepped into the room.

"Morning, Beth. I just wanted to check on Tip's work schedule."

"How's he liking the job?"

Sammy turned from the bulletin board and grinned. "About as much as any kid likes hard work. He'll be okay, though. Don't worry." He strolled toward the desk. "I understand you've got Brett Hall working on PR."

"How did you hear about *that* already?"

"Ol' Brett's a mover and a shaker...He knows everybody who's anybody on the circuits. Word gets around fast."

She smiled wryly, shaking her head. "I *guess*! Well, as long as you're here, you might as well sign up."

His chuckle sounded embarrassed. "Aw, he already got me yesterday...Square Dance With the Stars–pretty neat marketing idea, huh?" He grinned. "Gotta go. I have a cranky ride who needs some attitude adjustment."

His off-tune whistle echoed down the aisle, combining with the myriad sounds of a busy working barn. Horses whinnying, the metallic ring of horseshoes on concrete, the undercurrent of conversations. From outside, the banter of the construction crew boosted Beth's comfort level.

She focused on Connor's plan outline and shook her head. She'd been skeptical about his ability to round up the elite members of the equestrian community, and bring them all to Highover for an elegant open barn event. Obviously, she'd underestimated him.

She picked up the phone and dialed the Lexington *Herald-Leader*. "Rick? It's Beth Webb. I have a news release for you. Want me to fax it?...Of *course,* it's good news–I leave the bad stuff for you guys to make up."

Beth's thoughts raced as she stepped from the shower. Connor would be there in an hour. Her excitement faltered slightly with a nagging worry that she might be building the evening up too much. Closing her eyes, she took a sip of the white wine she'd brought into the bedroom with her, and focused on the hours ahead. *Don't be silly. This is going to be wonderful. Just relax and enjoy yourself.*

Thirty minutes later, she stood in front of the mirror, seeing herself in a new light. The rosy glow on her cheeks was not make-up, but the flush of anticipation and desire. Her sparkling eyes accentuated her full lashes, and soft pink stained her lips. The gown looked as beautiful as it had on the day she'd picked it out. Gold lamé and black faille bands wrapped around the fitted bodice at an angle, accentuating her trim waist. Delicate leaves of gold fell in staggered petals from the hip, forming the swishy skirt. She stuck one foot out so she could look at her black satin shoes. Gazing again at the image in the mirror, she smiled. *A whole new me.*

Connor rang the bell, then let himself in. He caught his reflection in the mirror over the side table in the foyer, and checked to see that his forest green dinner jacket hung perfectly from his broad shoulders. The black satin lapels neatly framed his crisp white tuxedo shirt.

Beth's voice drifted down the hall. "I'll be right there. Help yourself to the wine in the study."

He strolled into the cozy room and poured himself a splash of Pinot Grigio. Idly, he gazed about the room, picturing Beth in this chair, at that desk, browsing her bookshelf. A small rustle from behind interrupted the rambling thoughts. He turned around, and time snapped into a freeze frame. She stood quietly in the doorway, looking positively radiant, and a little shy.

He whistled softly. "You look absolutely *gorgeous*! I can't take you out in public looking like that. I'll have to beat off every guy that comes along."

She giggled self-consciously and stepped into the room.

"Considering the way *you* look, we might just have to stay in the car."

He set his glass down and moved quickly, pulling her into his arms, looking into her eyes, inhaling her perfume.

"I'm the luckiest guy alive."

As they drove along Ironworks Pike, Beth glanced over at him frequently. Never, in her wildest dreams, had she imagined how fabulous he would look, all dressed up.

He cleared his throat. "You know, I still owe you dinner at the Seelbach."

"I know. I'd decided you were going to weasel out of it." She cleared her throat, suddenly nervous. "My aunt's invited us for dinner tomorrow…Would you—"

"I'd *love* to." Reaching over and covering her hand with his, he murmured, "We can clear the record and start over."

Hearing the sincerity behind his words, Beth's heart swelled with adoration, her own dreams for a new beginning so much closer to reality.

A few minutes later, she gaped through the windshield as the car turned into Lucy's driveway. "Good grief! This is *hardly* a shack!"

"What do you mean?"

She explained Lucy's allusions to a "nothing special house," and pointed at the huge, elegant home ahead. "*I* wouldn't throw it away."

At the front entrance, a uniformed valet moved quickly to Connor's door and opened it. A moment later, Connor gently grasped Beth's elbow and helped her step out of the car.

"I don't know any of these people, so you'll have to stay real close for the whole evening." He grinned wickedly and slipped his arm around her waist, pulling her close enough to murmur seductively in her ear. "Of course, we *could* follow your suggestion, and stay in the car."

She giggled like a schoolgirl on a first date, but womanly desire stirred beneath the elegant gold skirt. Before she had a chance to respond to the suggestion, the ornate door opened.

Lucy looked positively glamorous in a brilliant green chiffon gown, heavily decorated with copper-colored bugle beads.

"Beth! You look fabulous! You can't come in here looking like that."

Beth's already warm face heated up even more.

Lucy turned to Connor and switched on her charm.

"And you! What will I do with all the love-crazed women in this crowd?"

He laughed and offered his hand. "Tell them I'm taken. Connor Hall. Nice to meet you, Lucy."

Jamie appeared, smiling broadly and exclaiming, "Let the people in, for Pete's sake! What, were you born in a barn?"

As they followed their hosts down the hall toward the sounds of merriment, Beth perused the spacious entry and hall, admiring Lucy's beautiful taste in décor. Highly polished oak wainscoting gleamed in the reflection of antique wall lamps, and lush Oriental carpeting shimmered with the rich jeweled tones of the Far East. The din grew as they moved into a large ballroom, complete with crystal chandeliers. Beth shook her head. Next to this, her own house looked positively plain.

She caught Connor's gaze lingering on her bare shoulders and she flushed with pleasure. In response, she pursed her lips slightly, sending a tiny kiss wafting across the space between them.

His hand tightened on her arm and he growled under his breath. "You won't spend much time at this shindig if you keep that up."

"Promises, promises," she murmured.

Lucy introduced Beth and Connor around to most of the guests, many of whom had traveled from far parts of the country to attend the party. A few minutes later, Jamie slipped his arm around Beth's shoulders and grinned.

"So, Partner, how's my investment coming along?"

"Very well, thanks to you, my dear. The driving concourse will be graded right after Thanksgiving. We might even finish before Christmas." She searched his dark eyes. "How is Timmy doing?"

Jamie's expression remained pleasant. "Hanging in there. One of these days, he'll open his eyes and start raising hell again."

The sobering turn in the conversation felt uncomfortable, and Beth looked away, her gaze snapping to another familiar figure in the crowd. Looking unbelievably dashing in a full kilt and dress jacket, Hal hovered over a gorgeous woman with deep auburn hair.

"Jamie, who's that with Hal?"

"Melissa Breton McTeague of Thoroughbred fame."

Beth didn't travel in racing circles, so the name meant nothing.

Jamie leaned close and whispered, "Cameron Farms in Richmond, Virginia. She's worth about thirty million dollars."

Beth stared. Was Hal personally involved with this woman? Or just doing business? Suddenly, she felt foolish. She'd never paid attention to the grapevine, and it amazed her that she knew so little about her friend.

Glancing up at Connor, she saw the amused look on his face, and tried to look innocent. "What?"

"Well, for one thing, your curiosity is showing." He grinned. "Don't get out much?"

She pulled an exaggerated pout. "Well, I'm not used to seeing Hal anywhere, but at the barn. Can you blame me?"

He took her arm again. "Let's go meet the object of his attention."

Somewhere between that conversation and ending up next to Hal, a glass of champagne had appeared in her hand. The bubbly nectar tickled her nose and sparkled down her throat, transporting her to another world.

She touched Hal's arm. "I didn't know you'd be here."

He slipped his arm around her shoulders and planted a fatherly kiss on her forehead.

"Likewise. An' I didn't know ye were a butterfly. Ye look fabulous, Lassie."

He turned to the beautiful creature beside him, and introduced her. Missy, as he called her, was charming and intelligent, and she clearly had eyes for no one but Hal.

Beth watched them for a moment. *I can't believe I didn't know about Hal's girlfriend.* A niggling inner voice intruded. *And why would you? You haven't taken time for anyone but yourself for years.* She glanced at Connor, deep in conversation with Melissa. *I really need to make up for lost time.*

She listened to their conversation, learning that Cameron Farms also bred Thoroughbreds for sport horses, as well as for racing. A few moments later, Connor had convinced Melissa to attend the Highover Open Barn. He was good–no doubt about it.

Lucy appeared and whispered, "Come with me, I want to show you something."

With a quick glance back at Connor, Beth followed her friend across the room, and into a small parlor. Lucy closed the door and turned around, the flush of excitement and mystery shimmering across her radiant face.

She held out her left hand. "Look."

She wore a magnificent square diamond surrounded by brilliant emeralds.

"Oh, Lucy, it's beautiful!"

The new bride-to-be nodded, bringing the ring up in front of her face to admire it. "He proposed about an hour before the party was due to start. We're announcing our engagement in thirty minutes." She reached over and squeezed Beth's arm. "I wanted you to be the first to know, since you were my very first friend in the area."

Beth's eyes burned with emotion, and she embraced Lucy. For the first time in her life, Beth felt a truly personal connection to the outside world around her. Where had she been all these years? It was like a dream–she had friends, was attending a fancy party with lots of interesting people, and she had devoted the attention of a handsome man. She didn't even realize that she hadn't included her successful business in the list of blessings.

Thirty-Seven

Energized by Lucy's happiness, Beth emerged from the parlor and eagerly scanned the crowd for Connor. She caught sight of him and shivers of anticipation ran across her shoulders.

Behind her, Lucy whispered, "Go for it."

Connor strode up as the beginning strains of a haunting melody floated from the small orchestra in the corner. For a lingering instant, he gazed into her eyes, then bowed gallantly.

"May I have the pleasure of this dance?"

She hesitated, glancing down at the cane in her hand. She hadn't danced since high school. Would she still know how? Did it matter? Smiling demurely, she curtsied, then hooked the cane over the back of a convenient chair. Wrapped in the safe cocoon of Connor's arms, she sank against his chest as he swept her around the ballroom, expertly guiding her through the maze of other couples, moving her in time to the music like a bough swaying in the wind.

She spoke softly. "I can't believe I've missed all this. I feel like a fairy princess."

"More like a goddess, *I'd* say."

His voice held a telltale husky edge, and she instinctively nestled closer. He responded instantly, holding her even more tightly, his warm breath tickling her ear.

"If you want to stay for dinner, you'd better behave yourself. I'm not warning you again."

She tilted her head back and laughed with delight. *So, this is what couples do.*

The music faded and Jamie's voice crackled through the speakers.

"Hey, everybody! May I have your attention?"

From the orchestra stage, he grinned out over the crowd while he waited for the chattering to stop and the guests to refocus their attention. Beside him, Lucy looked up at him with open adoration.

He slipped his arm around her shoulders and beamed at the audience. "Lucy's agreed to marry me!"

The enthusiastic crowd showed surprised approval with applause and a chorus of catcalls. The drummer pounded out a long drum roll, while Jamie and Lucy gazed at each other, their love radiating to every corner of the room. The orchestra started another set, and the happy couple moved out of the spotlight.

Connor's arm brushed lightly against Beth's while they listened to the announcement, and she chanced a quick glance at his face as he gazed across the room at the newly engaged couple. A far-away, thoughtful expression softened his features, and her throat tightened with the intensity of her own emotions.

"I'm so happy for both of them. Lucy's become a wonderful friend and, of course, Jamie is my best pal. He deserves to be this happy."

Connor looked down at her. "Yes, Jamie is a truer friend than you know."

The comment puzzled her, but he clearly didn't plan to explain himself. It didn't matter–she had forever to get acquainted with Connor Hall. After all, hadn't she learned a lifetime about *herself* in just this one evening?

To Beth's disappointment, Lucy had set up the dining tables with place cards, randomly mixing up her friends, and Beth wouldn't even be at the same table with Connor. She'd have to be content to watch him from the far side of the room.

Hal's ladyfriend was seated next to her, and she seized the opportunity to become acquainted, thinking she might even woo some of the woman's money for the next equestrian facility. After all, Virginia was big horse country, a perfect location for another "Highover."

Melissa's accent hinted at Scotland–not as strong as Hal's,

but definitely there. "Hal has told me so much about you, and your amazing recovery."

Beth smiled. "It may be, but it seems to have taken *forever*."

Melissa lightly touched the napkin to her lips. "When do you plan to return to eventing?"

Beth's heart missed a beat while her brain scrambled to put together a coherent response. "Oh, Melissa, I'm not sure I–"

"Call me Missy. Everyone does." Her tone changed. "Surely you're not thinking of *quitting*?"

Her accent emphasized the hard consonants of the word, and Beth floundered in her own sea of indecision. When she recovered from the brief trip over the edge, she laid down her fork and faced her inquisitor, giving her a cool smile.

"As a matter of fact, Missy, I've made the decision not to spend the rest of my life in a wheelchair. I will ride again, but it won't be over fences."

Surprise flashed across Melissa's aristocratic features, and she opened her mouth to speak, but someone at the next table rose to offer a toast to the happy couple. With the interruption, Beth's irritation faded, and she concentrated on how she could gracefully exit the conversation.

A minute later, Melissa touched her arm. "I'm sorry I was so thoughtless. I spoke hastily–a bad habit of mine."

"No problem. I tend to be a little trigger-happy when it comes to the subject of my riding."

After dinner, Connor materialized beside her as the dinner guests moved toward the lively music drifting through the hall.

He snaked his arm around her shoulders. "That was hell, seeing you over there and not being able to talk to you."

"Likewise."

In the ballroom, she slipped into the comfortable crook of his elbow, and looked up at the face she'd grown to adore. "I had a little sparring match with Melissa. She's a real livewire, I can see why Hal likes her."

Connor chuckled. "Yeah, her great mind–not to mention the fact she's *gorgeous*."

A flash of jealousy burned across Beth's face, surprising her.

"You certainly didn't miss *that*, did you?" Cheeks flaming, she looked away from his smirk.

"Now, now, let's not play games," he teased. "You were the brightest flame at that table, and you know it."

Two dances later, Connor slipped his arm around her waist. "C'mon. I think it's time to say our goodbyes. You look exhausted."

Gratefully, she leaned against him as they walked across the ballroom. The excitement and emotions of the evening had extracted their toll on a body unused to such sophisticated socializing. They said their farewells, and offered more congratulations to the radiant couple.

Lucy hugged Beth, then threw a meaningful look toward Connor. "Call me, okay?"

Beth's smile came from her heart. "I *will*. I'm so thrilled you're going to be part of the family."

Beth snuggled into the cozy seclusion of the car as they drove in comfortable silence through the dark Kentucky hills. Connor's warm hand caressed her fingers, and all the wonderful stimulations assaulting both her mind and body throughout the evening whirled through her head. Glancing over at his shadowed profile, she knew she'd finally found that elusive "special someone."

As he helped her up the steps to the front door, pain flashed through her thigh and she doubled over.

"Sweetheart! What's wrong?"

She closed her eyes, gasping with pain.

"Ohhh, my leg!"

He lunged to keep her from falling, then braced her up against the house, and slipped the key from her fingers. A moment later, he scooped her up into his arms like a billow of golden fluff, carried her inside and down the hall to her room.

She hugged his neck tightly, exhaling slowly as the painful twinge died away. When he set her down in the wheelchair, her leg twitched, then was quiet.

"I guess I overdid it."

"Yes, I thought you looked tired, even before dinner. Where's your pain medication?"

She motioned toward the dressing table, and he picked up the small plastic container. "I'll be right back. You get ready for bed." He headed for the door, then turned back, grinning lecherously. "You need any help with that dress?"

She giggled. "Not tonight, I have a leg-ache."

She watched him disappear into the hall, then eased off her shoes, pulled a nightgown off the hook, and rose cautiously to test her balance.

The fairy princess gown slipped to the floor.

She'd just settled back into the chair when Connor returned. He handed her the pills and glass of water, then knelt down on one knee to retrieve the beautiful dress. She watched, overwhelmed with emotion as he held it up to his face and inhaled, closing his eyes.

When he opened them again, tenderness colored his tone. "This has been the most wonderful night of my life."

Her fatigue disappeared and she wanted the night to last forever.

"I know—me, too," she whispered.

He carefully hung the golden gown in the closet, then turned back to her, his expression serious.

"You need to rest. I don't want anything to screw up dinner at your aunt and uncle's."

"Yes, Dr. Hall."

She steered the chair toward the bed, then stopped and spun it back around to search his face for reassurance. *Tell him.*

He stepped closer and took her hand. "What?"

"Would you help me into bed? I feel a little shaky." *Wimp!*

A minute later, she sank into the soft mattress and gazed at his features as he tenderly tucked the comforter around her. At that moment, she couldn't imagine her life without him. Their eyes locked, and his expression sent an avalanche of emotion soaring through her heart.

He leaned over and brushed his lips against hers.

"I love you, Beth."

Her breath caught in her chest and she closed her eyes. Without knowing it, she'd been waiting an eternity to hear him say those words. She opened her eyes again, afraid it was a dream, but his face was still there—open, vulnerable, waiting.

Meeting his gaze, she whispered, "And I love *you*."

He slipped his arms beneath her shoulders and pulled her to him, whispering her name. She felt his heart thudding beneath the crisp formal shirt, and knew immediately that he'd been as terrified of the moment as she. Holding him tightly, she savored the joyous release of telling him of her deepest emotions.

She gently pulled back. "Independence certainly has its pit-falls."

He stroked her hair. "Yes, sometimes you need to come up against a brick wall in order to stop long enough to see where you're headed."

She grinned mischievously. "And what was *your* brick wall?"

"*You*," he growled, pulling her back to him and planting a firm kiss on her forehead. "When I realized I could actually put the riding center together and give something back to society, I knew my lifestyle would have to change. I needed something more in my life–I needed *you*. I withdrew from the Dublin Grand Prix, and started looking for property closer to Lexington. Then, I decided that running back and forth from Louisville wouldn't be practical, so I leased an office building in Lexington." He grinned diffidently. "It was a pretty big gamble, considering you wouldn't even return my phone calls."

She studied the quiet determination on his face. The modifi-cations he'd structured into his life astonished her–changes made just on the chance the two of them might build a relationship. Her own thoughts had been on a parallel, but fear of the unknown had caused her to put up obstacles along the way, even to the point of convincing herself his attentions had been based on pity.

He eyed her with amusement. "And you?"

"Me what?"

"Your brick wall."

She thought for only an instant. "Losing my independence."

He squeezed her arm gently. "You lost your physical indepen-dence for awhile, but I certainly never saw any indication that you'd lost your independent personality."

She flushed with embarrassment. "Yes, I know–I'm sorry I argued with you about everything. I'm so used to making things happen, and having my own way." She smiled sheepishly. "Guess

I'll have to work on that, huh?"

He shook his head. "Don't change anything. I love you just the way you are, stubborn streak and all."

Thirty-Eight

S unday dawned like so many other October mornings in Kentucky, bright and crisp, the endless blue sky promising one last respite from winter. Beth sat on the terrace, wrapped in a heavy sweater, watching the steam rise off her coffee.

Since Connor's declaration of love, her thoughts had soared with exhilaration at the direction her life was taking. Gone were the morbid broodings that she'd never ride again, or that life was meaningless without riding. Her feelings of isolation and loneliness had disappeared. Connor Hall had stepped into her life and changed it, and she wanted to live every minute of the rest of it in the same way.

Her gaze moved to Paso's resting place, so far away. Raising the mug, she murmured, "To you, old friend."

The doorbell chimed and she prepared herself for new beginnings.

As the truck headed toward Lexington, Beth gazed out the window at the crisp landscape, catching a glimpse of a small herd of deer that bounded across a brown field and disappeared into a clump of trees. She had never felt so peaceful.

Connor patted her hand. "I want to stop by the ranch for a few minutes and show you something."

"We have plenty of time. Aunt Ida doesn't expect us before Noon."

Twenty minutes later, nickered greetings echoed through the

barn, and Connor chuckled. "This bunch always thinks there might be some food in the offing."

"Do you have someone come in to feed in the mornings?"

"Yeah, *me*. I did the chores before I came over to your place."

He unlocked the door to the office and ushered her inside, then over to a large chart tacked to the wall.

"Look at this." Excitement edged his voice. "We have thirty volunteers–enough for ten riders. We'll start our training sessions next week." A question danced in his eyes. "I was wondering..."

His indecision piqued her curiosity and she moved closer to touch his arm. "What?"

"Well, I wondered if you might be willing...er, interested in being one of the training riders."

She cocked her head. "What do you mean? What would I do?"

"The volunteers have to spend a certain number of hours in orientation, learning how to work with challenged riders. The national association requires certification on each volunteer before we can open for business."

She nodded, interested to hear what he had in mind.

His expression became a little wary as he continued. "I thought maybe you'd like to participate as a rider. You'd have a chance to start riding again under supervision, and it would help me out." Guarded optimism crossed his features as he hurried to explain. "This has nothing to do with you being my patient."

Her heart opened up to his deep commitment to the project. The possibility of getting back into the mainstream sent a surge of excitement through her head.

"I'd love to! When do we start?"

He exhaled relief through his smile. "I have a small group coming on Tuesday." He gazed at her seriously. "It'll be pretty intensive, since I only have six weeks before we open. Are you sure you have the time? We're probably talking three to four mornings a week right through the end of November."

She frowned slightly. *That's a lot of time away from Highover. I really want to do this, but...* She blinked. *But what? I decided I wanted to spend time with him on his own turf, and I've been dying to ride again.*

She smiled. "I'll make time. This is special."

"Fantastic! It'll be fun, you'll see." He glanced at his watch. "Wait here a minute. I have to run over to the house."

While he was gone, she looked through the titles on the bookshelf next to the desk. The collection of physical therapy books was interspersed with volumes on riding, jumping, and three-day eventing, but one entire shelf was jammed with publications specifically about therapeutic riding. She lifted one down and paged through it. *This is really interesting. I didn't know there'd been so much research on the subject.*

"Pretty boring stuff, huh?"

She looked up. "No, not at all. I'd like to read some of these, if you can spare them for awhile."

He grinned. "Hep yo'se'f."

As they headed back toward Lexington, Connor brought up the plans for the Highover Open Barn.

"I saw the news article about the square dance–you did a great job." He grinned. "Sounds like such a good time, I think I'll try to be there."

"That would be good." Her mind clicked into business mode. "How many celebrities are we expecting?"

"Including wives and significant-others, probably around a hundred." His face glowed with enthusiasm. "We'll keep it small, feature it as the 'place to be' if you're important in equestrian circles."

She shook her head. "I don't know how you can do all this along with your other projects. Are you managing all right with the PR gal? She can be a little pushy sometimes."

"Yeah, but she gets things done. That's what's important. She's hooked me up with an events coordinator in Louisville, and we're using all local services for the party itself." He smiled, a mischievous twinkle in his eyes. "All you have to do is look beautiful."

The tantalizing aroma of roast beef enveloped them as they stepped from the chilly porch into the warm kitchen. Beth's heart basked in the glow of family love as she made the introductions.

"Auntie, this is Connor."

Connor shook Ida's soft hand, then held out the bouquet of flowers he'd brought. "Thank you for sharing this day with me."

She smelled the flowers and twinkled up at him. "You're most welcome. I'm just delighted that Beth has finally found someone."

Beth groaned, her face hot with embarrassment. "Aunt Ida!"

Connor grinned, throwing her a conspiratorial wink. "Me too."

"Happy Sunday, Bethey."

She whirled around to face her Uncle Earl, then wrapped her arms around his neck and hugged him tightly. He chuckled and disentangled himself from her grasp, then turned to Connor.

"How about a little cider?" he rumbled, winking conspicuously.

Connor nodded and followed the energetic old man into the living room, leaving Beth to deal with her aunt.

"Auntie, *please* don't embarrass me. I'm only just getting to know him."

The elderly woman stroked her shoulder lovingly. "I'm sorry, Honey. I'm just so thrilled to see a glow on your cheeks from something other than riding horses out in the cold."

The afternoon passed quickly, filled with a meal fit for a king and the obligatory football game. In deference to the old couple's traditions, the women stayed in the kitchen with the dishes, while the men relaxed in the den.

Connor was fascinated by the old man's lifetime spent with horses.

"Do you miss being at the barn, Earl?"

"Yeah, I do. I retired 'cause I couldn't manage the heavy physical work anymore. My back, y'know..." His eyes took on a far-away look. "But, yeah, I miss it, all right."

Connor's brain went into overdrive and he leaned forward, elbows on his knees, and began talking about his riding program. The old man's face brightened and, soon, the two of them were deep in serious conversation.

Beth peeked out the kitchen door, then turned to her aunt. "Well, those two certainly hit it off."

She shivered with happiness. Things were going so well, it had to be fate–*she* certainly hadn't been much help. *I guess when the right person comes along, there's no question.*

"Bethey, when two people are right for each other, nothing can change the chemistry." Ida chuckled. "And I don't mean *those* two." A tender look came over her face. "Your uncle is the only man I've ever loved. He can be a real pain in the neck at times, but I wouldn't have it any other way. The key to keeping love alive is being willing to compromise when it's important."

Beth nodded thoughtfully. *Good advice. I'll need to keep reminding myself to follow it.*

As they headed down the road toward home, Connor glanced over at Beth.

"I've asked your uncle if he'd like to manage my barn."

"You *did?*"

"Yep. He can work part-time, stay involved, no strenuous activity."

"What did he say?"

"He said 'yes,' of course!"

She laughed and shook her head. "You sure are a mover and a shaker, that's all I can say."

"If something's important, you'd better believe it." He grinned wickedly. "So, watch out!"

He pulled up the driveway and turned off the engine, then took her hand and gazed somberly into her eyes.

"Beth, I want to talk about some *other* important things. Us."

His touch and change of tone sent a ripple of panic through her chest, and she looked down at her hands, wanting to postpone the conversation.

"I know, but this isn't a good time." She looked back up at him, apologizing with her eyes. "I'm really tired."

His expression remained neutral and he nodded. "No problem. We'll talk next week, after the open barn."

Beth lay on the bed in the dark, watching the tree branches move against the moonlit sky. Why did she get so nervous anytime Connor wanted to talk seriously? She wanted him in her life, but seemed incapable of actually letting it happen. Give her millions of dollars to handle, or a bunch of arrogant, wealthy investors to manage, and her courage was illimitable. Why was *this* so hard? Why couldn't things just stay as they were, at least for a while? She turned away from the night sky, and stared at the luminous face on the clock.

It was the middle of the night and her madhouse of thoughts was far too distracting for sleep. She flipped the comforter back, and Felix meowed his displeasure, angrily twitching his tail as he moved to another spot on the bed.

"Sorry, kitty cat."

She rose and padded down the hall, past the kitchen door, and into the study, where Connor's books sat on the table next to her favorite chair. She picked one up and began to read.

An hour later, she closed the book slowly and let it drop into her lap. The photographs she'd just seen had opened her eyes, and broken her heart. *There is so much suffering out there. I've only had a tiny taste of life as an invalid. I'm one of the lucky ones... there are so many for whom there is no hope.*

She thought about the amazing changes in Connor that were a direct result of his involvement in therapeutic riding. *He has a purpose, something deeper than earning lots of money, or making a name for himself in the world of competition.*

In the dimly lit room, she gazed at the dark television screen and knew, finally, what she wanted to do.

A nagging worry settled into Connor's head on his way home that night. Beth had declared her love, but was she still unsure about how far she'd let her feelings take her? She always seemed to find ways to avoid discussions of a future together. He clenched his jaw. *Dinner in Louisville is going to be a turning point–one way, or the other.*

Thirty-Nine

The next morning, Beth phoned Hal to tell him she wouldn't be in for a few days.

"Well, it's about *time* ye took some time off for yourself."

She grinned. "Did you enjoy the party?"

"Oh, Aye! Missy's good company, she is. And how about you?"

Beth heard the happy lilt in his voice, which she now recognized as the sound of a man in love. She resisted the urge to tease him, instead, bubbling with her own happiness.

"It was wonderful, just *wonderful!*"

After hanging up, she settled back in her favorite chair with Connor's reference books. Concentrating on the text, rather than the heart-rending pictures, she lost herself in the world of therapeutic riding.

Hours later, she set the books aside and leaned her head back against the chair. *I've been so insulated. I had no idea so many wonderful things were happening in the world. All I've ever thought about was business or riding.* Connor had figured out a way to do both. A rush of warmth flooded her thoughts and she picked up the phone.

He answered on the third ring. "Hope Ranch Therapeutic Riding Center."

A ripple of love raced through her heart. "Oooh. You sound so business-like."

He chuckled. "You expected otherwise?"

"Just checking to see what time you want me tomorrow."

"I want you *all* the time, my dear."

Her face warmed at his suggestive tone, even though her own thoughts spent plenty of time in fantasyland with him.

His tone became less intimate. "I'll pick you up about nine. We can have some breakfast before the crowd arrives."

Her pulse fluttered. "I'll be ready."

She hung up the phone, and moved to the desk to start outlining her new plans on paper.

The little car eased out of the garage. *Let's try again. No airs above the ground this time.* Beth drove down to the main road, her thoughts returning to her scheduling project. *I'll need to factor in the most crucial events at Highover, then plan the remaining time accordingly.* Her highly organized mind worked at peak, boosted by her intense interest in her new ideas, and energized by Connor's love.

Hal strode out of the barn, pinning her with an exaggerated scowl. "Ye said ye weren't comin' in."

"I know, but I need some information from the office. I promise I won't bother anyone."

He grinned. "Aye, well, see that ye don't. We're a very busy place, we are."

He climbed into his truck, and Beth smiled fondly as he drove up the lane. With such wonderful people helping her, moving into her new life would be so much easier.

Looking around at the magnificent grounds bathed in the late afternoon light, she appreciated just how fortunate she was. The completed jumping stadium looked like something from one of the most prestigious events in the world. She daydreamed briefly, envisioning splendid horses sailing gracefully over each elaborate fence. Enthusiastic cheering from the grandstand echoed through her visions. She slowly turned in a circle, scanning the entire area, absorbing the beautiful buildings, the perfect fences, the wide pastures beyond. The sounds of construction equipment drifted on the air from behind the rebuilt dressage barn, a comforting assurance that the driving concourse would be a reality before year's end.

In five days, Highover Gate would host some of the country's most famous and skilled riders. Connor's flamboyant idea for presenting Highover to both the equestrian community and the locals had been so attractive that, not only had each rider accepted, but the press had also snapped up the story. To her delight, the local papers had made daily mention of some positive tidbit about the event, and the larger newspapers and a couple of equine publications had picked up the feature story.

With one last look toward the jumping arena, she headed for the barn office. As she entered, she automatically looked at the work schedule on the wall, noting that Tip Ferra had evening stall duty. She hadn't given much thought to her new employee recently, so she scribbled herself a reminder to ask Cozy how the kid was doing.

Turning her thoughts to the task at hand, she pulled out a file drawer and located the folders for each scheduled event for the coming months.

"Evening, Miss Webb."

Startled, she flipped a folder onto the floor, and the contents flew in all directions.

Tip rushed over and knelt to retrieve the papers. "Oh, gee, I'm sorry! I didn't mean to scare you."

She closed her eyes and let out a breath. "It's okay. I just didn't think anyone was still here." She looked at her watch and frowned. "Are you just getting here?"

The boy looked up from the floor, his face a web of confusion. "Uh, I'm all finished. I was just leaving when I saw the light on in here."

"Oh, sorry. I, uh..." She stopped. She already felt stupid, and didn't want to make it worse.

He laid the folder on her desk and edged toward the door.

"Tip, stay a minute and tell me how the job is working out. Do you have enough to do?"

She affected a teasing tone, hoping to encourage the young man to stay in the den with the lioness. He sat down and hunkered his shoulders a bit, obviously uncomfortable about the unfortunate circumstances of his first business encounter with the boss.

"It's going good. You have some real nice horses here, especially that chestnut mare at the end." His face brightened with enthusiasm. "Man, she's beautiful! Does anyone ever ride her?"

Sadness crept into Beth's heart and she shook her head. "No, she's my horse, and I'm just not strong enough to ride her." She looked away from the earnest young face. "Maybe in a few months."

I wish I could believe that. The memory of her last ride on Lizzie hung fresh and frightening in her mind.

Tip stood up. "Well, I'd better head for home. Sammy wants me to go with him to look at a horse he's thinking about buying."

"Yes, Hal told me about that. I understand the horse was injured."

"Yeah. He was a real nice jumper, but he tangled himself up in some wire. His owner couldn't pay the vet bills, so Doc Allen kept the horse for payment."

Tip's manner grew more self-assured as he talked. "I saw the injuries. The cuts were pretty deep, but the doc sewed him up good. There'll be scars, but other than that, he's sound."

For a fleeting instant, Beth saw a glimmer of intensity and excitement in the boy's expression.

"Sounds like you're pretty observant."

He grinned. "Yeah, I really like horses. All animals, actually." His grin faded. "I don't have any at home. My mom's afraid of dogs and my dad has bad asthma."

Pain and frustration briefly swept across his features.

All that money and prestige–and all he _really_ *wants is a pet. What a shame.*

"Well, Tip, you can gorge yourself on horses and cats right here, anytime you want."

He grinned as he headed for the door. "Thanks, Miss Webb."

She moved over to the work schedule and traced his workdays with her finger. *I think I'll try to be around when he's here. There's more to this young man than meets the eye, and I'd like to see what it is.*

The barn was quiet in the early dawn hours as Connor tossed the last flake of hay into a stall, then ambled down the aisle toward the arena. He leaned his shoulder against the wall, gazing around the large area that would soon be filled with purpose. A contented sigh escaped, the cloud of breath curling on the crisp air. The

wonderful, love-filled day he'd spent with Beth and her family
had consumed his thoughts. *I've been waiting all my life for that
experience and didn't even know it.* With one last glance around
the arena, he focused his thoughts on the day's activities and left
the barn to head for Highover.

Beth eased into the seat of Connor's truck and grinned. "What
torture do you have in store for me today?"

He shook his head. "No torture, just a lot of hours in the saddle.
I hope you're up to it."

"You don't know me as well as you think, Mr. Hall."

A smile twitched the corners of his mouth. "Now *there's* an
understatement."

Thirty minutes later, she sat on a bench off to the side of the
Hope Ranch arena, watching Connor talk to a group of volunteers.
They were a mixed group of individuals, most of whom had some
experience with horses, and several whose backgrounds were strictly medical. While the assembled men and women concentrated on
Connor's instruction, Beth was profoundly moved by his dedication
and sharp attention to detail. No one was more right for the job.

His voice interrupted her thoughts. "Beth, c'mon over here.
We're going to start."

Feeling a little self-conscious, she walked slowly across the
finely sifted dirt. Her leg had been behaving itself lately, but fear that
the nerves would act up again simmered in the back of her mind.

He introduced her to the group, then outlined the plan. Select-
ing four people, he instructed them to go pick a horse and saddle it
up. Then he counted out another four, then another, giving the same
directions to each group. When he'd finished, only two volunteers
remained.

"Beth will be our rider, and I'll be one of the side-walkers."

He turned to her. "All you have to do is sit on the horse. You
don't have to guide it. In fact, I don't *want* you to try to ride the
horse at all. Just pretend you can't move or do anything. The purpose
of this exercise is to teach the volunteers to watch a rider carefully,
and see that he or she doesn't fall."

She nodded, disappointed with her passive role in the exercise.

He continued. "Okay, let's pick a horse and get started."

The barn aisle was crowded with the other groups saddling their mounts, and Beth smiled at the quiet school horses, patient and willing as they were tacked up for their work. Connor guided two volunteers in saddling a roan mare, his total absorption in the work again filling Beth with a burst of pride and love for him, and his dedication to the cause.

He checked the belly strap when the volunteers had finished. Satisfied that it was tight enough, he nodded and turned to address the group.

"The most important thing to remember is that the saddle *must* be secure. Most of our riders don't have the balance to stay on the horse if they start to slip, so we mustn't have a loose saddle."

He turned back to Beth. "Ready?"

A rush of apprehension made her voice shake. "I think so."

His gaze softened, and an encouraging smile softened his rugged features. "Everything will be fine. We're right here."

From her perch on a gentle gray mare, Beth studied him as he worked at his passion, then her thoughts turned to her own circumstances with him. *No matter how obnoxious or argumentative I've been, he's kept his calm, nurturing attitude toward me and my egotistical demands.* Why had she been so difficult, when he'd only tried to do what he thought best for her? Like so many other questions she'd asked herself over the past five months, the answers remained a mystery. Remorse burned her eyelids and she straightened up in the saddle. *It's time to give something back.*

Connor dumped the last dustpan of debris into the trash barrel, then tossed his work gloves onto the kitchen counter and surveyed the empty room. The tiny house was now at least clean enough to live in. As he wandered through the nondescript rooms, he realized that his excitement about living there had waned. He plopped down on a milk crate and stared at the worn carpet. *I can't expect Beth to live here.* He thought about the beautiful house at Highover Gate. *And I'm not living there, either.* It was clear some compromises were in the offing.

He ambled back to the barn, thinking about the great volunteer crew that had shown up that morning. He felt optimistic about his venture–and about Beth. She'd looked so lovely, sitting elegantly on the old gray mare. It had been obvious that she'd wanted to do more than just sit there, that she'd desperately wanted to *ride* the horse. But, amazingly, for the first time since he'd met her, she'd done exactly what he'd asked, with no arguments. Perhaps that was a good omen.

Forty

B eth opened her eyes to the dim light of dawn, casting its eerie glow around the edges of the window. She started to stretch, then groaned. Her legs had turned into dead logs, and her torso ached as though she'd been doing crunches. *I've been out of the saddle too long. By tomorrow, I won't be able to walk at all.* She closed her eyes again, forgetting her physical discomfort, and focusing, instead, on her riding experience. When the training session had finished, Connor had worked with her in the arena, allowing her to ride the gray mare under her own control. Only at a walk, but she'd been thrilled anyway. After so many months with no hope, she'd accept it with gratitude.

Connor showed up bright and early.

"Ready for another adventure on horseback?"

She pulled an exaggerated pain-wracked face and stooped over, holding her back.

"If I wasn't crippled before, I will be soon."

He laughed and wrapped his arms around her, hugging her tightly as she snuggled against his chest.

His voice vibrated against her cheek. "There's a method to my madness, Dearie. This may be the only way I can keep you under my control."

"I don't care. Control me all you want." *Nothing matters anymore except being with you.*

He sucked in a breath and pulled her closer.

Minutes later, he turned the truck onto the highway, then sat stiffly back in his seat, giving Beth the sense of something on his mind.

He cleared his throat. "I have another idea for putting Highover on the map."

She chuckled. "At the rate you're going, we'll need a bigger map."

He reached over and took her hand. "No, I'm serious. What I have in mind could be a major PR coup."

"I'm listening."

If he was nervous about his idea, he didn't show it. His voice was strong, his words well chosen.

"If the therapeutic riding program were to operate out of Highover, you'd not only have the support of the national equestrian industry, but you'd garner approval from the local community which, as it stands now, has no real connection with the facility."

She narrowed her eyes, digesting the basics of the idea. He was right–as far as the locals were concerned, Highover was simply another ambitious private endeavor to line the already-plush pockets of an elite few.

Connor looked straight ahead at the highway, his shoulders rigid with anticipation of her reaction.

"I like it. In fact, I love it!" She reached over and touched his shoulder. "I want Highover to be a year-around facility, and I've been wondering what to do with the winter months. This would be perfect."

Connor pulled off the highway, turned off the engine, and looked at her for a long minute.

"I was afraid you'd think I was horning in on your glory."

"On the contrary, your wonderful program would enhance Highover and make it even more attractive."

He nodded, his expression changing subtly to one of serious thought. "I'd been planning to expand my practice, even before you and I..." He glanced over and grinned. "Got together. I hadn't really thought about the influx of new clients Highover might bring in, but obviously, I'd better take that into consideration."

She tilted her head and chose her words carefully. "I have another idea along those lines. With your expertise in equestrian injury, why couldn't you develop a rehabilitation center at Highover? It would be another exclusive feature to make Highover the most complete facility of its kind in the country."

Connor's eyes widened with delighted surprise. "Lady, you are something!"

"Since you are going to modify your business plan anyway, provide an alternative scenario that uses Highover as the primary location. I think the board would welcome this opportunity." Her voice dropped, sounding like a whisper in her own ears. "I think we're a fantastic team...why not take advantage of it?"

Connor steadied her as she stepped down from the truck. "I think Hal will be here today."

She had forgotten Hal's participation in Connor's plans.

"What exactly will *he* do? The same as the others?"

"No, he'll be my counterpart. Any therapeutic riding program is required to have one qualified riding instructor and one physical therapist per so many students. If we get really busy, I'll probably have to look for one more instructor."

The volunteer group that morning was larger than the first one. As Connor moved amongst them, he held everyone's full attention.

"Okay, this morning we'll have some classroom time, then work with the horses and riders after lunch."

The group followed him to the farthest end of the arena, where chairs had been set up in front of an easel. Beth picked a seat toward the back that afforded her a good view of Connor.

A minute later, Hal strode into the arena, and Connor waved him over.

"Folks, meet Hal MacGregor. He'll be our instructor consultant. He's the one who will answer any of your questions about riding, or the horses. I'm the one to ask if you have questions about disabilities, or medical issues."

Hal took a seat, and Connor began his presentation.

"It's important to understand the types of riders we'll have here. Most will be children, but occasionally there may be an adult or two. Understanding the disability helps us determine which horse to choose, what type saddle to use, and so on. The service we provide here is known as hippotherapy."

He peeled back one of the large sheets of paper on the easel, revealing a list of disabilities and the problems associated with each one. Beth settled back into her chair and listened attentively as Connor commanded his world, but soon her thoughts wandered to a more personal plane. *I want to be part of this with him, feel the same sense of satisfaction from working in this atmosphere.* The plans to move the program to Highover would provide her with more than business benefits. It would also close the gap of busy schedules, and give them the opportunity to slip into each other's lives.

Connor's voice poked into her trance. "I lost you there for awhile, didn't I?"

Her cheeks grew warm with embarrassment at having been caught daydreaming instead of listening.

"Yes, I found myself thinking all sorts of things." She smiled wickedly. "Not all of them about riding."

He leaned down and growled into her ear. "You're not allowed to distract me while I'm working."

"Well, then maybe I'd better leave."

"You forget—*I* drove."

He took her arm, looking smug as he walked beside her toward the office, and she glanced at him from beneath her lashes. *I hope you're ready to have me in the middle of all this, 'cause that's where I plan to be.*

The following morning, Beth hurried down to the barn, hoping to catch Tip before he left for the day. She wasn't sure why she felt so compelled to talk to him again, but the urge was there, so she allowed it to direct her.

Cozy stepped out of the feed room just as she headed for the office.

"Mawnin' Miz Webb."

She smiled fondly at the lanky old groom who'd been such a help to her over the past few years.

"Good Morning, Cozy. Is Tip Ferra still here?"

Cozy nodded toward the back of the barn. "Yes'm. He down to the end, there." He grinned and shook his head. "Miz Webb, he's the hardes' workin' kid I ever seen."

The strong endorsement surprised her. "Really?"

He bobbed his head. "He kin do four stalls to my two."

"*Good.* It's about time you took it easy."

A worried look crossed the old man's face. "Miz Webb, you ain't thinkin' 'bout turnin' me out t'pasture, is you?"

"Oh, my goodness, no! I'm *so* sorry...I didn't mean it to sound like that."

She touched his worn flannel shirt-sleeve. "You're the glue that keeps this place together. I don't know what I'd do without you."

His weathered face relaxed a little, and she smiled.

"You'll have a place here for as long as you want it. You have my word."

His eyes glistened with emotion. "Thank you."

Beth watched silently for a few minutes, appreciating Tip's gentle manner as he stroked Lizzie's neck and talked to her in soft tones. As though he could feel her scrutiny, he turned and grinned.

"Hi, Miss Webb. Lizzie and I are just having a little chat. Boy, she's beautiful."

Beth smiled and stepped into the stall, remembering all her grand plans for the lovely mare. Lizzie nickered to Beth, then turned and nuzzled Tip's shoulder.

Emotion cracked Beth's reply. "Yes, she is."

They both remained silent for a moment, then Beth found her voice again. "Do you ride?"

"A little. I've ridden a couple of Sammy's horses." He threw her a quick look. "But I've never ridden anything special, like Lizzie. I'm not good enough to handle a really valuable horse."

How many teenagers would admit something like that? Not many. He's smart enough to know his limitations. She turned her attention to the horse beside them.

"Well, Tip, if you ever want to bring your riding skills up to par, we have plenty of horses here to practice on. If you progress *really* well, I might even consider letting you ride Lizzie."

The teen's face broke into a huge smile. "Wow! That would be so cool!" He turned and scratched Lizzie's jaw. "I guess I'll have to get busy, won't I, Girl?"

His tone changed. "Oh, by the way, that gray gelding at the other end of the barn—Poncho? I noticed a lump on his right foreleg this morning. It feels a little like a windgall, but you'll probably want the vet to have a look."

"Come, show me."

They walked over to the gelding's stall, and Tip moved the horse around so Beth could see better. Firmly, but gently, Tip moved his hands down the leg to locate the lump. When he'd found it, he nodded for her to check it out.

His assessment of the blemish was correct. She glanced sideways at the boy. His talent with horses was undeniable. The lump was so small it could have grown for weeks, without detection.

She straightened up and smiled at his fresh young face filled with confidence.

"Good job, Tip. I'll have Cozy call the vet today. You're right, it could be nothing, but in this barn, we don't take chances." She cocked her head. "What do you want to do when you graduate?"

She watched his expression closely as he considered an answer.

"I'm not sure. I hadn't given it too much thought, until recently. My mom wants me to go to college, but I haven't enjoyed school much…"

His voice trailed off and Beth jumped in. "What do you think would make you happy? Have you thought about that?"

His features reflected that he *had* thought about it, but he didn't reply.

"Tip, I can see your talent with the horses. You have the right temperament and touch and, most importantly, you care about their welfare." She smiled. "I'll bet you're the same way with kittens and puppies—I think you'd make a fabulous veterinarian."

His face lit up with a brilliant smile and she knew she'd hit home.

"Yeah, I've thought about that." The grin disappeared. "But I don't know if I'm smart enough for the college courses."

She took hold of his shoulders and looked him squarely in the eye. "Tip, if you want something badly enough, you'll find a way to make it happen. There are always people around who'll help you when you need it. You've certainly proven yourself *here*."

She dropped her hands and stepped back, startled by the intensity of her desire to guide the young man. "Would you like me to arrange a meeting for you with *our* vet? He's one of the best equine specialists in the country. He could tell you what life as a veterinarian is like, and what schooling would be required. He might even take you on as an apprentice."

Joy flashed across the boy's face and he nodded vigorously. "Yes! That would be *so* cool. Thank you, Miss Webb!"

As she watched him jog down the aisle and disappear through the barn door, she felt a deep new sense of responsibility.

She wasted no time in phoning Ken Fall, the Highover veterinarian. He'd appreciate Tip's obvious calling to veterinary medicine, and she was pretty sure that, if she asked, he'd take Tip under his wing.

Flushed with feelings of commitment and purpose, she allowed her mind to open to thoughts of life with Connor. Quite by accident, she'd discovered a niche in his riding program, a slot she could fill nicely. He'd made a chance remark about the hassle of juggling volunteer schedules and meshing them with rider needs. Her own organizational skills were perfectly matched to such a task. She could do that, and leave Connor free to do what he did best—interact personally with the people.

Warmth flooded through her heart. After such chaos, things were coming together nicely.

Forty-One

Connor strolled slowly along the bank of stalls in the Dressage barn at Highover.

"This will be perfect, but are you sure you can spare twelve stalls?"

Beth chuckled. "Out of four hundred? I think so." She moved closer. "As the program grows, you can add more."

He shook his head. "No, ten riders is the maximum number I want for any session. Each group will ride once a week, giving us the capability to handle fifty riders, Tuesdays through Saturdays. At that, I'm stretching the horses *and* the volunteers pretty thin."

"Not to mention yourself." She slipped her hand into the crook of his elbow and smiled up at him. "I'd like to help."

He barked out a laugh and swept his arm through the air. "And you think *this* isn't helping?"

"No, I mean with the actual program. Connor, I've made my living organizing things a lot more complicated than this. Let me take over the scheduling, so you can handle the rest."

He gazed at her for a moment, then pulled her into his arms. She nestled into the bear hug, confident of her new role in his life, and optimistic about the future.

"I'm meeting with my accountant on Monday to go over the financial aspects of moving the riding program here. One thing, though, you'll have to come up with a figure for the rent. Business is business."

She grinned. "I'll have my people talk to your people."

A few minutes later, they walked through the crisp morning air toward the main barn. She gazed around at the perfect setting, then glanced up at Connor.

"All ready for tomorrow night? Have all your hot-shot riders under control?"

He laughed, his rosy cheeks bright beneath his twinkling eyes. "Piece of cake. Horse people love a good party. Even Stephen Wegner's coming, all the way from California."

His expression became wistful and her heart lurched. *He misses the competition, the excitement, the goals.*

She laid her hand on his arm. "Have you thought about going back?"

"To California?"

His off-hand tone didn't fool her, but she didn't respond, just tilted her head, keeping her eyes locked with his.

He finally looked away and nodded. "Yeah, all the time. But I have more important things to do with my life right now. Riding can wait awhile." He cleared his throat, but his voice was still husky. "Let's get this party underway."

Bright and early on Saturday, Jamie phoned, his voice quivering with excitement and emotion. "Tim woke up this morning!"

Beth closed her eyes, relief crushing her chest, making it hard to breathe.

Jamie raced on. "He doesn't recognize any of us, but the doctor said that could change, probably *will* change."

"Thank God. Can he have visitors? I'd like to see him."

"It's still restricted to immediate family, but that should only be for a day or two. I'll fill you in this afternoon." He chuckled. "Lucy's beside herself with excitement after seeing the big newspaper story about your shindig."

"They made it sound like it'll really be something, huh?"

After hanging up, she read the newspaper article again. Square Dance With the Stars had been organized on two levels: the afternoon open barn would be by invitation only for the equestrian celebrities, complete with champagne and hors d'oeuvres. At five, the facility would open to the public with tours, a barbecue feast, and the evening's entertainment. Though the piece was written in a positive tone, it had an undercurrent of bridled resentment at yet another rich playground populated with untouchables. It would be imperative that she move quickly to follow up with the news of Connor's therapeutic riding center.

By ten o'clock, news crews from the major networks had arrived and begun setting up cameras and positioning reporters in strategic places. Beth turned from the window, scanned her checklist again, then stepped out into the main aisle.

Cozy and his crew had been working since before dawn, and it showed. The oak walls and stalls glowed with hours of elbow grease, the wrought iron had been rubbed to an ebony sheen, and the concrete floor showed not one wisp of bedding or dirt. Without checking, she knew that each building on the grounds had been given the same care.

Tip stepped out of a stall and waved. "Hi'ya, Miss Webb!" He set a grooming bucket down, and strode toward her. "I have three horses left to clean up, an' I'm done. What do you want me to do then?"

In the short time he'd been there, Tip had flourished, nurtured by the down-to-earth environment, and his responsibility for living creatures. Beth felt wonderful in the knowledge that she'd been instrumental in effecting his growth.

"Some of the VIP guests might like to see the horses. I want you to be responsible for that. Rather than having people inside the stalls, I want you to bring the horses out into the aisle. Less liability that way."

His face glowed with gratitude at her trust. "Yes, Ma'am! I brought some clean clothes to change into, just in case." He turned back toward the grooming bucket, then stopped. "Oh, I meant to thank you for setting me up with Doc Fall. He's great! And he's showing me how to do real stuff on his patients."

"That's wonderful, Tip. When you get your vet license, I'll hire you full time here."

The boy's eyes widened. "Cool!"

Beth smiled as she moved through the crowd, brushing elbows with riders she'd only seen on television. A brief shudder of yearning dampened her spirit, then disappeared as she caught sight of

Connor schmoozing with Nina Templeton, a former World Cup champion in Dressage.

Nina's bright eyes twinkled from her small face. "You've certainly got the right idea here." She gazed around the large dressage arena. "Once the word gets out about this place, you'll need to expand."

Beth groaned. "No, thanks, I've had all the growth I can stand for one lifetime."

Connor grinned. "Beth's ready to move in some new directions. You'll be hearing more about it later tonight."

Beth stared, speechless. Someone came up and distracted Nina, and Connor took Beth's elbow, steering her out of the earshot of bystanders.

She regained her voice. "What are you talking about? Hope Ranch?"

He held her shoulders and searched her face, his eyes shadowy with the effect of her attitude. "Is that a problem? Have you changed your mind?"

She looked down, suddenly embarrassed. "No, of course not. I just...we didn't discuss when we'd announce it."

"Can you think of a better time?"

"No, but you could have mentioned it to me."

"I intended to, but it slipped through the cracks with all the preparations for the party." He released her. "Beth, if we're going to be a team in this thing, there has to be some leeway for both of us."

He was right. Her obsession with control had tripped her up again–she needed to step back and let Connor handle his business the way he saw fit.

She reached out and touched his jaw. "I'm sorry, Love. Old habits are hard to break. I'll work on it."

He grinned, grabbing her hand and covering her fingers with kisses. "I'll help you–*guaranteed.*"

Hal appeared, his eyes sparkling with excitement. "You two love-birds better get your wits about ye. The crowd linin' up outside looks bigger than we expected."

Connor followed Hal down the aisle toward the door, and Beth hurried out to the exercise paddock where the barbecue was set up.

A burly black man leaned over the smoking pit, sweat glistening over his muscular arms and across his wide forehead, even in the chilly November weather. Large, deep vats of rich red-brown sauce, thick with meat, simmered on the grate over the fire. A mouth-watering aroma curled through the crisp air.

He looked up as she approached. "We're ready when you are."

"We might have more people than we expected."

He chuckled. "No problem. We always bring lots of extra. Free barbecue brings folks out of every nook and cranny for miles around."

Within minutes, the barn echoed with the din of an enthusiastic and curious crowd. Small groups gathered around some of the more well-known and recognizable celebrities who, to Beth's delight, settled comfortably into their star-status and entertained their admirers.

She clicked on her two-way radio to touch base with Hal in the main barn, and Tip in the hunter barn.

"Heads up, guys. There's a tidal wave of people headed your way. Tip, if anyone wants to see horses, it'll have to be later. With this many people, I don't want any mishaps."

A thin voice croaked beside her. "Miss Webb?"

A wizened old man with a beard squinted at her, hoisting a fiddle case up for her to see. Behind him, three bearded men of assorted heights gaped around at the building.

"Where do ya want us t'set up?"

"We're having the dance in the boarding barn. Follow me."

An hour later, she leaned against the wall and closed her eyes, taking a moment to catch her breath. She'd never imagined how strenuous a party could be. The music had started and strains of "Arkansas Traveler" drifted across the night air.

"Beth Webb?"

She straightened up, focusing on a trim man with dark hair and sharp features creased by a smile. Stephen Wegner, in the flesh.

She shook his hand, fearing she sounded gushy. "Hi, I'm so glad you could come! Are you having a good time?"

"Yes! This is such an incredible facility. You must be very proud."

She chuckled. "When I recover, I'll let you know how I feel. It's been a long, arduous project. I'm glad it's finally finished. And, with endorsements like yours, we should have no trouble filling up the events schedules."

He nodded, his expression turning more serious. "Yes, but the fact that you're providing part of the facility to Brett Hall's therapeutic riding program is even more impressive. You've proven that you're really a part of the local community."

She blinked in surprise. "We haven't even announced it yet... the locals don't know anything about it. How did–"

"Brett told me earlier." Wegner's smile became self-conscious and his tone softened. "I have a retarded daughter, Deirdre. Seven years old. We enrolled her in a riding program in Monterrey last year, and it has changed her life."

Beth reached out and touched his arm. "I know what you mean. I've seen that world in person."

He cleared his throat and squared his shoulders. "Well, I'm ready to kick up my heels, how about you?"

She grinned. "More than you know, Stephen."

"There you are!"

Connor slipped his arm around Beth's waist and pulled her tightly against his side. "What do you think? Have we made a splash, or what?"

"I'd say so. I just met Stephen Wegner...Funny, I thought he was taller."

"Sixteen hands of Dutch Warmblood makes *anyone* look tall!" He gave her a quick hug, then stepped back. "Time to talk to the masses."

He headed toward the small wooden stage they'd constructed for the musicians, and she followed, gazing proudly at his sure stride and relaxed posture, the confident set of his jaw. When all this craziness was finished, she would tell him she was ready to make a life with him.

The music faded and Connor stepped onto the stage.

"Hey! Is everyone having a good time?"

Enthusiastic applause and a chorus of "yeah's" resounded through the barn. Several horses whinnied, and everyone laughed.

"I'm sure many of you are involved in some way with the horse industry here in Lexington, but those of you who aren't must have some interest, or you wouldn't be here. Right?"

"Free barbecue!" someone shouted from the back of the room.

Connor laughed and continued. "The horse industry in the United States makes an economic impact of one-hundred-and-twelve *billion* dollars annually."

A deep murmur ran through the crowd.

"Here in Kentucky, we produce one-point-two billion of those dollars. With Highover Gate operational, we can attract another huge piece of the pie to our community."

Beth listened to the applause, again amazed at Connor's ability to gather a crowd and keep their rapt attention.

He crooked his finger at her and smiled.

"I'd like to introduce our hostess for this shindig, Beth Webb. She's responsible for providing this fabulous facility to the great Commonwealth of Kentucky, and the equestrian community."

More applause and whistles followed her onto the stage. She took the microphone from Connor and smiled out across the sea of faces. Jake Biggs gave her a thumbs-up.

"Thank you all for coming. We're very proud of Highover, and hope to see you at future events. Some of the things we have planned are strictly serious horse competitions, but we hope to have some festivals and fun-days for the local community, as our way of saying thank you for your support."

She scanned the audience as she waited for the applause to fade. A sharp jolt ran through her at the sight of a beady-eyed round face. Ken Barker's expression was one of extreme discomfort, and she wondered how he could have found the nerve to show up.

She turned her attention to the rest of the audience. "I'm sure many of you have followed the string of problems we've had while trying to complete Highover. I owe so much to Cincinnati Construction Company for their diligence and competence to stay on top of the project, and their cooperation with local companies and townspeople.

She looked directly at Barker. "They've been sensitive to and compliant with environmental issues–such as the protection of wetlands."

Barker's face turned deep crimson and his brows came together. She gestured toward Dan Cornell, standing in the front row.

"Please give our CCC site boss a hand."

While the crowd clapped, she saw Barker slither, like the snake he was, through the crowd toward the door.

"Thank you. And now, I'm thrilled to announce that Hope Ranch Therapeutic Riding Center will call Highover its home next month." She glanced at Connor's surprised expression and grinned. *Gotcha.* "Connor Hall–Brett Hall to those of you on the competition circuits–has dedicated his professional career to helping injured riders." She took a deep breath. "Including me. Without his strength and positive attitude, I'd be addressing you from a wheelchair."

She caught sight of Jamie and Lucy, standing to the side in the front row. Jamie smiled warmly and nodded, and Beth continued her unscripted speech.

"That same dedication to others is the foundation he relied upon to organize Hope Ranch–another worthwhile addition to our community." She turned to Connor and smiled. "Thank you."

From her other side, a hand reached out and took the mike.

"I'm Stephen Wegner. Some of you may know me."

A ripple of laughter moved through the crowd, and he grinned.

"Beth pretty much covered the important parts, but I'd like to add my own two-cents."

Connor slipped his arm around Beth's waist while they listened to Wegner mesmerize the quiet audience with the story of his own child, and the importance of riding programs like Hope Ranch.

"I ask each of you to put yourselves in my place–or Beth Webb's–and make a pledge to support this worthwhile program right here in your own hometown."

The crowd responded instantly, and Stephen smiled and nodded, waiting for silence. When the last whistle had faded away, he turned to Connor.

"I'd like to make the first donation to Hope Ranch. Best of luck."

He held out a check and handed the microphone over. Connor stared at the small piece of paper, then grinned and shook Stephen's hand.

"*Thank* you!" He turned to the crowd. "Hey, everybody, let's doe-si-doe!"

The fiddler drew his bow across the strings, and the audience swirled into an eddy of confusion and merriment. Wegner disappeared into the crowd, and Connor gazed at the check with delight.

"Two-thousand bucks," he whispered. "Enough for two more special saddles!"

Beth stepped outside into the sharp night air and inhaled deeply. Above, the black sky accentuated a fine spray of stars and the smooth flow of the Milky Way. Her gaze stopped on Cassiopeia, floating through eternity chained to her throne, forever a reminder of humility. Like the queen of the myth, Beth had been prideful to a fault, too confident that she needed no one. A murmur of sorrow ran through her chest, pain for the time she'd wasted, alone and oblivious to life's joy.

She looked away from the monumental heavens and exhaled, feeling her energy return. Optimism flowed into the newly opened recesses of her mind, and her pulse fluttered at the prospect of a new life.

Jamie and Lucy strolled around the corner, hand in hand.

Jamie crowed, "Hey, Bethey! We've been looking all over for you."

"Catching my breath. Party-girl, I'm not."

Lucy's radiant face strengthened Beth's resolve. *I want to glow like that, be consumed by love, and everything else be-damned!*

Jamie slipped his arm around Beth's shoulder. "We've set a date for the wedding–April First at the Horse Park."

"What a great idea! Cherry blossoms and horse manure."

Lucy chuckled. "I'd feel really out of place in any other setting." She reached out and touched Beth's hand. "I want you to be my Best Woman."

Forty-Two

On Tuesday afternoon, Connor stared at his reflection in the mirror.

"Well, Buddy-Boy. Are you ready for this?"

Thinking about his dinner plans with Beth, his heart thumped. Beneath his self-assured exterior, he still feared she wasn't ready for total commitment. As he straightened his tie, the face in the mirror mocked him. *You've been fooled before.* He scowled, flicking off the light as he walked out the door.

Beth opened the front door and caught her breath, her gaze roaming boldly over Connor's body, then snapping back to his face.

She smiled lecherously. "Boy, don't *you* look good. Come in here where I can see better."

She moved straight into his arms, nuzzling his neck, then lifting her face to be kissed. Her body ached with longing, and her thoughts ran wild. *So much catching up to do.* His kiss was long and deep, resurrecting images of another night they'd shared.

She struggled to free herself from his arms, gasping and laughing.

"Whew! If we're going to dinner, we'd better leave *now.*"

On the drive to Louisville, Connor's relaxed profile supported his confidence in Hope Ranch. "Did I tell you the mayor took me aside before he left the party? He's thrilled with the program. He has a niece with muscular dystrophy, and wants to sign her up."

A gentle look crossed his face. "You never know who's out there, needing you."

Beth's pulse thumped, and her voice cracked. "*I* need you."

His hand slipped across the space between them and covered hers, sending his warmth through her whole body and into her heart. *There's so much I want to tell you, but I don't know where to start.*

The glow of the city lights fanned across the horizon, the traffic thickened, and Connor squeezed Beth's hand before returning his own to the steering wheel.

"How's your young vet-hopeful?"

"Doing well. He may be the best employee I've ever had."

He laughed and glanced at her glowing face. "Boy, what a change! A few weeks ago, you wanted to boot his rich butt out of your barn."

"I know—I can't stand arrogance."

Connor listened to her enthusiasm and smiled, thinking back to his own youth, and the person who'd helped *him* make something of himself. Watching Beth talk, he saw a new side to her—a woman who seemed to have finally found something more important than her own ambitions.

"Connor, I'm going to make sure that Tip gets into vet school when he graduates. Money isn't the issue for him, but emotional support and motivation are." She hesitated. "Maybe with the proper role models around, he'll make a determined effort to dedicate his life to helping others."

"If anyone can guide him, it'll be you."

"I have *you* to thank for opening my eyes." She was quiet for a moment. "I haven't told you just how much I've enjoyed the training sessions with the volunteers."

He smiled, his thoughts running parallel to hers.

She shifted in her seat and continued. "I've had the chance to see you in action. You're a totally different person than when I met you."

"Yes, I am. The riding center has given me the fulfillment that all the money and trophies in the world couldn't."

There's only one thing still missing from my life.

In the dim light, Beth saw Connor's contented expression and, for a fleeting instant, anxiety coiled through her thoughts. *Will you make room for me in your new life?* She firmly pushed away any possibility that he might not.

The car pulled up in front of the grand old Seelbach hotel, and a flush of excitement replaced her misgivings. A liveried doorman appeared, offering her a gloved hand as she stepped onto the pavement. Connor slipped his arm around her waist, and they walked through the heavy doors and into the luxurious lobby of the hotel that had been the setting for F. Scott Fitzgerald's *Great Gatsby*.

"Our reservations are for eight, but we're early, so we might as well wait in the bar."

She slipped her arm through his and smiled, trying to reassure herself that he would care as much as she did about the things she planned to tell him.

Connor's heart suddenly thumped with anxiety as he held Beth's chair out for her in the dimly lit lounge. Now, more than ever, her love was the most important thing in his life. Her perfume wafted up, stirring his emotions. Leaning over, he kissed the top of her head and caressed her shoulder, then sat down in the chair next to her.

"You look beautiful tonight."

She smiled shyly and looked down, but he sneaked his hand across the table and lifted her chin.

She giggled like a little girl. "You're making me feel really self-conscious."

He winked. "Good. This is a special night, and I want you to enjoy it completely."

She cocked her head. "Special?...Oh, that's right. Celebrating my three steps." She narrowed her eyes, teasing him. "The three steps you gave me hell for."

He chuckled and relaxed back into his chair. "Yes, you're the most difficult patient I've ever had. I'm glad *that's* over."

She leaned forward with a solemn look. "Connor, I want to be serious for a minute. I have so many things to tell you, but I'm not very good at this, so bear with me."

Her tone startled him, but he nodded for her to continue.

"All these years, I've thought I had the perfect life. The life I wanted. A high-flying, fast lane, wheeling-dealing life, my *only* life. No outside distractions, no one to worry about but myself. No relationships, no love—except for my family and Jamie. Even finding myself in a wheelchair didn't make me recognize the emptiness of the life I'd been living. All I could think about was returning to the sameness and security of that life."

Her expression revealed her apprehension. "Then I met you, but when you didn't fall into my cookie-cutter plans, it annoyed me. I was so desperate to keep everything the way it had always been, that I couldn't see how good you were for me, how right you were about me and life in general."

He shifted in his chair, not daring to speak for fear of breaking her train of thought.

She paused, taking a small sip of wine, then set the glass down and gazed at it. "I've watched you grow, while I've stood still. You've turned into the man I always dreamed would come along, the someone special that everyone is supposed to have, once in his or her life." She stopped and took a measured breath. "Then you moved on past me, and I was suddenly terrified of being left behind."

She looked up, searching his face. "I want—"

He reached out and gently stilled her lips with his fingertips. "Beth, I haven't left you behind. I've tried to give you room to come to terms with yourself, and what you really want. I'm right here."

The maitre 'd appeared and the emotional moment ended. Connor's thoughts locked on Beth as she walked ahead of him toward a table in the corner. Everything she'd said had penetrated the deepest corners of his heart. *She doesn't know it, but she's grown so much since we met. Her ambitious and independent nature has softened, revealing a warm, caring woman. The woman I've always wanted.*

Beth felt Connor's gaze as she settled into the comfortable captain's chair. Worry surged through her head. Would she be able to pick up the thread of her thoughts again? The serious tone of their earlier conversation had evaporated, and dinner conversation turned to discussion of all the new happenings at Highover and Hope Ranch. The opportunity to return to her speech never presented itself.

Pushing his coffee cup away, Connor leaned forward, his voice strong and rich. "Ready to go?"

They walked out into the chilly night, and he slipped his hand into the crook of her elbow.

"Let's take a walk down by the river. It's such a beautiful night."

The city had already dressed itself in holiday lights, and the soft twinkling spots cast a romantic glow over every plane and angle of the historic buildings. Strolling across the street, they headed for a park that followed the riverfront for blocks. The breeze came from the south, promising a change in the weather. A half-moon shimmered on the lazy swirls of the Ohio River, as it moved eternally toward the Mississippi.

At the edge of the plaza, Beth leaned on the railing and closed her eyes, consumed by a feeling of peace. She no longer feared what the future might hold, if she could spend it with Connor.

His arm circled her shoulders and his soft drawl floated on the breeze. "You've told me what you want. Now, it's my turn."

He grasped her shoulders and gently turned her toward him, capturing her eyes with his own luminous gaze. The air around them hummed with expectation.

"I want *you*. Always. For my whole life. For *our* life."

His words flowed over and around and through her heart, his voice echoing softly through the night air.

"Will you be there?"

Without hesitation, she whispered, "I will."

Their lips met and her soul soared up and up, flying like the wind on a bay horse with wings, finally clearing the fences around her heart.

Can Love Triumph Over Ambition?
Ambition Overcome Prejudice?

In the risky world of showing high-ticket Arabian Horses, two professionals–with a great deal to lose– find out the hard way.

Young veterinarian, Liz Barnett, has moved her equine practice from Kentucky to rural California, excited by the chance to partner with an established clinic, as well as show her beautiful Arabian horses. She soon finds that she's living in an area by-passed by time and progress, as she butts heads with stubborn old ranchers who want nothing to do with a young female vet.

Hunky horse trainer, Kurt DeVallio, has spent the past ten years struggling with the deaths of his wife and infant son, and a horse-drugging frame-up that destroyed his professional career. His tunnel vision for finding a way to clear his name, and be "his own man" again, has thrown him into the midst of greedy folks who'll try to win at any cost.

When circumstances force these two together, they learn that winning has many meanings.

Outstanding Equestrian Fiction
from
Equine Graphics Publishing Group

Toni Leland

From the age of eight, Toni Leland nurtured an on-going love affair with horses. Every moment of every day was filled with fantasies of owning her very own horse, a dream that finally came true at the age of twelve. Her life has been graced by many of these beautiful creatures, so it only seemed natural that her careers would revolve around them, as well.

Graphic artist, advertising consultant to the equine industry, and publisher/producer of magazines, books, and videos about horses have consumed the past eighteen years of Toni's life.

The next step was obvious: equestrian fiction.

Toni lives and works in Ohio with her husband.

Visit her at
Romancing the Horse
http://www.tonileland.com

CPSIA information can be obtained at www.ICGtesting.com
Printed in the USA
BVOW071334171111

276302BV00001B/16/A